Double Cross

JAMES DAVID
JORDAN

Double Cross

A NOVEL

B&H
PUBLISHING GROUP

Nashville, Tennessee

978-0-8054-4754-5

Published by B&H Publishing Group,
Nashville, Tennessee

Dewey Decimal Classification: F
Subject Heading: MYSTERY FICTION \
PRIVATE INVESTIGATORS—FICTION \ PARENT-
CHILD RELATIONSHIPS—FICTION

1 2 3 4 5 6 7 8 • 12 11 10 09

To Allie and Johnathan.
I love you.
Dad

ACKNOWLEDGMENTS

I'D LIKE TO THANK my wife, Sue, whose love, patience, and editing keep me chugging along. Also I would like to thank my agent and publicist, Tina Jacobson, for her support and guidance, and my good friend, Dale Wills, whose knowledge of guns keeps Taylor Pasbury shooting.

CHAPTER
ONE

THE DAY MY MOTHER came back into my life began with a low December fog and a suicide. Mom was not responsible for the fog.

I hadn't seen her for twenty years, and the idea that she might show up at my door was the farthest thing from my mind on a Thursday morning, a few weeks before Christmas, when the music alarm practically blasted me off my bed. With the Foo Fighters wailing in my ear, I burrowed into my pillow and tried to wrap it around my head. I rolled onto my side and slapped the snooze bar, but smacked the plastic so hard that it snapped in two, locking in another minute and a half of throbbing bass before I could yank the cord from the wall socket.

It wasn't until my toes touched the hardwood floor and curled up against the cold that I remembered why I was waking up at 5:45 in the first place. Kacey Mason and I were meeting Elise Hovden at eight o'clock in a suburb northwest of Dallas. We would give her one chance to explain why nearly half a million dollars was missing from Simon Mason World Ministries. If she couldn't, our next stop would be the Dallas police.

Since Simon Mason's murder earlier that year, I'd been living in his house with Kacey, his twenty-year-old daughter. I had promised to watch out for her if anything happened to him. It wasn't a sacrifice. By that time Kacey and I were already so close that we finished each other's sentences. I needed her as much as she needed me.

I slid my feet into my slippers and padded down the hall toward Kacey's door. Chill bumps spread down my thighs in a wave, and I wished I'd worn my flannel pajama bottoms to bed under my Texas Rangers baseball jersey. Rather than turning back to my room to grab my robe, I decided to gut it out. I bent over and gave my legs a rub, but I knew they wouldn't be warm again until I was standing next to the space heater in the bathroom.

I pressed my ear to Kacey's door. The shower was humming. Of course she was awake. Had there ever been a more responsible college kid? Sometimes I wished she would let things go, do something wild. For her, that would probably mean not flossing before going to bed. If hyper-responsibility got her through the day, I supposed it was fine with me. After all, she was a markedly better person than I had been at her age.

By the time I met her father I was twenty-nine, and thanks to a decade of too much alcohol and too many useless men, I was dropping like a rock. But Simon Mason caught me and held me in place for a while, just long enough to give me hope. Then he did what he had to do, and he died for it. Some things are more important than living. He and Dad both taught me that.

So now I was changing. To be accurate, I would say I was a work in progress. I hadn't had a drink since before Simon died, and I'd sworn off men completely, albeit temporarily. Frankly, the latter was not a big deal. It wasn't as if a crowd of guys had been beating a path to my door. I simply figured there was no use getting back into men until I was confident the drinking was under control. One thing I had demonstrated repeatedly in my life was that drinking and men just didn't go together—at least not for me.

As for Kacey, after everything she'd been through, it was amazing she hadn't folded herself into a fetal ball and quit the world for a while. Instead, she just kept plugging along, putting one foot in front of the other. I was content to step gingerly behind her, my toes sinking into her footprints. She was a good person to follow. She had something I'd never been known for: Kacey had character.

I shook my head. I was not going to start the day by kicking myself. I'd done enough of that. Besides, I no longer thought I had to be perfect. If a good man like Simon Mason could mess things up and find a way to go on, then so could I. Even in his world—a much more spiritual one than mine—perfection was not required. He made a point of teaching me that.

I closed my eyes and pictured Simon: his shiny bald head, his lean muscled chest, his brilliant, warming smile. As I thought of that smile, I smiled, too, but it didn't last long. Within seconds the muscles tightened in my neck. I massaged my temples and tried to clear my thoughts. Soon, though, I was pressing my fingers so hard into my scalp that pain radiated from behind my eyes.

If only he had listened. But he couldn't. He wanted to die. No matter how much he denied it, we both knew it was true. After what he had done, he couldn't live with himself. So he found the only available escape hatch. He went to preach in a place where his death was nearly certain.

I lowered my hands and clenched them, then caught myself and relaxed. This was no good. It was too late. *Not this morning, Taylor. You're not going to think about Simon today.*

I took a deep breath and ran my fingers back through my hair, straightening the auburn waves for an instant before they sprang stubbornly back into place. *Today's worries are enough for today.* That was the mantra of the alcohol recovery program at Simon's church. It was from the Bible, but I couldn't say where. To be honest, I didn't pay attention as closely as I should. Regardless of origin, it was a philosophy that had worked for my drinking—at least so far. Maybe it had broader application: *Focus on the task at hand and let yesterday and tomorrow take care of themselves.*

At the moment, the first priority was to get the coffee going. I started down the hall.

When I turned the corner into the kitchen, I could see that Kacey had already been there. The coffeemaker's light was on, illuminating a wedge of countertop. In the red glow of its bulb, the little machine chugged and puffed like a miniature locomotive. Two stainless steel decanters with screw-on plastic lids waited next to the ceramic coffee jar, and the smell of strong, black coffee drifted across the room. I closed my eyes, inhaled, and pictured the cheese Danish we would pick up at the corner bakery on our way out of our neighborhood. That was plenty of incentive to get moving. I headed back down the hall.

When I reached the bathroom, I flipped on the light, closed the door, and hit the switch on the floor heater. I positioned it so it blew directly on my legs.

Within a minute the chill bumps were retreating. I braced my hands on the edge of the sink, leaned forward, and squinted into the mirror. Glaring back at me was a message I had written in red lipstick the night before: *Start the coffee!*

I wiped the words off with a hand towel and peered into the mirror again. I blinked hard and studied my face. No lines, no bags, no creases—no runs, no hits, no errors, as Dad used to say. I was beginning to believe the whole clean living thing. Zero liquor and a good night's sleep worked like a tonic for the skin.

It was tough to stay on the wagon after Simon's death. I had never been an every-day drinker. My problem was binge drinking. With all that had happened during the past six months, the temptations had been frequent and strong, but I was gradually getting used to life on the dry side of a bourbon bottle. There was much to be said for routine. Maybe that's why dogs are so happy when they're on a schedule. When everything happens the same way and at the same time each day, there's not much room for angst.

On second thought, the dog analogy didn't thrill me. I pulled the Rangers jersey over my head, tossed it on the floor, and turned to look in the full-length mirror on the back of the bathroom door. Standing in nothing but my bikini panties, I rocked onto the toes of one foot, then the other. My long legs were still lean and athletic. Fitness was something Dad had always emphasized—fitness and self-defense. There were times when I had hated him for it, but now I was glad for the benefits. It would be years before I had to worry about really showing age. I might have lived harder than most twenty-nine-year-olds, but I could still turn heads in a crowded room. No, the dog analogy was not appropriate. I had plenty of issues, but I was no dog. At least not yet.

I turned on the water and cupped my hands beneath the faucet. It was time to wake up and plan what we would say to Elise. After splashing my face and patting it with a towel, I turned around, leaned back against the sink, and crossed my arms. I caught a whiff of the lavender cologne I'd taken to spraying on my wrists before bed. The Internet said it would soothe me into peaceful slumber. For fifty dollars an ounce, it should have brought me warm milk and rocked me to sleep. I tried to recall how I'd slept the past few nights, then caught myself. I was just looking for ways to waste time. I needed to focus. The issue at hand was Elise.

Simon informed me about the missing money just before he left for Beirut. His former accountant, Brandon, had confronted him about it, thinking that Simon had been skimming. Simon wanted someone to know that he hadn't done it, someone who could tell Kacey that her dad was not a thief. That's why he told me. In case he didn't come back. And as the whole world knew, he didn't come back.

Elise was the obvious person for the board of directors to choose to wind up the business of Simon's ministry. She had been his top assistant for years. When I told Kacey about the missing money, though, she bypassed Elise and went directly to the board to demand an audit—impressive gumption for a twenty year old. It didn't take the auditors long to confirm that Simon had nothing to do with the missing money.

The accountants concluded that the board had assigned the cat to clean the birdcage. Elise had set up dummy vendor accounts at banks around the country in a classic embezzlement scam. Simon's ministries had major construction projects going, and Elise issued bogus contractor invoices to Simon Mason World Ministries from fake businesses with post office box addresses that she controlled. When the ministry mailed the payments, she picked up the checks from the post office boxes and deposited them in the bank accounts. Who knows where the money went from there.

The ministry had grown so quickly during the years before Simon's death—and Simon was so trusting—that controls were lax. When the invoices came in, the payables department paid them without question. By now the money was probably stuffed under a mattress in some tropical paradise. That was another thing I intended to pursue with Elise. She had developed a great tan.

Before I stepped into the shower, I wrapped myself in a towel and went back into the bedroom. I pulled my .357 Sig Sauer out of my purse and checked the magazine. It was full. I slipped the pistol into the inside pocket of my purse. Elise didn't strike me as the type to get violent, but people did weird things when backed into a corner. If I'd learned anything during my time in the Secret Service, it was to hope for the best—and prepare for the worst.

CHAPTER
TWO

KACEY AND I USUALLY didn't talk much before our first cup of coffee, and that morning was no different. By 7:15 I was easing my Camaro onto the Dallas North Tollway. A half-mile in front of us, the highway looked like a Christmas display. Taillights blinked and faded, then blinked again as early commuters tapped their brakes and squinted through their windshields into the fog.

I looked at Kacey out of the corner of my eye. "I'll have to get creative if we're going to make it to Elise's by eight."

Kacey nodded and yawned, but even in the dim light from the dashboard I could see her fingers clutching her coffee carafe. I gunned the engine, cut back across the entry lane, and veered onto the first exit ramp. Though my quick entry and exit from traffic would have made a driver's education teacher cringe, it wasn't the cause of Kacey's anxiety. In the months since Simon hired me to take charge of his security, she had ridden with me plenty of times—including once, after her kidnapping, when things were plenty dicey. She was not a nervous passenger; she was dreading the morning's meeting with Elise as much as I was.

Why shouldn't she dread it? Confronting a person with evidence of embezzlement was no small thing. When that someone was Kacey's father's most trusted employee, a woman Kacey had known since she was a kid . . . well, my knuckles on the steering wheel were as white as hers around the coffee carafe. I eased off the gas and turned left onto Northwest Highway. With any luck I could cut across to I-35E and take a straight shot north to Lewisville before traffic became completely knotted.

As I drove, I pulled out my phone and checked my office's voice mail from the prior evening. The first two were from clients I had been neglecting since Simon hired me to take over his security in March. In the months since Simon's death, I had been trying to work my security business back to normalcy, but I hadn't yet gotten to everyone on my client list. I made a mental note to follow up that afternoon.

The third message was from a private investigator friend, the one I'd hired to look for my mother. His message was garbled, and I couldn't make it out. Looking back, it was just as well. I learned soon enough what he wanted to tell me.

My mother had run out on Dad and me when I was nine, and for the next eight years Dad made excuses for her. In the meantime he did his best for me. Unfortunately the Army Special Forces didn't provide much training for raising girls. Besides, as much as he loved me, he had issues of his own. The battles he fought, both the Army's and his own, depleted him. He taught me what he knew how to teach—to move, to shoot, to take care of myself—but for the other things, girl things, I was on my own.

As for his excuses about Mom, I swallowed them for years. By the time I was seventeen, though, I had killed two men and cradled Dad's head in my hands as he died. Life had stopped allowing me the adolescent luxury of gullibility. I tossed out the excuses and faced the truth: Mom left because she had her eye on something better, plain and simple. Of course, that knowledge didn't make me want a mother any less. Anyone who doesn't understand what I'm saying should try being seventeen and completely alone. Your brain can tell you that you have no choice but to be tough, but that doesn't stop you dreaming of a safe home, a warm fire, and a mom and dad.

But that wasn't the reason I was looking for her. If not for Simon, I probably would have left things as they were. One of the last things he told me before he died was that he hoped I would find her, give her a chance to make things right. Considering everything he had done for me, I owed it to him. I owed it to myself, too. My mother was the last loose end in a long, sordid story. Or, at least I hoped she was.

Besides, in a strange way the search made me feel that Dad and Simon were still close by. After all, we were all connected—Mom and Dad and Simon and I. I liked that feeling. I hadn't had a surplus of connections in my life.

I hit the wipers to clear the layer of mist that the fog had deposited on the windshield. From the corner of my eye I saw Kacey run a finger under the neckline of her sweater, then cross her arms and stare out the passenger window. Along the side of the road, a cluster of unlit restaurants emerged from the fog like hulking ghosts creeping from a gloomy netherworld. After we passed, I watched in the rearview mirror as they receded into the mist.

I shivered. "Fog creeps me out."

Kacey merely shrugged. What was she thinking? She'd already been through so much. At some point a college kid should get to be a college kid, but I doubted that day would ever come for Kacey.

I wanted to touch her arm and tell her everything

would be all right, but I stopped myself. I was probably already bugging her to death, hovering over her like a den mother since I moved into the house. How could I not? I knew what it was like to lose a father, and I knew what it was like to love Simon Mason, although the way that I had loved him was still too complex for me to decipher. If I was oppressively protective of his daughter, then that was too bad. Maybe someday, looking back, she would appreciate the attention—attention I'd have given anything for when I was her age.

I lifted my carafe out of the cup holder and took a drink. On a morning like this, caffeine could only be good. Maybe it would jolt me out of the contemplative bog in which I'd been mired since the alarm went off.

North of town the fog had settled into the low places where the highway crossed creeks and drainage ravines. Each time we descended a hill we dipped into the haze and then climbed out of it on the other side with a gray slick on the windshield. I continued to work the wiper knob with my finger to keep the windshield clear. As we moved farther from Dallas, the rising sun gradually burned larger gaps in the haze, and by the time we approached Elise's neighborhood the hills and valleys were indistinguishably bright and crisp.

Elise's house was one of the first that had been built in a large new development on the outskirts of Lewisville. After turning into her subdivision, we

passed homes in various stages of construction—
some partially framed, some partially bricked, and
some nothing more than plumbing pipes extending
like plastic fingers from gray foundation slabs. Inter-
spersed among the construction were weedy lots with
colorful metal for sale signs that shook in the morning
breeze.

Even with our windows up, the scent of freshly
sawed lumber seeped into the car. I thought of Dad's
workshop in the old garage. He liked to build things, to
work precisely with his hands. I pictured him smiling
up at me from his workbench, a level on the table and a
hammer dangling from a loop at the waist of his jeans.
Some scents, I suppose, are really just memories in a
form that never fades.

We passed crews of construction workers as we
moved deeper into the subdivision. Some pulled tool
boxes from the backs of pickups. Others dangled their
feet from tailgates and crammed the final bites of fast-
food breakfasts into their mouths. One of the workers
put his fingers to his lips and wolf-whistled as our car
passed. Kacey laughed and waved. I pressed a little
harder on the gas.

At five minutes past eight, I eased the car to a stop
in front of Elise's two-story country French house. It
sat alone at the end of a cul-de-sac that backed up to a
tree-lined lake. It faced east, and the December sun was
just high enough to glare orange and gold off the front

windows, giving the first floor the look of a blazing brick oven.

I turned off the ignition and leaned toward Kacey. "Do you want me to do the talking?"

She ran both hands back through her hair, suspending it above her head until she gave it a flick that sent it tumbling, dark and shiny, over her shoulders. She chewed her lip, and I was impressed that a girl her age was even considering taking the lead in such a difficult conversation.

Just as I was about to suggest that she let me handle it, she opened the door and swung her long legs out of the car. "Be my guest."

I opened the car door and slung my purse over my shoulder.

The yard was a patchwork of newly laid sod, brown, dormant, and soggy. Though late fall had been mild even by Dallas standards, the lawn still smelled more like cold mud than warm grass. Only about three-quarters of the shrubs had been planted in the beds in the front of the house, and it was apparent that Elise had moved in before the elaborate landscaping was complete.

Smeared boot prints mottled the front walk, evidence of the most recent contingent of yard workers. On our way to the door, Kacey and I twisted our steps over and around the muddy blotches, like schoolgirls contending with a hastily chalked hopscotch board.

When we arrived at the door, a north breeze was skimming the front of the house, dipping and rebounding in the recessed entryway. After ringing the bell, I buttoned my jacket all the way to my neck and shoved my hands in the pockets of my jeans. Living in Texas had made a winter wimp of me.

There was no sound from inside. I rang again while Kacey cupped her hands around her eyes and looked through the door glass. "Everything's dark," she said.

"Maybe she's still in bed." I rang again.

Kacey dug into the oversized leather bag that hung from her shoulder and pulled out her phone. She checked for the number and punched it in, then put the phone to her ear and waited. After a few seconds she tapped a button and dropped the phone back into her purse. "Voice mail."

I motioned toward the driveway that stretched past the side of the house to the rear-entry garage. "Let's try around back."

We worked our way back up the muddy walk and around to the driveway, which we followed toward the back, stopping momentarily at the one window at the side of the house. I stood on my toes and peered through a slit in the blinds. A quilted day bed in the corner was smothered in red and beige pillows with embroidered cows. Against one wall was a desk painted off-white and accented with a red rooster lamp. "Nothing here but farm animals. Let's head around back."

As we approached the rear, Kacey stopped and held up a hand. "Do you hear that?"

"What?"

"It sounds like a car running. She must be in the garage."

"The little rat! She was trying to bolt before we got here."

Kacey looked at me over her shoulder. "Little rat?"

I shrugged sheepishly.

She smiled. "Do you think we should fill her full of lead with our Tommy guns?"

"Okay, okay. I've never called anyone a rat before. It just popped into my mind. I think I kind of like it, though. It's functional."

She rolled her eyes and continued down the driveway.

The three-car attached garage was in the back corner of the house. The garage door faced rearward, toward the lake. Behind the house, the driveway broadened into a large, square slab, which allowed a car to come down the driveway and do a U-turn to enter the garage. Just to the side of the slab was a huge backyard, enclosed in a black iron fence. The yard sloped for a couple hundred feet toward the lake. Through the fence

I could see that the back of the house opened onto a railed-in redwood deck.

As we got next to the garage, the sound of the car engine became obvious. Kacey rapped on the garage door. "Elise!"

Car exhaust seeped from beneath the door, and I covered my nose and mouth with my hand. "Surely she's not in there," I said through my fingers. I pounded the door with my fist. "Elise! It's Taylor and Kacey. Let us in!"

Kacey folded her arms. "Maybe she ran back into the house to get something."

"And left the car running? She may be weird, but she's not stupid."

"Then what do you think?"

"Let's listen for a second." I put my ear to the garage door. There was no sound but the car engine. I set my purse down on the driveway and walked over to the gate. It was unlocked. I opened it and jogged to the deck, where I peered through one of the picture windows into the back of the house. The light was on over the breakfast table, but there was no sign of Elise. I tried the back door. It was locked. I pounded on it. No response.

Kacey came through the gate and hurried across the deck toward me. "I've got a really bad feeling about this."

I took off my jacket and wrapped it around my hand.

She raised an eyebrow. "What are you doing?"

I balled my hand into a fist and pulled back my arm. "Hopefully, not ruining a good jacket. I'm going to pop the glass."

"What? You can't break into her house."

"What do you think the chances are that she's in that car?"

"Pretty good."

"That's what I think, too." I stepped forward and punched the door pane. Glass fell on both sides of the door. I waited for an alarm or a scream or both, but there was no sound. Reaching through the hole in the glass, I knocked away the shards with my jacket, doing my best not to tear the suede on the jagged edges. When I felt the dead bolt, I turned it. "You stay out here until I get the garage door open," I said over my shoulder. "I don't want you getting asphyxiated."

Kacey moved in close behind me. "No way! I'm coming with you." Her voice rose with each word. Her cheeks glowed and her eyes moved quickly left and right, scanning the family room through the hole in the glass. It was obvious that she thought this was exciting. We really should have been sisters.

I wagged a finger. "Okay, but take a deep breath and hold it, and cover your nose and mouth with your sleeve." I swung the door open and sprinted diagonally through the family room. I could hear Kacey's footsteps slapping the tile behind me. A short hallway led past the laundry room. In front of me was a door that appeared to lead to the garage. Throwing it open, I felt around the corner for the light switch, hit it, and then searched the wall near the door for the garage opener button. When I found it, I punched it. The door cranked open.

As daylight filled the garage, we got a look through the windshield of Elise's Nissan. It was empty. My eyes already stung from the exhaust. I motioned for Kacey to follow me. We ran past the car and out the garage door into the light. When we were ten feet into the driveway I stopped and inhaled.

Kacey did the same, her hands on her hips. "If she's not in the car, where do you think she is?"

"I don't know. Wherever she is, though, she's not going to be happy with me about the back door."

"I'll be sure to let her know that I begged you not to break it."

"Thanks a bunch."

"No problem. I've always got your back."

"Right." I looked back toward the garage, which was empty except for Elise's car. The concrete floor had been sealed, and practically sparkled. Her garage was cleaner than our kitchen.

"I'd better turn off the car." I took a few deep breaths.

Kacey moved past me. "Let me get it."

I smiled. "You enjoyed that, didn't you?"

Her dark eyes were shining. "It was a blast."

"Look, Kace, I can see this sort of thing gets your blood pumping, and that's okay. I don't want you to get the idea, though, that this is a—" Before I could finish my speech, she took a breath and ran back into the garage. When she reached the car, she lowered her head and yanked open the driver's side door.

She jumped back and screamed.

I took a breath and ran into the garage. When I reached Kacey, I grabbed her arm and spun her toward the driveway. "Get out of here and get some air!"

I turned to the open car door. Elise was slumped sideways across the console in a white terry cloth bathrobe. Her head rested on the passenger seat with one hand tucked beneath her cheek, as if she were napping. Her face and hands were bright red.

I reached around the steering wheel and pushed the ignition button, killing the engine. Then I nudged Elise in the side. "Elise!" No response. I grabbed her arm and tugged. It was locked stiff, and the movement twisted her whole body in the seat. Rigor mortis; she'd been dead for hours.

My eyes watered from the exhaust. Just before I backed out of the car, I noticed Elise's key fob in the cup holder beneath her arm. Attached to the key ring was a computer flash drive. I had to get out of there, but I couldn't take my eyes off the flash drive. It might contain information stored from her computer. I turned my head and looked at Kacey out in the driveway. She was bent over at the waist, vomiting. I reached back into the car and slipped the flash drive off the key ring, leaving the fob in the cup holder. I shoved the flash drive in my pocket and ran out of the garage.

When I got to the driveway, I locked my fingers behind my head and gulped air. After a few moments I took Kacey's arm and pulled her farther from the garage. Her face was pale. Her breathing was short and quick. "Stay back here," I said. "I don't want you getting poisoned, too. Sit down on the driveway if you need to."

After a few more deep breaths, I ran back into the garage. When I got to the car I grabbed Elise around the waist to pull her out. She was frozen in a nearly fetal position. If I pulled her into the driveway and sat her up, she would tip over like a grotesque piece of yard art. I leaned into the car and studied her more closely. Her eyes were closed, and her eyelashes contrasted like delicate black stitching against the bright red of her cheeks and eyelids. Beneath her robe she wore pink wool pajamas with red hearts. On her feet were fuzzy pink slippers.

Despite the unnaturally twisted pose of her lower body, from the shoulders up she appeared as peaceful as I had ever seen her; much different than when she was alive. She was a woman who had always fought an unsuccessful battle to be included. At that moment

I desperately wished I hadn't called her a rat. A curly lock of blonde hair dangled over her left eye. I reached across her and brushed it back, my fingers grazing her clammy forehead. There was no reason to disturb her now. I left her where she was and jogged back out to the driveway.

As I approached Kacey, she wiped her mouth with her sleeve. "Is she dead?"

I nodded. "She's been dead for quite a while. Are you okay?"

"I'm fine. Sorry, it was the shock that got me. I just wasn't expecting—"

I touched her arm. "Kacey, there's a dead person in there. I'd be concerned about you if you weren't upset."

"It never occurred to me that she'd do this. I feel awful. Maybe if we had handled it differently."

I placed my hand on her back. "Look, we didn't steal the money, she did. It's sad that she's dead, and I'm sure we'll feel even worse about this later, when we have a chance to think. But we didn't do anything, and we don't have any reason to feel guilty. So don't do that to yourself."

She nodded.

I walked over and picked up my purse from where I had left it on the driveway. I pulled out my phone.

"Why is she so red?" Kacey said. "It's awful."

"Carbon monoxide. That's what it does." I dialed 9-1-1.

When the operator answered, I said what seemed obvious: "I want to report a suicide."

CHAPTER
THREE

WITHIN FIVE MINUTES A white-and-blue Lewisville police SUV rolled into the driveway, lights flashing, and made a U-turn so it was facing the open garage door. A bowlegged, mustached officer stepped out onto the pavement from the passenger side. He held up a hand to shade his eyes against the sun, which had risen above the roof of the house. His partner, a heavyset woman with a dark, round face and remarkably large eyes, walked around the front of the SUV from the driver's side.

It quickly became apparent that the bowlegged one was in charge. "Hello, ladies. Did one of you place a 9-1-1 call about a suicide?"

I raised my hand. "I did."

"I'm Officer Ferrell. This is my partner, Sandra Jackson. Where is the victim?"

"In the car, there." I pointed toward the garage.

"Carbon monoxide?"

"Yes."

"Have you been in there?"

I nodded.

"Did you check for a pulse?" He took a step toward the garage.

"Rigor has already set in."

He turned back to me. "You a doctor?"

"I'm a security consultant. I've seen dead people before."

He put his hands on his hips and looked us up and down, but mostly up, since Kacey and I were both taller than he was. "Are you relatives of the victim?"

"Business associates," I said. "We were supposed to meet her at eight o'clock. When we got here, she didn't answer the doorbell. We came around back and heard the car running."

"Was the garage door open?"

"No. We opened it."

"How did you do that?"

I pointed toward the back gate. "We heard the car running in the garage and went into the backyard to look through the windows. We figured that she must be in the car, so I busted the backdoor glass. We went through the house to the garage."

He squinted at the vomit on the driveway. "Where'd that come from?"

Kacey, who by that time had color in her face again, lowered her head. "That was me. Sorry."

I nudged her with my elbow. "Would you please stop apologizing?"

Ferrell frowned at Kacey. "Were you in the garage, too?"

"Yes."

"You may have carbon monoxide poisoning. You'd better sit down until the paramedics get here."

She shook her head. "I didn't breathe when I was in there. I just haven't seen as many dead people as she has." She gave me a weak smile.

He turned back to me and cocked his head. "I recognize you from somewhere. Are you on TV?"

"I'm a security consultant."

He scratched behind his ear. "Yeah, you said that. I guess you must look like someone." He turned toward the garage. "I'm gonna take a look. Was the car turned off when you got here?"

"I turned it off." I moved my hand toward my pocket where I'd put Elise's flash drive, but I stopped myself.

"How long has the garage door been open?"

Kacey checked her watch. "Fifteen minutes or so."

Ferrell looked over his shoulder at a row of live oaks in the backyard near the lake. The tops of the trees swayed. "There's a lot of air movement around here. It's probably okay. Sandra, you stay out here and keep an eye on me. If you see me acting funny, hold your breath and come and get me."

"I think it would be smarter to wait for the paramedics to get here," Sandra said. "If there's already rigor mortis, she's been dead for hours. Let's let them check the air out first."

Ferrell frowned. "We've got a job to do here, Sandra. Just watch me, okay?" He jerked a thumb back over his shoulder. "You ladies better move back there a bit. I don't want any more casualties." He walked to the edge of the garage, leaned in, and sniffed.

"Carbon monoxide is odorless," Sandra said.

Ferrell straightened up and hitched his belt. "I know that, but we don't have any idea what else was going on in there."

I couldn't figure out what he had in mind. The garage was empty except for the car. It was not as if Elise had been running a meth lab.

Apparently Sandra couldn't figure it out either. She pulled a notepad out of her back pocket, flipped it open, and began writing something. "Whatever you say, Ed," she said, without looking up.

Ferrell took a couple of steps into the garage, stopped, and inhaled. He waited where he was for a few moments. Then he took a few more steps and breathed again. "It seems to be okay," he said over his shoulder. "Remember to keep an eye on me, Sandra."

Sandra sighed, softly enough that Ed couldn't have heard it. "Don't worry, I'm riveted." I had a hunch I had been wrong in my initial assessment of who was in charge.

Ferrell arrived at the open car door and leaned in. A few moments later he backed his head out again. "It's carbon monoxide, all right. She's red as a cherry."

"How are you feeling, Ed?" Sandra still didn't look up from her notepad, and I almost expected her to yawn.

"I'm fine. The air seems to be okay." He stuck his head back in the car.

A siren whined in the distance. Sandra looked toward the corner of the house and flipped her notepad shut. "Paramedics," she said, as the siren became louder. She walked to the edge of the garage. "Ed, why don't you come out for a minute and get some fresh air? The medics are just about here."

Ed straightened up and walked back out into the sunlight. "Good idea. There's no rush. She's not going anywhere." He breathed deeply. "You know, the scary thing is that you can't smell the stuff."

Sandra just looked at him.

My phone rang. I checked the screen. It was Michael Harrison, the FBI agent who had investigated Kacey's kidnapping earlier that year. Since Simon's death, Michael had taken an interest in Kacey's welfare. In the process we'd become friends, a result that even a casual observer would have found odd. Our backgrounds were as different as our personalities. While I was being raised by a decorated Special Forces officer, he was growing up poor and fatherless in Chicago's most notorious housing project. If anyone were to ask ten ordinary people walking down the street which of us was more likely to be a politically conservative workaholic with an economics degree from the University of Chicago, all ten would probably point to me.

Instead, I turned out to be a hard-partying mattress-back with the dubious distinction of being the only female Secret Service agent ever drummed out of her job because of extracurricular conduct. Michael, on the other hand, was so self-disciplined that he made accountants look exciting. He had become the youngest Agent in Charge of a major metropolitan FBI office.

I punched the button on my phone. "Hi, Michael. You're not going to believe what's happening in my world this morning."

"I can't wait to hear. First, though, confirm that you and Kacey are going to the gun range this evening at seven. I'm planning my schedule and I thought I'd drop by and let you kick my butt again."

I could just picture him sitting in front of his computer calendar, plugging in activities to fill each fifteen-minute increment for the rest of the day. "I doubt if we're going to make it to the range. We're over at Elise Hovden's house. She killed herself last night." I knew that would throw our conversation off schedule.

"Holy smoke." That was Michael's version of swearing. He must have had one heck of a mother. "How did she do it?"

"Carbon monoxide. Got in her car in her bathrobe and turned it on with the garage door shut."

"What time?"

Now there was a classic Michael question. Just the facts, ma'am. "I don't know. She was stiff as a board when we found her at around 8:30." I knew how his mind worked. He was already calculating an estimated time of death. I wanted to move the conversation along. "Sad, huh? Living here all alone and then to end it that way?"

"Yeah. I didn't have her pegged for being depressed or anything."

I lowered my voice and cupped my hand over the phone. "We think she was embezzling money from Simon's ministry." Officer Ferrell looked at me out of the corner of his eye. I turned my back to him.

"Why are you whispering?" Michael said.

"The police are here. I don't want to spread around the embezzlement thing."

"They'll get to it sooner or later anyway, unless they're incompetent. How did you happen to be over at her house?"

"Kacey and I were supposed to have a meeting with her to discuss—" I paused and looked over my shoulder at Ferrell. He was walking toward the corner of the house to meet the ambulance. "To discuss the embezzlement. We were going to give her a chance to explain. It appears she didn't want to have that conversation."

"How's Kacey taking it? She can't get a break, can she?"

"She seems to be doing okay. She and Elise weren't close."

"And how are you taking it? Everyone always assumes you can handle everything." He paused. "I worry about you sometimes."

Michael could drive me crazy, but every once in a while he said something that made me want to hug him. "I'm fine. Thanks for asking."

"I think I'll come by. Where does she live?"

I raised an eyebrow. A detour like that could throw his whole day out of kilter. "Lewisville. You don't need to come all the way out here, though. What about your schedule?"

"I can shuffle some things."

I heard him tapping keys on his computer, and I knew he was changing appointments as we spoke. "I'll text you the address," I said. "There's really no reason for you to do this."

The key tapping continued. "It's okay. I want to do it. Just a second . . . here. You don't need to text me. I already got her address from my directory. The map's coming up. I can be there in thirty to thirty-five minutes."

I couldn't resist. "You'd better make that thirty to thirty-seven minutes, in case there's traffic."

He didn't seem to get it. "I assume you'll be there a while," he said. "Have the cops talked to you yet?"

"Not much. I'm sure it's coming." The siren on the ambulance rose to a screech then abruptly died as the paramedics pulled into the driveway. "The paramedics are here, I've got to go."

"I'll be there soon." The call clicked off.

I stuck the phone back in my purse just as two med techs jumped out of the ambulance. One ran to the back of the truck and pulled out an oxygen canister and mask while the other approached us.

"Is she in the garage?"

The man with the oxygen trotted up behind him, and Sandra pointed at the canister. "You can put that away. She's been dead for hours—carbon monoxide."

"Suicide?"

"Looks like it."

The med tech took a deep breath, walked into the middle of the garage, and held up something that looked like a pocket calculator. He watched it for a few seconds, then walked to another part of the garage and did the same thing. After repeating it on the other side of the car, he exhaled and shoved the device into his pocket. "Air's okay."

Officer Ferrell, Sandra, and the other med tech walked into the garage, leaving Kacey and me standing in the driveway. I walked to the edge of the garage. "Do you need us for anything?"

Ferrell was reaching into the driver's side of the car near the floorboard. He pulled the lever to pop the trunk. The lid thunked. He stood up straight. "We'll have some questions. We'll get to you as quickly as we can." He walked around the door and lifted the trunk lid.

"It's okay. Take your time." I nudged Kacey and whispered, "Let's take a look in the house."

"Do you think we should?" She inclined her head toward the garage.

I knew the police wouldn't want us rummaging around in Elise's house, but there was nothing but boredom and a chilly wind out there in the driveway. Besides, I was curious to see the final surroundings of a woman who had somehow convinced herself to leap into an abyss that most of us scratch and kick and claw to avoid. So I looked Kacey in the eye and said four words that nearly always lead to trouble: "Nobody said we couldn't."

CHAPTER
FOUR

WITH ONE EYE ON the garage, I edged across the driveway toward the gate. I raised the latch and we side-stepped as quietly as possible into the backyard. Once I had eased the gate shut, we crossed the short expanse of lawn to the deck and the back door. When we reached the door, we tiptoed to minimize any crunching on the broken glass. Swinging the door open, we stepped into the house.

The family room was large and high-ceilinged, and stretched seamlessly into the kitchen on our right. A person standing at the kitchen sink could look directly across the family room to the stone mantle of the fireplace on our left. A blue-and-white checked couch faced the fireplace, with red upholstered wing chairs on each side. In the middle was an oak coffee table.

Looking around, it was easy to understand Elise's sparkling garage. She must have been a clean freak. The room smelled of pine needles, but with three weeks until Christmas, there was no tree in sight. Everything was in perfect order, with not so much as a magazine or newspaper lying around. The Spanish-tile floor was spotless, and even the cream-colored throw pillows sat fat, happy, and perfectly positioned on the couch. If she had had a more upbeat personality, she would have been a great match for Michael Harrison. They could have had a riot comparing electronic calendars over dry Chardonnay.

In the corner to the left of the fireplace, next to one of the huge windows that looked out over the deck, was a white pine secretary with a computer monitor and docking station for a laptop. In the center of the table lay what looked like a sheet of computer paper, with a pen resting on top of it.

I set my purse on the couch and walked over to the table. Part of the typed sheet of paper had been scored and torn off precisely along a straight edge. I bent over to read it.

By the time anyone reads this, I will be gone. I know that everyone will be disappointed in me. That's nothing unusual. People have looked down on me my whole life. Never mind, that's not the point. I didn't set out to do something bad. I know that in my heart.

Mom, I love you. Please don't agonize over this. I think you'll understand why I had to go this way. Please remember that all my life I've done things the way you taught me. Until now.

Kacey, despite what you will probably think, I loved your father very much and would never have done anything to hurt him. I want you to know that the bad part of what I did came right at the end, after his death.

The paper was torn after that. There was no signature.

I motioned to Kacey. "She left a note."

She put a hand on the corner of the desk and read while I checked the wastebasket on the floor for the missing half of the page. The trash can was as clean as the rest of the room. On the tile beneath the desk was a printer, but there was nothing in it but blank computer paper. I opened the single desk drawer, which contained only yellow Post-Its, paper clips, and a mechanical pencil, arranged precisely in a built-in tray.

Kacey lifted her hand from the desk. "It's so awful."

"I guess she couldn't handle the thought of jail time."

The door that led to the garage opened and closed. A moment later Sandra walked into the room.

She crossed her arms. "What are y'all doin' in here?"

Kacey rubbed her hands together. "It was cold out there."

"We didn't dress for being outside in the wind." I crossed my arms and shivered.

Sandra's expression softened. "I suppose you two got more than you expected on this trip to Lewisville. I'm sorry about your friend out there."

"Thanks," Kacey said. "We weren't really such good friends, though. I think that Elise didn't have a lot of good friends. That makes it even sadder."

Sandra stuck her hands in the back pockets of her dark blue pants. "Yeah. Look, you may as well make yourselves comfortable in here. Ed should be ready to talk to you in a few minutes. Let me just prepare you. He can be kind of intense, but he's an okay guy. Just go with the flow and you should be out of here in an hour or so."

"We found a suicide note," I said.

"Where is it?"

I pointed toward the desk.

She walked over to the note. "Is this where you found it?"

"We haven't touched it," I said. Kacey nodded.

"Who tore it off?"

"I don't know. That's the way it was when we found it."

"Did you look for the rest of it?" She bent over and looked in the wastebasket.

"It's not in there. We already checked."

When she finished reading the note, she shook her head. "Her poor mother. I'll be right back." She walked out to the garage.

I turned to Kacey and touched the lump in my pocket where I had put Elise's flash drive. "I found something in Elise's car."

Her eyebrows narrowed. "What do you mean you found something?"

I pulled the flash drive out of my pocket and held it up.

"Where'd you get that?"

"It was on Elise's key chain in her car. I thought it might have some computer files that could have something to do with the missing money."

"Isn't that tampering with evidence?"

I pictured Officer Ferrell pushing my head down as he shoved me into the backseat of the police SUV. I shook the image out of my head. "This isn't a crime scene, it's a suicide. Besides, her computer files belong to your father's ministry. You've got a right to them." I stuck the flash drive back in my pocket. "Maybe this will help us figure out what she did with the money so we can try to get it back."

I walked over to the couch, picked up my purse, and held it out to her. "Would you mind doing me a favor by taking this out to the car? It's got my gun in it, and I don't want that to cause a problem with the police. I want to look around for Elise's laptop before they come back in from the garage."

Her eyes widened. "You brought your gun?"

"People can do unexpected things when they're cornered. Did you expect what we found in the garage?"

She slung my purse over her shoulder and put her hands on her hips. "You missed my point. I just want to know why I didn't get to bring mine."

I tapped a finger on my cheek. "Well, let's see. You're not twenty-one, you don't have a permit to carry it, and you don't have a single reason in the world to be carrying it even if you did have a permit. Do you need to hear more?"

"I'm a better shot than half the guys at the range."

Actually she was a better shot than ninety percent of the guys at the range, but I wasn't about to let her redirect the argument. "That doesn't change the fact that you don't have a permit to carry—and don't get a big head about your shooting. You've still got a lot to learn. Now, do you mind? I'd like to get that gun out of here before they come back in."

Kacey headed for the front door. I went back to the desk in the corner. A docking station and printer, but no laptop—so how did she write the note? I looked all around the desk, and opened and closed the drawer again. Then I walked across the room, through the kitchen, and into a hallway that ran from the back of the house to the front. The first door was the master bedroom. I stepped onto the cream-colored carpet and looked around.

I felt as if I had walked through a mirror into Barbie's bedroom. To my right was a canopy bed with a pink duvet, a frilly white dust ruffle, and layers of lacey pillows. Beyond the bed was a bay window with a built-in pink cushioned love seat. The curtains were white lace. I assumed that the window looked out onto the lake, but the blinds were drawn. To the left of the door was a pink-and-white painted dresser with a mirrored back; against the opposite wall was a tallboy in the same colors. Beyond the tallboy was the door to the master bath.

On the floor next to the tallboy sat a pink nylon laptop case. I walked over and unzipped it. No computer. I looked in the closets and even opened the dresser drawers. Nothing. Glancing toward the bed again, I noticed a cell phone plugged into its charger on the end table. I went over, picked it up, and checked the screen. No messages. I made quick mental ledger entries of the pluses and minuses of taking the phone. The biggest plus was that it might have phone numbers and information that belonged to Simon's ministry. The biggest minus was that even though this was a suicide scene, I was still uneasy about the whole evidence thing.

I got over it by assuring myself that it was an employee's phone, probably issued by the ministry. We were entitled to it. Besides, it wasn't as if we were going to throw it away. If the police ever needed it, we'd still have it. In fact, the same was true of her flash drive. Legitimate or not, that line of reasoning made me feel better.

I looked over my shoulder at the bedroom door. Everything was quiet in the house. I unplugged the phone and stuck it in my jeans pocket with the flash drive. Just in case the police came in and looked around, I unplugged the charger from the wall and put it in the drawer of the end table. No sense inviting questions.

As I was about to leave the room I noticed a picture of Simon and Elise in a silver frame on the dresser. They wore jeans and Texas Rangers baseball caps. Behind them was Rangers' Ballpark in Arlington. For a man in his forties with a ridiculously busy schedule, Simon had always kept himself fit. His gray T-shirt strained against the lean muscles of his chest and arms. He looked as if he could have walked into the ballpark, slipped on a uniform, and trotted out to center field.

I picked up the frame and touched his face. If only he had listened, he would still be here. Kacey would have a father, and I would have . . . well, whatever he was to me, I would have that. I focused on Elise. She was beaming, thrilled just to be standing beside him.

She'd have given anything if he would have loved her. But he didn't, and what difference would it have made if he had? He was gone.

I recalled the evening that I met Simon. It was in Chicago at the Bulls' arena, and he had only recently received terrorist threats. That was the night he hired me; the night the kidnappers took Kacey. I tried to picture him standing there in his corduroys and denim shirt, so casual, so unassuming, yet such a great man. That I had loved him, I was certain. The question was in what way.

My father used to tell me that the most dangerous places were the ones where he felt most comfortable. Those were the places where he relaxed and lost track of what was happening around him. It doesn't make sense, I know, that I could have felt comfortable standing there in Elise's bedroom. After all, not a hundred feet away, she was lying dead in a car that was being swarmed by police and medical technicians. I was in a comfortable place, though—a quiet place in my mind. I was with Simon in Chicago, the place I most wanted to be.

I suppose that's why I was so startled when a man's hand clamped hard onto my shoulder.

Instinctively, I reached up, grabbed the hand, and yanked it down hard over my shoulder. I pivoted on my left foot, bent at the waist, swung my right foot up, and lifted with my back. It was a leverage move, and it worked perfectly. In less than a second I was standing over my attacker, who was on his back on the carpet, red faced and puffing.

It was Officer Ferrell.

CHAPTER
FIVE

FERRELL SHOOK HIS HEAD. "What in the—"

I let go of his hand. He reached for his holster and unsnapped it.

I took a step back. "Whoa, wait a minute. I'm sorry. That was reflex. Let me help you up." I held out a hand.

He rolled onto one knee and swatted my arm away. Reaching for the edge of the dresser, he pulled himself to his feet. Before I could say anything else, he was spinning me around. "Hands against the wall!"

I tried to turn to face him. "Look, I'm really sorry. I didn't know it was you."

He jerked my arm hard and slapped my hand against the wall. "Shut up! Hands on the wall!"

I leaned forward and extended my arms. He kicked my legs apart, so I was standing spread-eagle, then he pulled one of my wrists back to cuff me. He was grabbing my other wrist when Kacey and Sandra walked into the room through the door just to our left. Behind them, his tie loosened and the sleeves of his button-down shirt rolled up over his thickly muscled forearms, walked Michael Harrison. His charcoal suit coat was slung over one shoulder.

Ferrell looked at Michael and dropped one of my arms.

Michael pushed his black-rimmed glasses up on his nose. His face brightened. "Excuse us. Are we interrupting something?"

I twisted my neck toward him and scowled.

Michael lost the smile. "What is going on here?" His voice was a full octave lower than when he thought he was being funny.

Ferrell grabbed for my wrist again, but missed, which made him even angrier. "She attacked me! Tossed me on my back!"

I rested my forehead against the wall and felt like banging it. "I did not attack you. You grabbed me from behind. Besides, I already apologized."

I tilted my head and looked up at Michael. His eyebrows narrowed to a point. A vein bulged in the side of his neck. I'd seen that look before. Now I was the one who smiled. I lowered my head and waited.

Michael took a step toward Ferrell. "Get your hands off her." His voice was clear and hard, and if I hadn't known him so well, I'd have been terrified. He pulled his coat off his shoulder, reached inside it, and pulled out his badge. He held it up toward Ferrell.

Ferrell squeezed my wrist. No one moved. I wondered how long it would take Ferrell to figure out that Michael was not a person to be trifled with—and I wondered how long Michael would give him to do his figuring. I was enjoying the moment immensely.

Ferrell's feet shuffled on the carpet behind me. He loosened his grip on my wrist, but still didn't let go. "Who are you?" Ferrell's voice wobbled, and I knew that our little encounter was just about over.

Michael took another step forward and held the badge closer to Ferrell's face. "Michael Harrison, Agent in Charge of the Dallas FBI. I'm going to say this one more time. You need to let the lady go."

Ferrell's grip on my wrist loosened even more. "I'm a Lewisville police officer," he said, the last few syllables trailing off in retreat.

"I don't care if you're Elliott frickin' Ness." Michael reached back into his inside jacket pocket to put his badge away. As he moved his arm, his bicep flexed. The cotton of his shirt stretched tight.

I was impressed, and apparently Ferrell was, also. He dropped my arm and stepped back, putting more distance between him and Michael. Nevertheless, he attempted a verbal rally. "The FBI doesn't have jurisdiction here. This is local. It's just a suicide."

Uh-oh. I turned my head and raised an eyebrow at Michael.

He crossed his arms. "Yes, but I'm, uh . . ." He looked down at me. I pulled my hand up to where my body blocked it from Ferrell's view. Then I rubbed my fingers and thumb together rapidly. Michael's eyes lit up. "I'm following a money trail. Investigating the movement of illegally acquired funds—across state lines, that is. You know—in interstate commerce. That makes it a federal offense—moving funds in interstate commerce." He cleared his throat.

I was surprised he didn't finish the sentence by holding a finger in the air and saying, "Yeah, that's it!" Michael's mouth turned up, and he gave a nearly imperceptible shrug, but he didn't look at me.

Ferrell scratched his head. "What funds? What are you talking about?"

Michael quickly found his rhythm. "That's still confidential at this point, but Ms. Pasbury has been assisting me with the investigation. I need to talk to her, and that's going to be hard for me to do with her spread-eagled against the wall like that." He paused. "Besides, she's modest. I know that it must offend her sensibilities."

I rolled my eyes.

Apparently Sandra determined that it was time to bail her partner out. She walked over and touched my arm. "You can turn around, Ms.—what did you say your name was again?"

"Pasbury. Taylor Pasbury." I straightened up and brushed at the front of my blouse. I turned around to face Officer Ferrell. "Look, I really am sorry. I was trained in the Secret Service. It was just an instinctive reaction."

Kacey took a step forward. "An awful lot has happened to her during the past year."

My mouth practically dropped open. A lot has happened to me? "Oh, Kace, you're such a sweetheart." I walked over to her and gave her a hug. Within a few moments I was wiping a tear with the back of my hand.

Sandra shook her head. "Are you crying?"

I shrugged. "I do that a lot. It doesn't take much."

In unison, Michael and Kacey said, "It's true, she does."

Ferrell mumbled something under his breath, and I caught the last couple of words: ". . . crazy chick."

Sandra stepped in front of him. "I think we can all just forget about this and get back to business. We have a suicide in the garage out there."

Ferrell shook his head. "Forget about it? I'm not—"

She looked him in the eye. "Ed, we're forgetting about it."

Ferrell mumbled again and stuck the plastic cuff band back in his pocket.

"Can we go take a look at that suicide note, now?" Sandra said.

Michael stepped out of the way and we all filed past him. When I got next to him, he whispered, "You tossed him on the floor?"

I turned a palm up and shrugged. As I moved past him into the hallway, I heard him chuckle.

CHAPTER
SIX

BACK IN THE FAMILY room I recalled the reason I had been in the bedroom in the first place: the missing laptop. There was one obvious place I hadn't been able to look. "Did either of you find a laptop in Elise's car?"

Sandra looked at Ferrell, who shook his head.

"Did you look in the trunk?" I said.

"Lady, we scoured every inch of that car," he said. "Even the engine compartment."

Sandra frowned at him. "Her name is Ms. Pasbury, not Lady."

Ferrell acted as if he hadn't heard. He walked over to the desk in the corner, picked up Elise's note, and read it. Then he motioned to us. "Have a seat."

Kacey and I sat on the couch. Michael stood behind us, his hands braced on the back of the couch.

Ferrell leaned against the fireplace, the torn note in his hand. "Did you know Ms. Hovden well?"

"She managed Simon Mason World Ministries," I said. "Kacey's known her for years. I've known her for less than a year."

He pointed at me. "That's how I recognized you. You were Simon Mason's security guard. I remember you from television."

I gave him as much of a smile as I could muster, considering that a few minutes earlier he had thrown me against a wall.

"You were the one who tried to rescue him over in Lebanon. Boy, I'd like to hear that story." He seemed already to have forgotten our little dance in the bedroom.

I touched Kacey's leg. "This is Simon Mason's daughter, Kacey."

He straightened his back. "You were the one who was kidnapped?"

Kacey nodded.

"You're a brave kid. I'm sorry about your father. He was a good man. My wife and I used to watch him on TV whenever we played hooky from church on Sunday morning. He seemed like a regular guy."

Kacey's face reddened. She looked down and rubbed her hands on the legs of her jeans. By the time she looked up and spoke, her voice was steady, polite, and uncharacteristically formal. "Thank you. My father *was* a regular guy. I miss him very much."

No one spoke for a few moments. Ferrell cleared his throat. "Okay, uh, let's get back to Ms. Hovden, then. Had she been depressed?"

"Not that I know of," Kacey said. I could see her face relax as the conversation moved to another subject.

I held up a hand. "Before you get too far along, I think we know why Elise did this."

He seemed irritated that I was cutting short his interrogation. "Okay, why?"

"Elise was responsible for winding up the business affairs of Simon Mason Ministries after Simon's murder. The auditors found that nearly half a million dollars was missing. It looks as if she was embezzling money. Two nights ago I called Elise and told her what the auditors had found. We agreed to meet here this morning at eight."

He rubbed his jaw. "So, she got caught with her hand in the collection plate, and she knew it."

"It looks that way."

Sandra, who had been standing to the side with her hands in her pockets, stepped forward and nodded toward the note in Ferrell's hand. "Okay, so the note she left makes sense. I have to ask this again, though. Did either of you tear the bottom off of it?" She watched us intently.

Kacey sat up straight. "Of course not. We didn't even touch the note. Why would we do that?"

"Hold on, Ms. Mason," Sandra said. "Nobody is accusing you of anything. I'm just trying to figure out what happened. The fact is that you two found the note, and part of the paper is obviously missing. Do you know where the bottom half of the sheet is?"

"We have no idea," I said. "We never even picked it up off the desk, and neither did you. Officer Ferrell was the first person who touched it."

Sandra looked at Ferrell, whose neck reddened. He shot me a sideways look, and I knew our roller-coaster relationship was back on the down track.

"So what?" he said. "It's not like this is a murder scene. No one's going to be dusting for prints or anything."

I was sure happy to hear him confirm that.

He walked over and placed the note back on the desktop, then leaned back on the desk's edge. "I'd say your church has got itself a scandal brewing, Ms. Mason. I guess that's your business, though, not the Lewisville Police Department's."

Kacey stood. "If our auditors can't find the money, we'll be the first to issue a press release. The financial affairs of Dad's ministry have always been transparent, and that's not going to change now. Do you need us for anything else?"

Behind us, Michael muttered, "Atta girl."

Sandra smiled. "I guess not."

Ferrell straightened up. "But I'd like to—"

"That will be all, Ms. Mason," Sandra said. "You two are free to go." She turned her back on Ferrell. "We'll call you if we need any more information. By the way, did Ms. Hovden have any relatives in the area? She mentioned her mother in the note. Someone will need to notify her or some other next of kin."

"I think her mom lives in the Fort Worth area," Kacey said.

Sandra took her notepad and pen out of her shirt pocket. "Do you know how to contact her?"

"I can call the ministry's offices. They probably have her listed on personnel records as a contact person." Kacey pulled her phone out of her pocket. Within a few minutes she had a telephone number. She clicked off the phone. "Who makes that sort of call to her mother under these circumstances?"

"That's up to you. You can call now, or we can take the body to the hospital morgue and they'll call her. If you call now, she might want to make arrangements for having the body taken straight to a funeral home. I doubt if there will be an autopsy unless the mother requests it. It's not required in this country."

I turned toward Kacey. "Have you ever met her mom?"

"A couple of times at the church. She was very proud of Elise. I remember that. This will kill her."

"It's up to you, Kace. Maybe you should just let the morgue call."

She tilted her head back and closed her eyes. "Elise worked for Dad. Her mother should hear this from me rather than from a complete stranger." She turned and walked toward the back door.

I couldn't have been prouder. "Do you want me to come out with you?"

"No, I'll handle it." She moved around the broken glass, opened the door, and stepped out onto the back deck.

Through the windows we could see her pacing for a couple of minutes, her lips moving as if she were rehearsing, before she raised the phone and tapped in the number.

While Kacey was outside, I revisited the laptop issue with Officer Ferrell. "You said you checked the trunk of Elise's car. Did you look under the seats? Maybe she had her laptop on the floor and it slid under somehow."

Ferrell sighed. "I told you before, there wasn't any laptop. We went over the interior, the trunk, everything. Why is her laptop so important to you?"

I leaned forward with my hands on my knees. "Do you think it's odd that we found a computer-generated note, but no computer?"

He shrugged. "Not really. She must have printed the note somewhere else—at the office or anywhere, for that matter."

As we spoke, Michael walked around the couch and over to the desk. He leaned over to read the note.

When he finished reading, he rubbed his ear between his thumb and forefinger and looked out the picture window. I wondered whether he was thinking the same thing I was.

It struck me as odd that Elise would print a suicide note at the office and then bring it home to kill herself. On the other hand, she had a logical motive to kill herself, and there was no sign at all that anyone else was involved. Everything except the note made perfect sense. I shook my head. I needed to stop trying to create drama where there was none.

"I was curious about the laptop because it belonged to Simon Mason Ministries, and it could have ministry records on it," I said. "We'd like to recover it if we can."

Sandra scribbled in her notepad. "I'm making a note. We'll let you know if it turns up."

Kacey came back into the house chewing her lip. "Well, that was pretty awful." She turned to Ferrell. "Do you know where they're taking her body?"

"Lewisville Memorial, I assume. She should be at the hospital within a half hour or so."

"I'll call her mother back in a few minutes and tell her. She's pretty confused. It's probably best if they do just take Elise to the hospital morgue for now."

"You know," Ferrell said, "before you leave, I want you to tell me the whole story one more time—about how you found her. We need to be sure we've got this straight." He pointed toward Sandra's notepad. "Would you take some notes, Sandra?"

Sandra frowned. Her eyes said, *Take your own notes*, but she said nothing.

Ferrell pointed to the glass on the floor by the back door. "Let's start with that. Tell me one more time how the door got busted."

Kacey recounted how she had heard the car engine running and took them through the entire story. Meanwhile, my eyes focused on the writing table in the corner. A computer-generated suicide note with the bottom torn off, and no computer anywhere to be found. It all seemed so—

"Ms. Pasbury, how did you break the glass without cutting your hand?"

I shook my head. "The door? Oh, I wrapped my jacket around my hand. I don't want to give you the wrong impression, but I've popped windows before."

Over by the writing desk, Michael, who was still looking out the window, coughed into his hand.

Ferrell raised an eyebrow.

"I run a private security company," I said, projecting my voice toward Michael.

From that point Ferrell directed his questioning toward me. I kept my answers short, because I wanted to get out of there. I needed time to think.

Elise was dead, and despite my rocky relationship with her, it was a sad thing. She had always struck me as the type who never quite fit in; the one who never got called on the phone to go out with the girls. I wished I had made more of an effort, but I suppose that was what everyone said in this type of situation.

Despite my unease over the laptop, the rational side of my brain knew that her suicide made perfect sense. Still, as Ferrell continued to beat me down with a monotonous string of questions, something in my stomach told me there was more to this story than what we had found on Elise's writing table.

CHAPTER
SEVEN

KACEY AND I MET Elise's mother at the hospital at one o'clock that afternoon. In the meantime Michael went back to his office and told me to call him if I needed anything. We were at the hospital until 3:30, and we did our best to help Elise's mom get started on the arrangements for the funeral. During the drive back, Kacey and I made an effort to reminisce about our times with Elise but without a great deal of success.

We wanted to show her respect. In fact, we wanted to be heartbroken. If nothing else, it would have made us feel better about ourselves. Elise, though, was the type of person who made others want to duck and run. Each time Kacey and I tried to conjure a wistful memory of her, our thoughts scattered in the opposite direction.

From a practical standpoint, since Elise had been in charge of winding up the affairs of Simon's ministry, her death placed a new burden on Kacey. She would have to report about the embezzlement to the ministry's board. The board members had historically served in a purely advisory capacity, because Simon and Elise ran everything. Now that both of the top executives were gone, the board would have no choice but to play a bigger role.

We agreed that it would be best to enlist Brandon Henckel, the ministry's former accountant, who had discovered the missing money in the first place, to help wind up the ministry's affairs. He had the training and the knowledge. Though a brilliant guy, Brandon had more neuroses than Bart Simpson. He had recently given up accounting and was now leading what he euphemistically liked to call "a less structured life." He was essentially a full-time computer gamer and part-time inquisitive hacker.

Like me, he was a recovering alcoholic and served as my recovery partner in the church's rehabilitation program. By 5:30, Kacey and I had called him and filled him in on Elise's death. We then made the necessary calls to inform key employees.

When we finished the calls, we realized that we

hadn't eaten since breakfast. We made a quick run to the wing shop around the corner for some takeout. Once back, we finally had a chance to sit down and kick off our shoes. I had just turned on the television when the doorbell rang.

Kacey sighed and licked her fingers. "I'll get it." She placed a half-eaten wing on her plate.

"If it looks like a reporter, either shoot him or don't answer it."

She gave me a thumbs-up and headed for the front door. As I watched her walk out of the room, I thought of how many times her father had given me the same thumbs-up, and I wondered for the thousandth time how a daughter could be any more like her father than Kacey was like Simon.

I heard the front door open and close, and then muffled voices. A few moments later I was gnawing the last few bits of meat from a chicken bone when Kacey came back into the room. "It's for you."

I set my plate on the coffee table and wiped my hands on a paper napkin. "Who is it?"

She shrugged. "Some lady. She said you would be happy to see her."

"Are you sure it's not a reporter?"

"She didn't look like a reporter to me."

Rather than walk down the hallway to get to the door, I circled through the dining room, in the hope that I could get a glimpse of a car through the front window. I stopped by the dining room table and squinted out into the fading sunlight. In front of the house was a blazing red Cadillac coupe. I didn't recognize it, but whoever owned it sure had a cool car.

I turned the corner into the foyer, where a tall, slender woman with unnaturally black hair stood with the back of her cashmere overcoat toward me. She had picked up a lamp from the credenza near the front door and was holding it upside down, studying the base, as if searching for a price tag. Even from ten feet away, I picked up her perfume, which could best be described as flowering talc.

I cleared my throat.

She set the vase down and turned to me. "I was just admiring your lovely house. My, you've done well for yourself, haven't you?" She smiled, revealing off-white teeth that were the slightest bit crooked in front. She appeared to be about fifty years old. Her heavy eye shadow and thick blush gave her a creepy Bette Davis look, but as I studied her face I noted her strong jaw and slender nose. With an hour or so of makeup instruction, she could be strikingly pretty.

Her gray eyes met mine for only the briefest instant before flitting away to continue their survey of the house's furniture and fixtures. "You don't have a clue who I am, do you, honey?" she said.

"No, I don't."

She reached in the pocket of her coat and began to pull something out. Instinctively I took a step sideways. It's crazy, I know, but Dad had drilled into me that when I wasn't sure what was happening, I should always move—harder to hit that way. She followed me with her eyes as she pulled from her pocket a shiny digital camera. She held up the camera and peered into it. "Honey, hold still, I want to make sure I get this one."

Just before she pressed the button, she said, "Smile, baby, I'm your mother!"

CHAPTER
EIGHT

THERE IS NO WAY to plan for the reappearance of a mother after twenty years—especially a mother who bolted without even saying good-bye. I had struggled since I was nine to understand why she left and how she could have forgotten us so completely. No calls, no letters, no nothing.

The saga had moved from sad to surreal, though, when I was twenty-nine and Simon Mason told me he had known my mother years before he and I met. "Known her" in the biblical sense, that is. Although I wasn't aware of it at the time, that was why he had hired me—as opposed to the hundred other security professionals who would have leaped at the chance to take charge of security for a religious leader as well known as the pope.

As she clicked away at me with her digital camera, I had no idea what to say or how to feel. I had mentally pictured this reunion a thousand times and in a variety of settings. No matter where or how we came together in these fantasies, one thing was consistent: She always threw her arms around me, cried, and asked me to forgive her, begged me to let her be my mother again.

Now it was happening, right here in the foyer of Simon's house, but she wasn't holding me, or crying, or demonstrating any obvious interest at all in being my mother again. Instead, she was checking the price tags on Simon's pottery and flashing away with a camera, like a tourist whose bus had just stopped in front of a decorative fountain.

I waved at the black spots that flickered in my eyes. Before I could do anything else, she dropped the camera into her purse. "I just had to get a picture of your reaction the first time you saw me!" She held her arms out. "C'mon now and give your mother a hug."

After a twenty-year absence, she was asking me to run to her. That struck me as something a real mother would never have done—certainly not the mother of my fantasies. Blood rushed into my neck and cheeks, and something else rushed up behind my eyes. I was not going to allow it to happen. I was not going to cry, not here in front of her. Not until she earned it.

My body moved forward and hugged her, but felt nothing warm or caring—or motherly—about her touch. It was a social hug, or a business hug, but not a mother's hug. It was over in an instant. My shoulders sagged, but I forced them back and stood up tall.

She loosened her grip. "I was so excited to see you that I took two wrong turns on the way over here. Had to stop at a Seven-Eleven for directions."

My effort to keep my lip from trembling seemed to trip a switch that transferred the unwanted motion to my knees. My legs wobbled. I felt for the stair rail behind me and sat on the second step.

"Is there something wrong, baby?" Her eyes fixed on me for the briefest instant, then moved up and around to the stairway, then to the living room to her left, and finally to the dining room to her right. She was surrounded by unfamiliar architecture, unfamiliar furniture, and an unfamiliar daughter, and her glance made it clear that she had prioritized her interests in that order.

Just then, Kacey came around the corner, a dribble of barbecue sauce clinging to the corner of her mouth. "What's the ruckus? Did you win the publishers' sweepstakes?"

I realized my hands were clenched. I relaxed my fingers and pointed. "Kacey, meet my mother."

Kacey did a double take.

"It's true."

Kacey took a step forward and held out her hand. "It's nice to meet you, Ms. . . ." She looked at me again.

"You'll have to ask her. I don't even know her name."

My mother took Kacey's hand in both of hers and shook vigorously. "Hillary Venable. You can call me Hil. By the way, honey, you've got something on your mouth." She pulled a wadded tissue out of her coat pocket and reached for Kacey's mouth. Kacey took a quick step back and wiped her mouth with her hand.

My mother shrugged and wiped her nose with the tissue. Kacey's eyes followed it all the way back into the pocket, and I knew she was wondering if it had been used before.

"Barbecue?" my mother said. "I'm the worst with that. Always end up with it all over me."

"We had wings for dinner." Kacey let her arms fall to her sides. They stood looking at each other.

I usually can't bear an awkward silence, but I was willing to ride this one out. I had plenty to occupy my mind.

My mother put both hands in her pockets. "So, are you two a couple?"

Kacey laughed out loud. "A couple of what?"

"It's all right, honey. Live and let live, I always say."

"Kacey is Simon Mason's daughter. I've been living here for the past few months, since her father was killed."

Kacey turned to look at me as I spoke. Her inattention cost her. My mother stepped forward and wrapped her arms around Kacey's neck. "Oh, you poor dear. I read all about your father and you. It was awful."

Kacey's eyes widened, and she looked at me as if to say, *She's your mother, aren't you going to get her off of me?*

"Simon was a great man," I said. "And his daughter is pretty great, too."

When my mother finally released her grip, Kacey backed away slowly, like a hiker who has stumbled onto a bear in the woods. She spoke rapidly. "Well, I've got to go study—test tomorrow. I'm sure you two have a lot to catch up on. It was nice to meet you, Ms. Venable."

"Call me Hil."

"Yes. It was nice to meet you, Hil."

"The pleasure was all mine. You're a real sweetheart." Before my mother finished the sentence, she had already moved her eyes away from Kacey and was looking at the dining room chandelier.

As Kacey walked out of the room, her shoulders shook, and I knew she was stifling a laugh. We would have a lot to talk about before bedtime.

I put my hand on the step beneath me and pushed to my feet. "After all these years I don't know what to say."

"Why, you don't have to say anything. I've just got so much to tell you about what I've been doing."

I shook my head. "What *you've* been doing? How about what I've been doing? Since I was nine, remember?"

She took off her overcoat and draped it over her arm. "Of course, I want to hear all about that, too. Is there somewhere I can hang my coat? You keep it warm in here, don't you?"

I took her coat and hung it in the entryway closet. "By the way, how did you find me?" I said.

"You were the one who found me. Your investigator friend called and told me you were looking for me. I asked him where you lived and decided to come see you."

"Where do you live?"

"Southlake."

"Southlake, Texas? You mean that you've been living twenty miles from me all this time?"

She waved a hand in the air. "Don't be silly. I just moved to Southlake about a year ago. I married a professor at the University of Texas at Arlington." She winked. "I hooked myself a good one this time, honey. He's a chemical engineering genius and a real big shot. I can't wait for you to meet him."

"You're married?"

"Yes, and why I keep doing that, I don't know. There just aren't many men as good as your father,

God rest his soul. Believe me, I've found that out the hard way."

"So, you knew Dad was dead?"

"How could I not? It was all over the news. What a terrible thing. You were a real hero, though, shooting those men who killed your father. I was proud of you."

"Those men tried to rape me, you know. Did you ever think it might be a good idea to come to the funeral, or to call me up and see how I was doing?"

She pulled a lipstick out of her purse. "My life was such a mess at the time. I wouldn't have been any help to you. I had my hands full just taking care of myself."

"Taking care of yourself? I was seventeen—and you were taking care of yourself?"

"I was going through a divorce, and everything was falling apart." I watched her closely, unable to believe that she would actually apply lipstick while we were talking about this. She lifted the lipstick, but when our eyes met, her hand stopped halfway to her mouth. She lowered it again and dropped the lipstick back into her purse.

"How did you marry someone else when you were still married to Dad? He never told me you two had divorced."

"Let's not dwell on that. It's water under the bridge." She dug in her purse again and pulled out a pack of Salems.

"You can't smoke in here."

"Oh, you're part of that crowd."

My hands clenched again. "I'm not part of any crowd. This is not my house, and I don't think you should smoke in it."

She nodded toward the hallway that led to the back of the house. "Have you got a back porch? How about we go sit outside for a bit?"

"It's forty-five degrees outside."

"Gracious, are you that thin-blooded? Why, up north they would consider this a balmy day."

"How do you know what they would think up north?"

"I lived in Chicago for three years with my second husband."

"What number are you on now?"

"Stanley is number three."

I shook my head. "Let me get your coat."

"I don't need it. I've got this sweater. That should be fine." She smoothed the front of her white turtleneck.

"Well, I'm wearing a coat." I opened the closet and pulled out my ski jacket. Then I led her down the hallway, through the family room, and out the back door.

The Masons' porch was Southern all the way: white wood floorboards, white rail, and white rocking chairs. We sat side by side in the rockers and looked out over the rectangular pool toward the stand of cedar elms by the back fence. She pulled a silver-plated lighter out of her purse and lit her cigarette. She threw her head back and inhaled. Then she puffed smoke out of her mouth in three short bursts. "Whew, I needed that. This is so stressful for me."

I leaned forward with my elbows on my knees. "Did it occur to you that I've had some stress, too?"

"Why, of course you have, honey. Who hasn't? But until you've had a marriage go south on you, you don't know what stress is, believe me." She stuck the cigarette back in her mouth.

The sky had turned gray since the morning, and the wind had picked up. It cut across the porch and from time to time gusted enough to puff my hair off the top of my shoulders and set it back down again. I pulled the collar of my coat tight. "Why did you come here?"

She flicked the ash off her cigarette. I watched it fall to the wood floor and wondered whether it would leave a burn mark.

"You were looking for me, remember?" She reached over and gave my arm a squeeze. "I'm glad you found me, though. Now we can get to know each other again."

"So, is that it? You just walk through my door one day and it's as if you never walked out on Dad and me? You think we can just pick up as if nothing happened?"

She flicked another ash. "Wait a minute. Don't think I'm going to let you hold that against me. I was sick. At one point I was living in the streets in downtown Houston. I ate out of a few garbage cans, too." She looked at me for an instant but turned away. "Does that make you proud of your mother?"

I leaned back in my rocker. "What happened?"

"Back then, even the street people said I was crazy; and, believe me, when that crowd's calling you crazy, you've got a problem." She laughed, but her eyes weren't smiling. She studied the back of her hand. "The Lord took care of me, even when I was in hell. He got me some help. Some medication, that's all. It doesn't seem like much of a miracle, but it was."

This was my first glimpse of my mother's incongruous relationship with God. I blew right past it, and who could blame me? She had run out on her family, was on her third husband, and still had not shown a lick of interest in me, her only daughter. Not exactly the type of person I would turn to for theological advice, even if I were looking for it. But faith and theology are two different things. I understand that now. My mother had figured out something worth knowing, something practical that a troubled life had taught her. Dad had hinted at it the night he died, but I didn't understand him then, and I didn't care about her ramblings as we sat there on the back porch. I just wanted her to be a real mom.

"How long ago was it that you got treatment?"

I thought I had spotted a flaw in her version of events, and I was wasting no time drilling down on it.

"About a year after I left your father."

"It wasn't just Dad. You left me, too, you know."

"I know, and, believe me, I still feel terrible about it." She took a drag from her cigarette and tilted her head back.

I waited for her to exhale, but she just sat there, holding the smoke in her lungs for what seemed like a full minute. Finally she exhaled through her nose. I exhaled, too, and realized I'd been holding my breath along with her.

"So, you've been on your medication for, what, nineteen years? You didn't miss Dad and me enough to come back once your meds kicked in?" I folded my arms.

She cleared her throat. "Well, I wasn't all the way better back then. It was just recently that I really got things straightened out."

I wasn't about to let her off the hook. "A few minutes ago you said you got your medicine within the first year after you left."

She waved a hand in the air. "Honestly, I'm not really sure how much good the medicine even does." She took a last drag, held the butt up, and examined the ring of lipstick on the filter. "What about you, though, honey? We've been spending all this time talking about me."

She hadn't answered my question, and I didn't want to let it go. For the first time, though, she was asking about me, even if it was just because she wanted to change the subject. There would be other chances to get my answers. I put a foot up on the porch rail. "I went to Texas A&M, graduated in three years with honors, took a job with the Dallas Police, then got lucky and got a job with the Secret Service in Washington. Protecting VIPs, that sort of thing."

"That sounds interesting. You know, the Secret Service was founded in 1865 to battle counterfeiting."

I gave her a sideways glance. "As a matter of fact, that's right. How did you know?"

"Oh, I read things. They sort of stick in my mind; I don't know why. I've got loads of useless information floating around up here." She tapped her head with her finger.

I rocked my chair and looked at a charcoal-colored cloud that the wind was steering over the backyard. The weather was darkening quickly. "Anyway, when I got out of the Secret Service, I started my own security business here in Dallas. That's how I began working for Simon."

She flicked the cigarette butt over the porch rail into a shrub, and it occurred to me that I should have given her something she could use as an ash tray. Now I could only hope that she wouldn't catch the landscaping on fire.

"You know, I dated a security guard one time in New Mexico," she said. "He was the surliest man I think I've ever met. He gave me a black and blue eye, right here." She pointed just beneath her right eye.

"You mean he hit you?"

"With a ladle. We were making tortilla soup. I prefer the tortilla soup in Texas to the New Mexico style. More substance to it."

I was detecting an attention deficit issue. I didn't have a clue how to respond to her tortilla soup analysis, so I picked up where I'd left off. "Simon called me and said the FBI had warned him about some terrorist threats. He asked me to take over his security operations."

"I heard. Who hasn't heard? Why, Taylor, you're famous. You and that Simon Mason fellow."

"Would you please stop it? I know about you and Simon. He told me just before he left for Beirut that he'd had an affair with you. He told me about your son, too."

She pulled the pack of Salems back out of her purse. "He did, huh?" She tapped the pack against the back of her hand until a cigarette slid out. "He was nobody then, just an assembly line worker in an auto plant." She lit the cigarette and puffed. "He wasn't even a preacher yet. Did he tell you that he knocked me up and then dumped me flat?"

"Not in exactly those terms. He said his wife had had an affair, and he was looking to get even."

"Oh, he said that, did he?" Color rose in her cheeks. I wished I hadn't said it.

"He said you were brilliant and troubled," I continued. "He didn't know if the affair meant anything ʻo you or not."

"Brilliant and troubled; resilient and muddled," she muttered.

"What did you say?"

"Nothing. Sometimes I make rhymes. Silly habit."

"Why did you abandon Chase? He's your son."

"How did you know his name?"

"I've met him. So has Kacey. We went to see him in Houston after Simon died. So, why did you abandon him?"

"Do you badger Simon about why he abandoned him? Chase is Simon's son, too, you know. That's how it works."

I studied her face for a hint as to why she would say something so bizarre. Her expression didn't change. "Simon's dead, remember? I can't badger him about anything."

She brushed at a hair that the wind had blown over her face. She seemed irritated to be reminded that Simon was no longer subject to interrogation the way she was. "Nevertheless, you'd think I'm the only person ever to do anything wrong," she said. "Everyone is always so high and mighty with me." She stood up, turned around, and leaned back with her hands braced behind her on the porch rail. The glowing tip of her cigarette was a fraction of an inch from the rail. I opened my mouth to tell her to be careful, but she lifted her hand and took a drag before I could say anything. Then, although the cigarette was only half gone, she flicked it into the same shrub as before. I didn't know what was making me more nervous, the conversation or the fire risk.

"Chase has been adopted," I said. "Did you know that? He lives in Katy, a suburb of Houston. His parents are nice people, an older couple."

"They're not his parents."

"Yes, they are his parents. Didn't you hear me? They adopted him. And as far as he's concerned they're the only parents he's ever known, or at least can remember. What do you expect?"

"You don't understand. I couldn't keep him. It was impossible. If you knew how bad I was back then—" She straightened her back. "I've got to go."

I held up a hand. "Wait. I'm sure you had your reasons for letting Chase go. I didn't mean to sound so critical." Actually, I wasn't so sure at all, but there was another subject I had to discuss with her before she left. "There's something else you need to know about Simon. Someone was trying to blackmail him. He told me about it before he left for Beirut." I watched her eyes. No noticeable reaction.

She bent over to pick up her purse from beside the rocker. "Why are you telling me that? I was nothing to Simon, remember?"

"He never said you were nothing to him—and I'm telling you because he was being blackmailed about Chase. They told Simon that if he didn't pay them, they would go public with the information that he had an illegitimate son. It could have ruined him." I continued to watch her face. Still no reaction. "I wondered if you knew anything about it."

"Oh, please, dear, if I wanted my pound of flesh from Simon, I would have gotten it years ago."

"I didn't say you were involved. I just wondered if you knew anything."

"Well, I don't." She walked toward the back door.

"So this is it? Will it be another twenty years before I see you again?"

"I certainly hope not," she said. "In fact, I would like for you to come over for brunch a week from Sunday morning. You can meet Stan the man."

I cocked my head.

"I told you I like to make little rhymes."

"Is Stan the man husband number three?"

"Yes. And I don't like your judgmental tone. You apparently haven't hooked even one husband yet."

I got up out of the rocker. "Judgmental tone? All I asked was—"

"How about it? Say, 9:30?" She pulled a pen out of her purse. "I can write down some directions for you."

By that time the swings in the conversation were making my brain hurt. I was thankful for a timeout. To be honest, though, I was also thankful to know that I would be seeing her again. "I'll be there. Just give me the address. I'll get the directions off the Internet."

She put her hand on the back doorknob, then stopped. She turned toward me. For the first time that day, her voice softened. "Taylor, I know I haven't been much of a mother. In fact, I haven't been any mother at all, but that doesn't mean I haven't loved you." She took a step forward and hugged me.

At first I just stood there, my arms at my sides. She held me for quite a while, though, and eventually I put my arms around her, too. By the time she let go, I was squeezing her far tighter than she was holding me, and she was the one who seemed to want to get away.

When she turned to walk into the house, I wiped my eye with the sleeve of my ski jacket and hoped she hadn't seen.

CHAPTER
NINE

THE NEXT MORNING, FRIDAY, I was jogging on the treadmill at my fitness club when my phone rang. I toweled the sweat from my face and pushed the button on my earpiece. "Hello."

"Taylor Pasbury?" It was a woman's voice.

"Yes?"

"This is Katie Parst. I'm a reporter for the *Morning News*."

I hit the down-speed button on the treadmill and slowed to a walk. "What now?" It seemed that we'd lived the entire past year with the press at our heels.

"Is this a bad time? You sound breathless."

"The whole point is to be breathless. I'm on a treadmill." I had never figured out how Simon could be so patient with these people.

"I'm sorry to interrupt your workout. I'm calling because I've obtained information that a substantial amount of money is missing from Simon Mason World Ministries. I was hoping we could talk for a few minutes."

I stopped the treadmill and hopped off. "I'm not part of the management of the ministries. I was just Simon's security chief." I picked up my phone out of the cup holder, slung my towel over my shoulder, and walked to the exercise mats in the corner.

"I know, but other than his daughter and Elise Hovden, I understand that you were the person closest to him during the last few months of his life. I've been doing a series of reports on an extortion ring that I think is run by a crime organization in the Dallas area. I thought you might have information that could help me."

I sat on one of the mats, spread my legs into a V, and bent forward at the waist, stretching my hamstrings. "If, for the sake of argument, you were correct that money was missing from Simon's ministries, what makes you think extortion is involved?"

"If you'll meet me somewhere to talk, I'll tell you."

"Look, I'm not going to bargain with you. You're the one who wants to talk to me. Besides, I don't have any authority to speak for the ministry."

"I'm not asking you to speak for the ministry. I'm just asking what you know."

I did a flash analysis of the potential costs and benefits of talking to her. News of the missing money was bound to become public soon anyway, and she might have information about who was blackmailing Simon. The upside of the interview could outweigh the downside. "I can meet you for a few minutes when I'm finished working out, but I can't promise any information that will matter to you."

"That's fine. The worst that happens, then, is that we get acquainted. Where do you want to meet?"

"I'll come to you." As boring as Kacey and I were, the gossip photographers wouldn't give up on us since Simon's death. I didn't want them to get the idea that anything was brewing.

"I live in Coppell and I've got a meeting near my house at lunch. Can you come out here and meet me at around ten o'clock this morning? There's a Starbucks just north of Sandy Lake Boulevard."

"Fine, I'll see you there at ten."

"I'm five feet five and have auburn hair."

"We must be related. I'm five nine and have auburn hair."

"Maybe there's another story here."

I chuckled. "One thing I've learned in the past year is that where Simon Mason is involved, there's always another story." I had to admit, she seemed likable enough.

As soon as I hung up, I called Michael at the FBI. He had a lot of experience dealing with local reporters. As usual, he picked up the phone before the third ring.

"Michael, I need to pick your brain about something."

"That shouldn't take long."

I laughed. "Don't worry. I'm going to use a lobster fork."

"Do they make a utensil smaller than that?"

"Not for use by adults."

"That shouldn't limit you, then, should it?"

I laughed again. "You're on today. Did you have a second cup of coffee, or what?"

"I'm on my third."

"That explains it. You're high."

"Buzzing."

I grabbed my toes and stretched. "Have you got a minute?" I made an effort not to grunt as I tried to touch my nose to my knee.

"Yes." I heard him tapping on his keyboard. "I've got a meeting coming up in, let's see, eight minutes."

I sighed. "I'll try not to go more than seven."

"It's fine. My meeting can wait."

I held the phone out and squinted at it. His meeting could wait? Had I dialed the wrong number? "I'm supposed to meet a *Morning News* reporter in about an hour. Her name is Katie Parst. Do you know her?" I let go of my toes and pushed myself to my feet. A woman with biceps bigger than my thighs dropped to her back on the mat next to me. She started doing crunches at a furious pace, emitting something between a moan and a growl each time she came up.

"Are you jogging or something? You sound out of breath."

"I'm at the fitness club." I took a few steps away from crunch lady and lowered my voice. "There's a woman here who's trying to work off the steroid shake she had for breakfast. You're probably hearing her roaring. I'm not quite that dedicated."

He laughed. "Nevertheless, you're making me feel guilty. I just ate a sausage biscuit from McDonald's."

"Why do you think I do this? You've seen me eat."

"Now that you mention it, I have seen you eat. You must have some great genes to put away food like that and stay as svelte as you are."

"Was that a compliment? It sounded like a round-about way to say that I eat like a horse."

"There's no upside for me on this subject, so let's get back to the point of your call. You were talking about Katie Parst?"

"Yeah, do you know her?"

"Best reporter at the paper, as far as I'm concerned. Does that help?"

"It depends on what you mean by best reporter."

"She's honest, gets her facts straight, and if you tell her something's off the record, you can be sure you won't see it in print. For reporters, that's the trifecta."

I walked over to the hamstring machine and lay on my stomach on the bench. "Well, well. Is there more to this story about you and Ms. Parst?" I pulled the weights up with my legs and tried not to groan.

"She's married and she's about fifteen years older than I am, so knock it off. She is very attractive, though, since you mention it. Why does she want to talk to you?"

"I can't tell you yet." I clenched my jaw and did ten more reps with my legs.

"Okay, wait a minute. You call me and ask for my advice, and then you won't tell me why? You disappoint me. I didn't think there were any secrets between us."

I pushed myself up and sat on the bench. "My life is an open book, but it's not my secret to tell." By that time I was panting.

"What are you doing now, splitting logs?"

"Actually, I'm making my legs firm and fine."

"Well, from what I can see, you've been doing a great job. Keep up the good work. By the way,

Katie Parst's got a lot of guts. She's been doing some stories knocking around the periphery of what appears to be an organized crime ring in Dallas. A lot of reporters would have avoided that one and gone on to something a little less risky. I know the Dallas police have asked her to share some of her info with them."

I stood up and toweled sweat off the back of my neck. "Interesting. Hey, I've got to run if I'm going to make my meeting with her. Thanks for the info."

Before I could click the phone off, he said, "Wait a minute. When are you and Kacey going shooting again?"

"We'll be there Tuesday at seven o'clock. She's getting good, isn't she?"

"She's amazing. Last time I saw her over there she nearly beat me. You'd better watch it. She'll be in your league before long." I heard the computer keys clicking. "I'm calendaring it right now. Seven o'clock sharp. I'll see you there, as long as I can get out of here early enough."

"Michael, you work too hard."

"I always make time for you and Kacey."

"And we appreciate it."

When I hung up, I reran the conversation in my head. *I didn't think we had any secrets between us . . . I always have time for you and Kacey.* Every once in a while I caught myself wondering . . .

Nah, couldn't be.

As I walked to the locker room, I tried to envision Michael and I sitting in a dark room in front of a fireplace. It just didn't work. And it wasn't the racial thing—at least, I didn't think it was. How could a person really know? He was just such an Eagle Scout. Of course, my tendency to pick the bad boys hadn't exactly worked well for me to this point in my life. Maybe a responsible type was what I needed.

I shook my head. Even if it were, it would never be Michael Harrison. There was a difference between responsible and neurotically responsible. I would have enough trouble with the former. I could never deal with the latter.

After I pulled off my workout clothes, I wrapped myself in a towel and sat on the bench in front of my locker. It was a weekday morning, so there were only a couple of other women in the locker room. I decided to call Kacey before I got in the shower.

I caught her on her way to her economics class. "I just got a call from a reporter at the *Morning News*. She knew about the missing money. She wants to talk. What do you think? I told her I'd meet with her, but I can still cancel. I checked her out with Michael. He thinks highly of her."

"That depends," Kacey said. "What did she tell you?"

I stretched one leg out on the bench and massaged my calf. "Nothing much. Just that she heard some money was missing and that she's been investigating an extortion ring in Dallas. I'm sure she's wondering if the two are connected."

"How did she know about the missing money?"

"I was thinking about that. Only a handful of people knew about it: your father, Elise, you, me, and your father's accountant, Brandon. We know you didn't tell, and we know I didn't tell, and we know your father didn't tell. It's a safe bet that Elise didn't, since she was the one taking the money."

"That leaves Brandon, but why would he talk to the *Morning News*? By the way, where are you? Do I hear water running?"

"I'm in the locker room at the fitness club. I'm getting ready to take a shower." I stood up and slid my feet into my flip-flops. Just as I was about to shut my locker door, I stopped. "Wait a minute. The Lewisville cops knew, remember?"

"You're right. That's where she found out. It has to be. Good old Officer Ferrell. What a charmer he was."

I closed the locker and spun the dial on the combination lock. "Well, if she already knows about the money, the story's going to be out soon anyway. Since she's been investigating an extortion ring, I thought she might have some information that could help us figure out who was blackmailing your dad."

"I agree. I don't see any big reason not to talk to her."

"I'll do my best to get more information out of her than she gets out of me. I've got to go if I'm going to make it to our meeting."

"Okay. Give me a call when you're finished."

I realized I had closed my locker without putting my phone and earpiece in it, so I had to open the door again and drop them into my shoe. Then I closed the door and headed toward the shower. Once in the shower, as the warm spray hit my face and I massaged shampoo into my hair, I worked through the issues that Katie Parst would likely want to discuss.

Since she was investigating an extortion ring, she must have a suspicion that the ring was somehow connected to the money missing from Simon's ministry. That made some sense. Simon was a world-famous guy with a secret. What Kacey and I knew, though—and what Katie Parst didn't—was that Elise Hovden had taken the money, not Simon. That would be a great disappointment to Parst, if I decided to tell her at all.

As I stepped out of the shower, I thought that this meeting should be okay. After all, Katie Parst was the one who had most of the information, not me. All I had to do was drink my coffee, ask some questions, and listen. I smiled.

For once I was going to have a pleasant meeting with a reporter.

CHAPTER
TEN

IT WAS 10:05 WHEN I walked into Starbucks. Coming from the cool December air into the warmth of the shop was the olfactory equivalent of sticking my head in a bag of coffee beans. I felt as if I'd gotten a caffeine jolt from merely breathing. I scanned the room and spotted Katie Parst in the back corner, sitting with her back to one of the floor-to-ceiling windows that encased three sides of the cafe.

Michael was correct. She was a pretty woman. Even though she was sitting, it was obvious she took good care of herself. Her auburn hair was darker and straighter than mine, and cut shorter, above the shoulder. Hard to believe Michael was right about her age. She looked ten years younger than the fiftyish description he gave. She sipped iced tea from a straw. When she saw me, she smiled and waved.

I went to the counter and ordered a grande drip. After paying and taking a sip, I headed over to the table. Parst stood and brushed crumbs from her navy wool pants. She took a quick look down at her pale yellow blouse and seemed relieved that she hadn't spilled on it, too. She was still chewing her last bite when she held her hand out across the small, round table. "Sorry, I didn't have time to eat breakfast at home, and I'm really making a mess. This stupid muffin crumbled all over the place. I'm Katie Parst."

"What did you have?"

"Blueberry. It was good. I usually don't spill my food all over me, though. Honest."

Anybody who could make a mess of her meal and laugh about it was someone I could relate to. I had to be careful. I was beginning to like her. "Listen," I said, "you never have to make excuses for how you eat around me. I'm not the most graceful sometimes. In fact, I may get one of those in a minute. My workout made me hungry."

"You know, I've admired you from a distance for quite a while."

"Just my luck. I work out to attract men, not women."

She laughed. "I meant that I've admired your work. Although whatever you're doing, I'd keep it up. You look great."

"It's been an active year."

She shook her head. "I'll say. I don't know anybody else who's led a raid on a terrorist hideout this year."

"An unsuccessful raid. And I wasn't the leader until everybody else got shot." That sounded so amped up that I was embarrassed. "Actually, the guys I was with were real pros. They just let me come along because I was the only one who could positively ID Simon." From habit, I moved around her and took the seat at the far side of the table, where I could see both of the doors.

She sat across from me and rested an arm on the table. "I'm sorry about Reverend Mason. I understand you were close."

"He was sort of like a father . . . or big brother." I waved a hand in the air. "To tell you the truth, I still don't know how to describe our relationship. I guess you said it best. We were close. He was a great man."

"How is his daughter doing? You're living with her at the Mason house?"

"She seems to be handling everything remarkably well. I mean, if you think I've had an extraordinary year, just think about what Kacey's gone through. She's an amazing girl."

"I remember her from the press conference at the hospital after the kidnapping. She was poised beyond her years."

I sipped my coffee. "I worry about her—that she's holding everything in. That's the way she is." I immediately wondered why I was sharing thoughts like that with this stranger. A reporter, at that. I had to watch myself.

"I imagine she's had to grow up in a hurry," she said. "It's a shame. She should be enjoying college. She's at Southern Methodist, right?"

"That's right, SMU. A sophomore."

She smiled. "Good gosh, when I was a sophomore in college, my biggest worry was whether so-and-so would ask me to the football dance."

I couldn't see any upside in making Kacey part of this conversation, so I decided to change the subject. I pointed to Parst's iced tea. "A little chilly out for that, isn't it?"

"I know. My husband thinks I'm crazy. I drink this stuff the year round; the colder the better." She gave her clear plastic cup a shake. "I don't like coffee. This is how I get my caffeine."

I held up my cup. "Well, here's to caffeine." I took a sip. "What does your husband do?"

"He was general counsel for Challenger Airlines for years. A few years ago he moved into the U.S. Attorney's office. Now he's a prosecutor. Sort of a midlife change of focus."

"A lawyer in the family, huh? That must come in handy in the journalism business."

"Not really. He's always more worried about my

safety than about the story. If it were up to him, I'd be covering fashion shows and Easter egg hunts."

"I wouldn't complain. It sounds like you married a good one."

"Yeah, I did." She leaned back in her chair. "So, how did you end up working for Simon Mason, anyway? I mean, I know from the newspapers that you were with the Secret Service, but I've never heard how you and Reverend Mason connected."

"When I quit the Service, I came back to Dallas and started my own security agency. In March Simon called me out of the blue. I'd never met him. He told me he'd received terrorist threats. He said that a church member had recommended me to him. It wasn't until later that I found out—" I caught myself and took another drink.

"Found out what?"

I took off my white pea coat and hung it over the back of my chair. When I turned back to her I said, "Found out how exciting working for Simon Mason was going to be."

"I'd say that's an understatement." She leaned forward. "It was a tragedy about Elise Hovden, wasn't it?"

"Yes, it was."

"Were you close?"

I shifted my weight in my chair. "I wouldn't call us exactly close. We did work together quite a bit, though."

She pulled a notepad and pen out of her purse. "Do you know of any reason why she would kill herself?"

"Are we on the record now?"

"Yes, we're on the record unless you tell me otherwise."

"So that's the way it works, huh? A few minutes of small talk and then swoop in for the kill."

She lowered her notepad. "Had some bad experiences with reporters?"

"Not really. I just don't trust them much."

"Believe it or not, some of us are honest. All I want to do is ask you some questions. If you don't want to answer something, just tell me. I try to be straight with my sources. That way they continue to be my sources."

She was ruining my reporter stereotype, but I wasn't ready to be anybody's idiot. I crossed my legs. "Why don't we do it this way? You're the investigative reporter; you tell me why Elise would kill herself. You must have some idea or you wouldn't have asked me here."

She placed her pen on the table. "Okay, but it all depends."

"I don't get it. What depends on what?"

"Why Elise Hovden might kill herself depends on whether a half-million dollars is really missing from Simon Mason World Ministries."

A man in a navy blazer, gray slacks, and an open-collared shirt walked over and sat at the table beside us.

He looked at his watch and then opened the *Wall Street Journal*.

I lowered my voice. "What gives you the idea that money is missing?"

"A source in Lewisville told me."

I rapped my knuckles on the table. "I knew it! That creepy Officer Ferrell. Are you going to do a story on it?"

"Wouldn't you, if you were me? By the way, I didn't say it was a police officer who told me."

I shrugged. "I've never been a reporter, so I don't know whether I'd do a story—and I know it was Ferrell. Nobody in Lewisville could have known except the police."

She looked at me steadily and apparently decided not to get bogged down in an argument over who her source was. "I've been investigating a bunch of thugs who extort money from high-profile people. I want to find out if there's any connection here. So, how about it? Will you confirm that the money is missing?"

I watched the man in the blazer put his paper down on the table and walk to the counter. When I turned back to Parst, I said, "Okay, yes. The money is missing. That won't be a secret for long anyway. Simon had nothing to do with it, though. He told me that himself, and the auditors have confirmed it. Simon was not a thief."

"I don't have any reason to believe he was. So, auditors have already gone over the books?"

"Yes."

She picked up her notepad and wrote for a few seconds, then looked up at me. "Does this have anything to do with Elise Hovden's suicide?"

"A minute ago, you said it depends. I'm waiting for you to tell me."

"I heard there was a suicide note and that Ms. Hovden admitted taking the money."

"You seem to know this story pretty well already. I don't think it's my place to be talking about whether there was a note. Elise has a mother who lives in the area. That's pretty personal stuff. I will tell you that it looks as if Elise was embezzling money from the ministry. That won't remain a secret for long either."

"That's fine. What I'm really interested in is whether Ms. Hovden was being blackmailed. I'm trying to expose some pretty bad people. You may have information that can help."

I hadn't expected that. Simon had been famous and an obvious target, but I couldn't think of a single reason why anyone would want to blackmail Elise Hovden. "Why don't you tell me something about these bad people and the way they operate? Then maybe I can tell you something you might want to know."

"Have you read any of my stories lately?"

"Sorry, I've been pretty busy."

The man in the blazer came back to his table sipping a cup of coffee. Right behind him was a slender blonde, maybe half his age, who sat at the table with him. He touched her hand and began talking, an earnest look on his face.

Katie leaned toward me. "These extortionists are well organized. Whether they are part of a larger criminal organization, I'm not quite sure yet. They must at least have some contact with a larger organization. They've become too big not to. They prey on prominent members of the community."

"How?"

"Vice. That's their hook. They run prostitution rings, gambling, and drugs. When they find out that a prominent person is, so to speak, patronizing one of their operations, they tighten the screws on him—or her. They threaten to expose the person publicly if they don't get their money. You can imagine that certain high-profile people are willing to pay quite a bit to keep their names off the front page, especially in connection with drugs and prostitutes. And who knows what sort of influence they're coughing up besides just money? Anyway, the people are too terrified to tell anyone, so it doesn't adversely affect business for the bad guys. My story last week was about the football coach of a suburban high school. One of the best football programs in the state. He'd been betting significant money on his own team's games—sometimes he even bet they would lose. These guys hit him up for ten thousand dollars. He was hocking school equipment to pay them off, then buying the equipment back out of hock with money he borrowed from family members."

"Poor jerk. He paid them the money and got outed anyway."

"Yeah. Unfortunately he couldn't give the police a single name of anyone involved. Or he was too afraid to."

"Well, I can't imagine Elise was into any serious vices. She was a straight arrow. In case you're wondering, I can tell you Simon wasn't involved, either. You might not think highly of televangelists as a group, but he was the real deal. As I said earlier, he was a good man."

"What did the auditors find?"

I leaned back in my chair. "I wouldn't stay in business long if I went around blabbing about my clients' affairs."

She put her notepad on the table and pointed to it. "You don't have to talk for attribution. You can be an anonymous source."

I studied her face and tried to think of any way Kacey and I could benefit from my telling this woman more than she already knew.

"Look," she said, "let's get it all out on the table. I know about Simon Mason's son, too. I know his name and I know where he lives. I've known about it for several weeks. I haven't written about it, because it's not news, it's personal. If I were just trying to dig up a scandal, don't you think that story would have run by now?"

I put my hands on the table. "Who told you that?"

"I wouldn't stay in the reporting business long if I went around disclosing my sources."

I smiled. "Touché. However, you're the one who needs information from me. I don't need anything from you. And if you don't tell me who your source is, you're not going to get your information."

She turned her head and looked out the window. "Let me make a call." She got up, weaved her way through the tables, and walked out the front door.

Through the window I could see her talking on her cell phone and pacing the sidewalk. While she was outside I tried to figure her angle. So she knew about Simon's son, and she must have been suspicious that somehow the blackmailers had gotten to Simon. Was it really possible, though, that both Simon and Elise were being blackmailed at the same time? That seemed to defy the law of averages.

As I watched her pace the sidewalk, a black Honda Accord with tinted windows slid up beside her and eased to a stop. The back window rolled down just as Parst hit the button on her phone and reached for the door to come back into the shop. The window rolled back up, and the car drove away.

When Parst got back to the table, she opened her mouth, but I spoke first. "Did you see that car?"

"What car?"

"A black Honda. It was right beside you."

She shook her head. "I was talking on the phone. What about it?"

I looked out the front window and scratched my head. "Never mind."

She folded her arms on the table. "All right, my source about Simon's son was Simon's former accountant, Brandon Henckel. He gave me permission to tell you. He said you knew him."

"Brandon? How would he know about Chase?"

She raised an eyebrow. "So, you do know about Simon's son. You're right, his name is Chase and he lives in Katy, Texas."

I mentally kicked myself. There was no use trying to backtrack, though. "Okay, Kacey and I have met him. We went down there a few weeks ago."

"Did Simon know about him?"

I was getting in too deep. I needed to think. "You know, I'm going to get that muffin now. I'll be right back. Do you want anything?"

"I'm fine, thanks."

I got up and headed for the counter. As I walked, I tried to process the information I had. Simon was being blackmailed. Elise was embezzling money. Simon had an illegitimate son. Simon's former accountant knew that Simon had an illegitimate son and knew that money was missing. Katie Parst was investigating a group that blackmailed prominent people who got involved in vices.

I shook my head. Too many moving parts. And wouldn't it be an amazing coincidence if they were all unrelated? What were the odds? There had to be a connection. No wonder Parst was so interested.

I stepped up to the counter and pointed at a muffin, but by that time I wasn't a bit hungry. I didn't have enough information yet to put the puzzle together. Katie Parst might, though. The question was whether I should trust her. Michael said I could, and my gut told me he was right. I paid for the muffin and headed back to the table.

She nodded toward the bag in my hand. "Did you get the blueberry?"

It occurred to me that I'd been so deep in thought that I didn't know. I ignored the question. "Can we go off the record?" I said, as I sat.

She set her pad and pen on the table. "Okay, we're off the record."

I looked around the table to make certain that no one could hear. "I'm going to trust you. Please don't make me regret it."

"I won't."

I took the lid off my coffee cup and swirled the liquid. "Simon knew about Chase. He'd known since just after Chase was born." I set the cup aside, leaned forward, and clasped my hands in front of me. "There's more, though. We're way off the record here, okay?"

"You've got my word."

"Someone was trying to blackmail Simon, but it had nothing to do with gambling, or prostitution, or drugs. It was about Chase."

She sat back in her chair. "Wow, when you go off the record, it's worth listening. How do you know Reverend Mason was being blackmailed?"

I took a drink of my coffee. "He told me not long before he left for Beirut. Back in March, a few days before Kacey was kidnapped, Simon found a note on the windshield of his car. All that it said was, *I know about the boy.* He didn't know what to think of it, but shortly after he found it he received a call from a man who demanded that he pay two hundred thousand dollars. He said that if Simon didn't pay, he'd go public with the information."

"Did Reverend Mason know who was blackmailing him?"

"He had no idea."

"What did he do?"

"Nothing. Within a few days, Kacey was kidnapped. All the publicity around the kidnapping must have spooked the blackmailer. Simon never heard from him again."

The blonde at the table next to us stood. The man

in the blazer grabbed her wrist and said something I couldn't make out. She shook his hand off and marched out of the shop. The man tilted his head back and closed his eyes.

Katie looked at him, then back at me. She dropped her voice to a whisper. "I wonder what that was all about."

"You might get a better story over there."

She smiled. "So, did Simon tell the FBI about the blackmail?"

"No. It was obvious that the Muslim terrorists who kidnapped Kacey weren't also trying to blackmail Simon about his illegitimate son." The man at the table next to us glanced my way. I lowered my voice. "So Simon kept it to himself."

"Who else knew about the boy?"

I ran a hand back through my hair. "Well, that's where it gets even more complicated. The boy's mother and Elise were the only ones who knew, to the best of Simon's knowledge."

"What's so complicated about that?"

I leaned as far over the table toward her as I could. "Chase's mother is my mother."

Her eyes widened. "What?"

"Simon and my mother had an affair. It was eighteen years ago, before Simon's wife died and before he became a minister. You know Simon's background. The whole world knows. He was just an auto worker. He and my mother were working on an assembly line together, a year or two after my mother ran out on Dad and me. Simon had learned that his wife was having an affair. It crushed him. He had the affair to get back at his wife. My mother was convenient. It was brief, but long enough to produce Chase."

"That's unbelievable."

"Simon's wife got sick shortly afterward. Then she died. Simon loved his wife very much. It tortured him that he'd done it."

"So Kacey and you are almost related."

"Chase is our half-brother."

She leaned back in her chair. "And Kacey knows?"

"She does now."

"Why are you telling me all of this?"

"There are too many things going on here for it all to be coincidence," I said. "Somehow there's a connection. You have information I don't have. I'm hoping you can help me figure it out."

"I hate to be so blunt, but isn't it obvious that your mother was behind the blackmail?"

I waved a hand in the air. "Believe me, when it comes to my mother, you should never be afraid to be blunt. She would seem to be the obvious suspect, but Simon didn't believe it and neither do I. If she wanted to blackmail him, she could have done it years ago. She gave Chase up for adoption when he was small. Besides, why would she leave a note on Simon's windshield saying, 'I know about the boy'? She was in a position to be much more direct. And a man called Simon with the demand, not a woman."

"She could have been covering her tracks and she could have had an accomplice."

"True. As I said, though, Simon was convinced it wasn't her. I feel the same way. There's no way yet to be sure."

"Where does your mother live?"

"Southlake. She came to Simon's house yesterday. I had an investigator find her. It was the first time I'd seen her in twenty years."

She shook her head. "What a story! I'm happy for you. It must be nice to get your mother back after all those years."

I frowned. "I'm not yet prepared to jump to that conclusion."

She studied my face but must have decided not to follow up on that one. "So, if it wasn't your mother, it had to be Elise. She was the only other one who knew, besides Brandon."

"There could have been others. We don't know who Elise told, or Brandon, or my mother for that matter. I do know that Brandon was upset with Simon for firing him. Brandon had a drinking problem. I told you it was complicated. Are you following all of this?"

Without so much as a smile, she said, "Not at all."

I laughed. The man in the blazer gave me a dirty look. It was apparent his day wasn't going as planned.

"Too bad this is off the record," Parst said. "I guess it doesn't matter, though. I'd need a flow chart to keep 'his story straight. Maybe Brandon should be suspect number one, but if he was blackmailing Simon, why would he give the information to me? You would think that he wouldn't want anyone to know that he knew about the boy."

"No one sticks out as a clear favorite. There's more, though. A couple of things about Elise's suicide don't add up. For one thing, she wrote the suicide note—"

Katie raised an eyebrow.

"Yes, you were right," I said. "There was a note. It was typed on computer paper. The bottom of the sheet was torn off."

"That's odd."

"I thought so. The police weren't nearly as inquisitive. It gets even odder. We found the note on the desk in her house, but we never found her laptop. It wasn't in the house and it wasn't in her car. There was a printer and a docking station for the laptop, but no computer."

"What a great feature story this would be."

"Remember, I'm counting on you not to print it."

"I can dream, can't I?" She took a sip through her straw.

I glanced out the window. The wind had picked

up. An empty Wendy's bag flipped and bounced along the curb like a suburban tumbleweed. As I was turning back to Katie, the black Honda that I had seen earlier edged around the front corner of the Starbucks and down the narrow street that ran parallel to our side of the cafe. I watched it from the corner of my eye. As it came up beside us, it slowed.

Katie must have seen my expression change. She moved her straw away from her mouth just as the car stopped, not ten feet to my right. "What is it?" she said.

She was turning to look when the rear window of the car slid down. I couldn't see into the backseat. But I did see a long, black silencer extend through the open window. It was pointed straight at Katie.

Katie's eyes opened wide when I dove across the table. My shoulder slammed into her chest, flipping her plastic glass into the air. A cold shower of tea and ice sprayed my face and neck and back as we hurtled toward the floor.

Just before we hit the tile, I felt one more thing—something hard and hot slamming into my side.

CHAPTER
ELEVEN

IN THE TWELVE YEARS before I met Katie Parst at Starbucks, I had served on a Dallas SWAT team, protected heads of state in the Secret Service, and even taken a piece of shrapnel in my rear end. I had watched my father die in my arms, raided a terrorist hideout in Beirut, and killed four men. But I had never been shot.

I suppose that's one more reason not to hang out with reporters.

When the tables and chairs stopped cartwheeling and the glass stopped breaking, I was lying face-to-face with Parst, my right hand mashed between her head and the tile floor. Her eyes were still as wide as they'd been when I dove across the table.

Besides the burning in my side, the first thing I felt was a stabbing pain in my middle finger. I didn't want to move, because I had a strong hunch that the pain was only going to get worse. I turned my head to look out the window. The Honda was gone.

I looked back at Parst. "Are you okay?"

"I think so." Her voice was high-pitched but steady. That was good. The less she panicked the faster I could figure out how badly we were hurt.

I took a deep breath and let it out. "Okay, listen to me. I want you to move your head slowly to the right, before you move anything else."

She lifted her head slightly and moved it, freeing my hand from beneath her.

My middle finger above the first knuckle was bent at a grotesque angle. Blood dripped from it, and as I turned my hand to the side, I saw something white jutting from the bloody spot. I assumed it was a bone. I resolved that looking at it was not going to do me a bit of good. I turned my head away and forced myself to think.

"Okay, I'm going to roll off of you now." The pain was so intense that my voice was barely more than a whisper. I fought hard to keep it a steady whisper—no sense scaring her even more. "Before you try to get up, I want you to wiggle each of your major body parts, one at a time, starting with your feet and toes, to make sure you don't have anything hurt in a major way. Take your time. We won't be going anywhere for a while."

I gritted my teeth, braced my good hand on the floor, and pushed myself off of her. Pain exploded from my finger and shot up my arm all the way to my neck. I must have blacked out, because I don't remember how I ended up on my back with the manager of Starbucks kneeling over me and staring into my eyes.

The woman's long blonde hair fell from her shoulders and dangled to my cheeks, tickling my nose as she spoke. "We've called 9-1-1. Just lie still. They'll be here in a minute. Do you want some water?"

I swiped her hair from my face with my good hand. "Where's Katie?" I tried to prop myself on an elbow, but the pain jerked me down.

"I'm right here." Katie leaned over me. "Don't try to move. You've been shot."

"But I don't get shot." Granted, not the smartest thing I'd ever said.

Katie placed a wet napkin across my forehead. "Apparently you do now. It looks as if you caught a bullet intended for me. Thank you."

I tried to lift my head just enough to see my side, which felt as if someone had taped a hot curling iron to it. I couldn't see it, but I could see the floor. There wasn't too much blood there. I took that as a good sign. My finger seemed to be the bigger problem. The pain alternated between deep throbs and stabs so vicious that I envisioned some horrible little creature gnawing at my skin from the inside, trying to burst free and scamper toward the door. That would have been fine with me. If he was causing pain like this, the sooner he left the building, the better.

The room began to float. I found Katie's face again and fought to keep her in focus. "Anybody hurt?"

"It doesn't look like it. Just you."

I closed my eyes and found that made it easier to think. A woman and child were crying near the front of the store. Without opening my eyes, I said, "Scary, huh?"

Katie patted my shoulder. "Less scary than it would have been. You're a brave woman."

I almost said, "Or a stupid one." For once, though, I gave myself a break. Even I could see that I'd done something good. I'd tried to save Dad and he died; I'd tried to save Simon and he died. This time, I'd done my job. I'd saved Katie Parst. She was right here, alive and breathing—because of me. Despite the pain, I allowed myself to smile.

Within a few minutes sirens were blaring and para- medics and cops were everywhere. I must have blacked out again, because the next thing I knew, they were wheeling me into the back of an ambulance parked in front of the Starbucks. Katie stepped in behind the gurney.

The paramedic held up a thick hand. "I'm sorry, ma'am. You'll have to meet us at the hospital."

"She saved my life. I'd like to ride with her."

By that time they had given me a shot for the pain. I was feeling woozily talkative. "Can't she ride along? She's my sister. Mom will want to know what's going on."

Katie looked at me and raised an eyebrow. I raised mine right back at her. Then, if that hadn't been enough to red-flag my lie, I gave her an exaggerated wink.

A crowd of people had gathered on the sidewalk, and two police officers were doing their best to hold them back. The pain medicine was great stuff. I lifted my head and waved with my good hand, as if I were homecoming queen. The crowd clapped and whistled. A man in the back shouted, "Way to go, lady. You're a hero!" The crowd clapped again.

The paramedic looked at the crowd and then back at Katie. "Sister, huh?" He smiled. "Hop in."

Katie jumped in the back just before he closed the doors. The inside of the ambulance began to whirl, and I remember Katie squeezing my good hand and saying, "Whether you like it or not, from now on I'm part of your life."

Days later Katie told me that I responded, "Thanks. I love you, Mom."

CHAPTER
TWELVE

IN THE HOSPITAL I learned that the bullet wound would be more of a nuisance than anything. The bullet had sliced through the skin just above my hip and lodged in the base of the table next to where Katie and I had been sitting. The man in the blazer had left just in time. A second bullet smashed into the espresso machine behind the counter, showering beans everywhere, but missing the barista, who had bent over to pick up the luckiest straw she'd ever dropped.

The doctors slapped a bandage on my side and gave me a tetanus shot. If that had been all of it, I'd have been on my way that day. My finger was the bigger problem.

It came between Katie's head and the tile floor. When the bone snapped, it sliced through the skin. By the time the doctors surgically rearranged things, it was clear my shooting hand would be out of commission for at least ten weeks. They insisted on keeping me in the hospital overnight while they dripped antibiotics into me to hold off infection. The pain was nauseating. Fortunately, though, they introduced me to an amazing painkiller that had a remarkably brightening effect on an otherwise miserable day.

Kacey arrived shortly after I came out of surgery. She and Katie Parst sat with me until nearly eight o'clock that evening. Kacey and I had been through a lot together during the past nine months, but this was the first time I'd seen her so rattled. I supposed that after losing her father, she figured I was basically all she had left. That would be sufficient to rattle anyone.

She was crying before she even got through the door of the hospital room, something I had never seen her do, not even after her father died.

In my entire life, I couldn't recall a single person who had ever cried for me. In retrospect I recognize how sad that was. My mother left when I was nine, and even when she was around she was too emotionally bedraggled to cry for anyone but herself. My grandparents had died by the time I was six, and I barely knew them anyway. Dad loved me, but he was a Special Forces officer. They don't cry much. Besides, by the time I was seventeen, he was dead and I was alone. There simply wasn't anyone else.

So, I'm not too embarrassed to say that I enjoyed it when Kacey sobbed over me. In fact, I cried, too, which is no big scoop, because I've always cried at the drop of a hat. Heck, I cry when I read the lost dog notices on the bulletin board at the vet's. Tough girl, easy crier: that's me. It used to drive me crazy, embarrass me. After all, it's not exactly the type of image that sells security services. But I've come to peace with it.

In this instance, though, I had every reason to bawl. If someone finally cared enough to cry over me, the least I could do was join her. I remember seeing a movie once where three men were dying of thirst in the desert. When they stumbled onto an oasis, they cried like babies as they waded in the water, splashing their blistered tongues and sun-baked faces. Same principle I suppose.

And I was glad that Katie Parst was there in the hospital room with us. She was just the right age to do some desperately needed mothering—for Kacey and for me. Before Katie left for the night, she asked me if I wanted her to call my mother. I thought about it for a second and told her no.

Katie gave my good hand one last squeeze and promised to come by in the morning to see how I was doing. As I watched her walk out the door, I wondered if she had a daughter and what it would be like to have

Katie for a mother. I imagined that it must be good, really good.

Within a half hour, Michael Harrison appeared at the door. When I looked up, his brown eyes brightened.

"Are we going to have to get your license revoked to keep you out of trouble? Did it occur to you to call me? I heard about it on my car radio."

I held up my splinted finger. "Doctor's orders. No dialing."

"Last time I checked, you had two hands."

I shrugged.

He walked up to the bed, lowered the metal rail, and sat on the edge of the mattress with his hip against my leg. "You got shot in the finger?"

"No, the shot was here." I pointed to my side. "Grazed me. The finger was just my general klutziness." I flexed my knee and jabbed it into his hip. "By the way, make yourself at home. You're practically sitting on me."

He patted my foot. "I knew you wouldn't mind."

"She saved Katie Parst's life," Kacey said. "She acts like that's nothing."

Kacey had a way of making me feel good about myself. I wanted her to keep talking, but Michael picked up my good hand. "What about this one? Is it busted, too?" He gave me a little hand massage, his thick fingers working with surprising gentleness. It wasn't bad.

When he placed my hand back on the bed, he folded his arms across his chest. "So give me the inventory. A busted finger and a nick in the side. Anything else?"

"Not just busted—open fracture."

"Ooh, baby, that hurts." He grimaced.

"And what do you mean *nick in the side*? It was a bullet! That's hot metal that kills people, remember? If it's such a small thing, why don't you try it sometime?"

"No thanks. Already have."

"You've been shot?"

"Twice. Once in the old hood in Chicago when I was growing up." He pulled one foot up to the mattress and lifted his pant leg, exposing a calf muscle the size of a grapefruit. There was a cream-colored, nickel-sized scar that stood out like a bleached spot against his dark skin. "That one was meant just for me. Went right into the muscle. Some gangbangers didn't like the way I looked at them. The other time was a bullet fragment—ricochet during a drug bust. One of our own guys." He took off his sport coat and rolled up the sleeve of his blue, button-down collar shirt. "You have to look real close to see this one. It was just a nick, like yours." He stuck his forearm under my nose.

I made a show of squinting. "Oh, I think I see it. It's hiding under that hair."

"You're a riot."

I felt that I had an advantage and I pressed it. "Were they using pellet guns?"

"What did they give you, laughing gas? Don't let me interrupt you. You seem to be having a great time being around yourself."

I stifled a laugh—didn't want to give him the satisfaction of knowing he'd said something clever.

He rolled his sleeve back down. "Besides, it's not that tiny. One thing I can tell you for sure is that little sucker burned like crazy. I'll bet yours does, too. I'm proud of you."

"She's a hero," Kacey said.

I could feel my neck getting warm, so I changed the subject. "Anybody bring a deck of cards?"

As if on cue, a chiseled, suntanned giant in a gray Adidas T-shirt knocked on the open door of the room. All three of our heads turned. I don't know about Kacey and Michael, but my eyes must have become wider than the wheel covers on my Camaro. The visitor flashed a smile, and his perfect white teeth practically lit the room. Though I had never met him, I immediately knew who he was, as would every other person living in North Texas.

Rob Morrow had been quarterback for the Dallas Cowboys for three years and was one of the hottest sports celebrities in the country. He obviously had the wrong room.

"Is this where the hero is staying?" he said. He once again bathed us in the light of that smile.

It's important to note that I'm no fawning sports groupie. In fact, I'm generally unimpressed by celebrity, but I will unequivocally state that this was the most gorgeous man I'd ever seen. I was glad I was lying down, because I have no doubt that my legs would have failed me if I'd been standing. Kacey took a half-step backward, and she may as well have grabbed her heart. He'd only been in the room for thirty seconds, and Kacey and I were both in grave danger of humiliating ourselves based on nothing more than our facial expressions.

Michael, on the other hand, took a step toward my bed, positioning himself partially between Morrow and me. He placed his hand on the bed rail. We were all so flabbergasted that no one responded to Morrow's question. We just sat there looking at him.

With the confidence of a man accustomed to being adored, he pulled a bouquet of yellow roses in a small crystal vase from behind his back. "Taylor Pasbury?"

Kacey couldn't speak; she merely pointed at me.

"These are for you. Should I put them on the nightstand?" He took two giant steps and was across the room.

"You're Rob Morrow," I said. Pathetic, of course, but it was all I had at the moment.

"That's me. I want to explain why I'm here and then I'll get out of your hair. I don't mean to be rude by dropping by like this, but I've wanted to do this for a long time."

I reached up and touched my hair. "You mean you've wanted to bring me flowers in the hospital for a long time?"

He laughed. "No, I've wanted to meet you." He had to squeeze past Michael, who didn't budge, to get to the nightstand to my right. He put the vase on the stand, then held out his hand to Michael and smiled. "I'm Rob Morrow. Nice to meet you." He sounded natural and friendly, as if he really was happy to meet him.

Michael shook his hand. "Michael Harrison." He finally stepped sideways, allowing Morrow to supplant him next to the bed. Michael looked around for a moment as if he didn't know what to do with himself. Then he walked over and stood in the corner, out of the way.

"Michael's a family friend." As soon as the comment left my mouth, I felt how awkwardly unnecessary, even demeaning, it sounded. But Morrow flashed that smile again, and I figured I could worry about Michael later.

I pushed the button to move the bed up to a full sitting position while I tried to catch my reflection in the metal bedpan that rested next to the vase on the nightstand. I touched my hair again, trying to flatten out some waves that I imagined were sticking straight out from the side of my head.

"I've admired you for a while, and then I saw the news reports today on TV. I already thought you were something, based on the whole Simon Mason thing. Now, I'm convinced that you must be the bravest woman on earth. I just decided to jump in my car and come over here to tell you how much I respect you."

I wanted to fan myself.

Morrow turned toward Kacey. "You're Simon Mason's daughter. I remember you from TV, too."

Kacey just sat there and blushed.

"I'm sorry about your father." Morrow sounded sincere. "Some of the guys on the team went to his church."

Kacey finally mustered the strength to speak. "Thank you."

Over in the corner, Michael cleared his throat. "Well, I guess I'll be going now."

Morrow held up a hand. "Don't even think about going because of me. I'm butting in here, and I'm leaving right now." He turned back toward me. "I was hoping that maybe we could get together for dinner sometime."

It had to be a dream. I tried to act nonchalant, as if I got date offers from NFL superstars all the time. "Sure, I'd like that."

He waved. "I'll see you, then." He turned around and was gone.

Kacey and I looked at each other. "Did that really just happen?" we screamed in unison.

"He's a big dude," Michael said. "Bigger than he looks on TV."

I didn't even look at Michael. "How sweet of him to bring me flowers. And he doesn't even know me." I tilted the vase and smelled the roses.

"He didn't ask how you were doing," Michael said.

I frowned at him. "He probably thought it was none of his business. There is such a thing as medical privacy."

Michael took a breath and let it out. "Well, I guess I really do need to be going."

Kacey was already on the phone with one of her sorority sisters. "You're not going to believe who just came to Taylor's hospital room!"

"Be sure to tell her about his smile. What great teeth," I said.

Michael moved across the room to the door. "I'll come by and see you tomorrow," he said.

"Yeah, that would be great." I gave him a quick wave and turned back to Kacey. "He wants to take me to dinner! You've got to be kidding me!"

When I looked back toward the door, Michael was gone.

For the next hour Kacey and I acted like two middle-school girls as we relived Morrow's visit at least twenty times. Eventually, though, the pain meds caught up with me. Kacey hugged me and told me good night.

I was asleep within a few minutes. Whether it was the medication or the trauma, I don't know, but I had a stressful dream that night, and it was not about Rob Morrow. I've never been a believer that dreams mean anything more serious than the spicy foods that induce them. This one, though, stuck with me.

My dad and I were sitting on logs near a campfire. Nothing special about that—in fact, even in my sleep I thought I knew exactly what was coming. During the past twelve years I'd had hundreds of dreams about that fishing trip in West Texas on my seventeenth birthday, the night Dad died. Most of the dreams were like digital videos of what happened; almost journalistically true to the story. They always begin with the two drifters entering our campsite with shotguns. They tear at my clothing. Dad fights them off while I run for the truck. One of them blasts Dad with the shotgun just before I reach the pistol under the dashboard. With a single shot, I drop the guy holding the shotgun, the little one with the snake eyes. The other one, the big one, whom Dad has hurt badly, tries to crawl away. I stand over him, and then I shoot him. That's the way it happened, and that's the way I've dreamed it, over and over.

The dream always ends the same way. I'm looking down, directly into the closed dead eyes of the big guy. Then his eyes pop open and he laughs in my face.

When I was younger, the dream was horrifying. It would jerk me straight up in bed. I've had it so many times now, though, that even in my sleep I know what's coming. So I stand over him expecting the eyes to open, as if waiting for the final shock at the end of a low-budget slasher movie.

During my night at the hospital, however, the dream had a twist that once again sat me up in a sweat. Everything was the same: the campfire, the drifters, the shootings. I stood over the big one, watching his eyes, waiting for them to open so I could get out of the dream and get back to sleep. This time, though, when the eyes opened, they weren't the drifter's eyes, they were Dad's eyes, and it was Dad's face. I leaped back with my hand over my mouth. When I looked again, it was no longer Dad's face, but Simon's. His throat was slashed from ear to ear.

I sobbed into the hospital sheets that night, long after I bolted up in bed, and long after I called the nurse to bring something to help me get back to sleep. I sobbed because I loved my dad, and I sobbed because I loved Simon, and I sobbed because I didn't want to be a killer. And, to tell the truth, I sobbed because my mother hadn't even bothered to call to see if I was okay.

I knew I was being unfair. She probably didn't know what had happened, but that didn't matter to me. Somehow, for once in my life, she should have found a way to be there. But she wasn't.

And I was alone again.

CHAPTER
THIRTEEN

BY THE NEXT AFTERNOON I was home, but my body felt as if I had spent the night in a clothes dryer. I decided that getting shot really wasn't so bad, because my finger and various bumps and bruises acquired in the thrill ride down to the Starbucks floor hurt far more than my side. The pain from my finger moved up and down my arm in bursts, like electric shocks.

The painkillers did wonders, though. Besides, I was still basking in the glow of the visit from Rob Morrow, and that helped take the edge off. It was almost as if his shiny white teeth had followed me home to light the Mason house for the approaching holidays. Kacey and I spent a ridiculous amount of time talking about whether and when he would call.

The weather was cold and damp, and all-in-all I figured if I had to be laid up for a while, I had at least picked the right day to start. A fire blazed in the fireplace, and Kacey had put up the Christmas tree and made clam chowder. There was little reason for either of us to go outdoors since Kacey's finals wouldn't begin for a week and a half. We sat in our flannel pajamas and sweatshirts on opposite ends of the couch, facing the fire, with our legs curled up beneath us. With chowder bowls in our laps, and Amy Grant Christmas carols floating in the background, I was enjoying the family feeling I'd had when Simon was alive.

I had retrieved Elise's cell phone and flash drive from my room before we sat down to eat. When we finished our chowder, I pulled out the flash drive and stuck it into a port on my laptop. The g-drive came up on the screen. The only things on it were copies of Elise's tax returns for the previous two years.

I scrolled through the returns. Everything seemed normal, though I was surprised that her salary at the ministry was so low. Whatever her social problems, there was no doubting that Elise could have made far more money working for a business. According to the returns, she donated ten percent of her pay right back to Simon's ministry. Not exactly the picture of an embezzler.

I pulled the flash drive out of the computer. "There's nothing on this but Elise's tax returns."

Kacey set her bowl on the end table. "How about her phone?"

I pulled it out and scrolled through her incoming and outgoing phone books.

"Anything interesting?" Kacey said. She popped a cracker in her mouth.

"I don't know. It will take some time to check out these phone numbers. She's got a bunch of them."

"You really think she didn't kill herself?"

I ran my good hand through my hair. "She probably did, but as long as we have some information, we may as well check it out, right?"

"I guess so, but that's her phone. Don't you think it's kind of private?"

"Sure it is, but if Elise was murdered, and she's up in the clouds or whatever watching us, do you think she's saying, *Hey, what about my privacy rights? Or, yeah, yeah, check the phone. Go find the jerk who killed me*"?

Kacey smiled. "Good point. By the way, it's heaven, not *up in the clouds or whatever*."

I held up a hand. "Wait a minute. I don't believe this."

"You don't believe in heaven?"

"No, I don't believe what I'm seeing in her outgoing calls directory."

"What's that?"

I eased myself off the couch and limped over to my purse, which was hanging over a chair at the breakfast bar. I pulled out my wallet, found a plain white business card, and checked the number on it. "I thought so."

"You thought what?"

"It's Brandon."

"What's Brandon?"

"Elise called Brandon three times within twenty-four hours after I told her the auditors had discovered money was missing."

Kacey leaned toward me. "You mean our Brandon? Dad's accountant?"

"Yep." I turned the phone off.

"Interesting. Brandon's one of the few people who knew that Dad had a son. Why would she be calling him? Do you think he could be the one who was black-mailing Dad?"

"I don't know. Even if he was, what would that have to do with Elise?" I tapped my finger on her phone as I ran the possibilities through my mind. "One thing's sure. It's time we paid Brandon a visit."

"Now?"

"Why not?"

"Well, for one thing you got shot thirty hours ago."

I pulled up my sweatshirt and checked the gauze bandage on my side. It was barely spotted. With the painkillers, I was feeling fine. "I'll be okay for a while. Let's go."

"You're crazy, but I'll get my keys."

I could tell by the way she hopped out of her chair that she couldn't wait to get there.

CHAPTER
FOURTEEN

ASIDE FROM SIMON, BRANDON had been the person most responsible for helping me face my drinking problem. He cheerfully took calls from me in the middle of the night whenever a bottle beckoned me. I owed him, and I hoped like crazy that he wasn't involved in Elise's death.

One of the great things about Brandon was that if you needed him, he was always at home. Since he gave up on accounting, the guy lived like a cloistered monk. All he did was play in video-game tournaments, sleep, and hack into computers for fun (and sometimes, I supposed, money). He was the perfect friend for me, because he was one of the few people in the world whose social life was even more blighted than mine.

Once Kacey and I were in the car on the way to his apartment, I called him to let him know we were coming. He asked what it was about, and I told him I needed to talk. In the 12-step program that was essentially the same as telling him that I wanted a drink and needed support.

"Have you been drinking?" he said.

"I can drive."

"Not if you've been drinking."

"I've got a ride."

"I'll put on some coffee."

I hated to mislead him. Technically, though, I hadn't lied, and I didn't want to tip him off, so I let him think what he wanted to think.

While we were driving to Brandon's apartment, Michael called to check on me. I assured him I was feeling okay, but I had to rush him off the phone because we were pulling up in front of Brandon's building.

"I'll call you tonight," he said.

"Sure, great." I clicked off the phone.

Within a couple of minutes, Kacey and I were standing in the lobby of Brandon's mid-rise apartment building just north of downtown Dallas. We called up from the lobby, and he buzzed us through. When we stepped off the elevator on the sixth floor, Brandon was waiting in the hall with his door propped open.

His belly hung like a thick sausage over the belt of his cargo pants. He waved, then pushed his glasses up on his nose when he saw Kacey step out of the elevator behind me.

"Hey, you look pretty good," he said as we approached the door. I made a conscious effort not to limp.

"From the phone call I thought this was going to be an emergency." His eyes again moved to Kacey.

"I think you've met Kacey Mason."

He stepped aside and let us walk past him into his apartment. He nodded to Kacey. "Sure, but you were only in high school. You've grown up very nicely." His voice was practically whistling.

I looked over my shoulder at him. His eyes were all over her. I stopped and put a hand on my hip. "Don't be creepy, Brandon."

His face reddened. "What?"

Kacey didn't seem to give it a thought. With her long legs and olive skin, she probably had guys scoping her like that several times a day at SMU.

"I read about your run-in at Starbucks. How long do you have to wear that thing?" He pointed toward the gauze-wrapped splint on my finger.

"Eight weeks minimum; maybe ten."

"I thought you got shot?"

"That was here." I pointed to my side. "It's nothing."

He shook his head. "Taylor, you are one tough b—"

"Don't even think about using that word on me."

He held up a hand. "Okay, okay. But has anyone ¬ver told you that you should stay away from guns for a while?"

"Believe me, I'd love to. It wasn't my fault. Whoever did the shooting was after the reporter, not me."

"What's she doing for protection? The reporter, I mean."

"The cops are hanging around her house for now. Other than that, I don't know. I just met her that day, so it's not as if we're close friends."

"Katie's really nice," Kacey said.

Brandon gave her a glance but seemed gun-shy because I'd called him creepy. He fell in behind me as I walked through the entryway to the cramped living area of his apartment.

I had only been to Brandon's apartment one other time, about three months earlier. It didn't appear that he'd cleaned it since then. Two couches and a leather reclining chair were arranged into something resembling a triangle and planted in front of a giant flat-screen TV hanging on the wall. With all that theoretical seating space there was not a single place to sit. Faded clothing, an empty pizza box, and several video-game controllers littered the furniture. The television was off-level by at least an inch. The room smelled syrupy, and empty soda cans littered the floor beneath the television.

I waved my hand around the room. "So many choices. Where do you want us to sit?"

"Just a second," he said, without a trace of embarrassment. He walked over to the tiny breakfast bar and pulled a couple of tall, narrow bar stools out onto the carpet in front of the television. "Here you go."

Kacey looked at me as we took off our jackets. I placed a hand on my side, just over the spot where the gauze was, and eased myself up onto the stool. Kacey climbed onto the one next to me, still watching my hand. I'm okay, I mouthed.

With Kacey in a pink sweater, and me in a yellow sweatshirt, we must have looked like a couple of exotic birds on perches in the center of the room. Brandon looked more like a walrus. He sat on the floor with his back to the couch, one flabby leg folded beneath him, the other stretched out straight on the floor. He watched me get up on the stool. "Are you sure you're okay? You look like you're moving kind of slowly."

"I'm fine. My side's bothering me a little." I wanted to change the subject, so I nodded at the pizza box on the floor. "You didn't have to clean the place for us."

He shrugged. "Believe, me, it was worse than this a few minutes before you got here. Do you want coffee or a Pepsi or something? I've got some chips and stuff."

I noticed Kacey squinting at the half-chewed pieces of pizza crust in the box. Something bluish-green and fuzzy was growing around the edges. She crossed her arms. "No thanks, I'm fine."

"Me, too."

Brandon must have seen Kacey eyeing the pizza box. He reached behind him, closed the top of it, and put it on the floor next to him. "These things take up so much room in the waste can."

We nodded.

He ran a hand through his hair—which did not appear to have been washed for several days—then wiped it on his pants. "So, what's this about?" he said.

I cleared my throat. "One of the things we got from Elise Hovden's house after her death was her telephone."

"Yeah?"

"She called you several times during the two days before she died."

Now he was the one crossing his arms. "So?"

"So, I didn't know you and she were so close."

"What are you doing, Taylor? I don't have to explain to you why I was talking to Elise or anybody else. She called me. What am I supposed to do, hang up on her?"

"Actually you called her, too. Twice."

"You probably noticed, then, that she called me first."

"I did."

"Just a second." He jumped up and walked out of the room. When he came back, he was screwing the lid off a plastic Pepsi bottle. Maybe it was my imagination, but it sure seemed he was stalling.

"I don't know why I should even tell you this," he said, as he lowered himself back to the floor. He kicked off his tennis shoes. The bottoms of his socks were filthy gray. "She asked me for help. She wanted me to find someone for her—more accurately, identify someone."

"Who?"

"Some guy she'd been calling at an Internet Protocol phone number—a computer phone number. She didn't know who he was. She knew that I do some hacking and thought maybe I could help her."

I cocked my head. "Why was she calling someone she didn't know?"

"She didn't say. I figured she was hooking up. You know, meeting somebody online. Happens all the time. I've done it."

I raised an eyebrow.

"Not a lot—actually, just once." His neck reddened.

I could have had a field day with that one, but we were there on serious business. "Look, Brandon, regardless of whether other people do that sort of thing, we're talking about Elise Hovden here. I don't really see her doing it." I turned to Kacey. "Do you?"

She just laughed.

Brandon took a drink of Pepsi and wiped his mouth on his sleeve. "Hey, I didn't know her that well. She asked me for help, and I helped her. That makes me a good guy, doesn't it?"

"Yeah, it does. Did you find the man she was looking for?"

"In a sense."

"What do you mean, in a sense?"

"He used an online service to set up a temporary phone number that was an automatic forwarding device. He gives someone the temp number. They call, it goes to the online service and gets forwarded to a regular number he gives the service. He could use it both ways, too. If he wants to place a call, he gives the online service the other person's number as the forwarding number. Then he calls the temporary number and his call is forwarded to Elise's number. A pain to trace, especially if they use multiple layers of forwarding numbers."

"So, how did you trace it? Have you got some sort of computer program?"

He laughed. "Nope. I did it the old-fashioned way."

"What's that?"

"I bribed somebody. One of the two major service-providers for that sort of thing is based in Dallas. We got lucky. The man she was looking for was using the Dallas service. I called a guy I knew over there and gave

him a hundred bucks to give me the forwarding numbers. One of them was Elise's cell, one of them was the
guy's number. And here's the really interesting thing:
one of them was Simon Mason's." He looked at Kacey.
"That was an old forwarding number, from back before
your father was murdered."

"You mean the guy she was trying to locate had
been calling both Simon and her?"

"At different times, yeah."

"And Elise didn't tell you what this was all
about?"

"Nope." He took a drink of his Pepsi, cupped a
hand over his mouth, and belched.

"C'mon, Brandon!"

"Hey, it's my apartment."

I sighed. "Okay, so you paid a guy a hundred dollars to get this information for her and you didn't even
ask what it was for?"

"Didn't figure it was any of my business."

"What was the guy's name who'd been calling
her?"

"I didn't get a name. Just a phone number. But it
was the originating phone number. That's what she
wanted so much." He scratched one leg with his other
foot. His sock was so dirty I was surprised it didn't leave
a streak.

I coughed. "My throat's kind of scratchy. Can
I take you up on that Pepsi now?"

"Sure. Just a second." He got up and went into the kitchen.

I leaned toward Kacey and cupped my hand to my mouth. Before I could say anything, she whispered, "It was the blackmailer!" I moved away from her just as Brandon came back in with a plastic Pepsi bottle in his hand. He handed it to me and sat back down on the floor.

"Thanks." I braced the bottle between the splint and my thumb while I unscrewed the cap with my left hand.

Brandon smiled a closed-lipped smile, hiding his crooked front teeth. "Need some help?"

"I've got it." I finally wrestled the cap off and took a drink, then set the bottle on my leg. "Simon was being blackmailed. Did you know that?"

He reached up and adjusted his glasses. "No, but I can't say it surprises me. Did someone find out he was embezzling money from his own ministry?"

Kacey frowned. "Dad wasn't embezzling money."

Brandon shifted his weight on the floor. It was clear he'd blurted it without considering who Kacey was. She glared at him, and he looked toward the TV, like a dog that thinks it can make something unpleasant disappear by not looking at it.

By this time Kacey had been taking self-defense classes for nearly eight months. A good athlete and a quick learner, she could have taken Brandon apart in about thirty seconds if she decided he merited it. After what he'd just said, I thought I might let her. She seemed composed enough, but if her eyes had been pistols he'd have been dead where he sat.

I turned back to Brandon. "That's a bunch of bull, Brandon. You know Simon wasn't embezzling. You've talked to the auditors."

He pushed his thinning hair behind his ears, but didn't respond.

I decided to move things along. "Katie Parst told me she'd talked to you. She said you knew about Simon's son."

"Yeah, I know about him."

"How did you find out?"

He put a hand on the couch cushion behind him and pushed himself up to his feet. "Look, Taylor, I don't know who you think you're talking to, but I don't have to sit here and let you grill me as if I'm some sort of criminal defendant. What I do and what I know is really none of your business."

He had a point. I owed it to him to lighten up a bit. "I didn't mean to give you the third degree." From the corner of my eye, I saw Kacey looking at me, her mouth open. "It was nice of you to answer as many questions as you did," I said. "We're just trying to figure some things out about why Elise would kill herself. We'd better get going."

He stuck his hands in his pockets. "If you want my opinion, she was one messed-up chick. I never even got reimbursed for the hundred bucks I paid to my friend."

I tapped Kacey on the leg and she hopped down from her stool. I knew I would hear from her when we got outside. I eased down from my stool and headed for the door. Just before I got there, I turned back to Brandon. "By the way, would you give me the phone number you found for the guy Elise was calling?"

"I would, but I can't."

"Why not?"

"I didn't keep it."

"You mean you didn't even write it down?"

He shrugged. "Yeah, I wrote it down, but it didn't mean anything to me. I called Elise and left the number on her voice mail. She'd been calling me every four or five hours, so I called her again to make sure she got it. Then I threw the number away."

"Can you call your friend and get the number again? I'll give you another hundred bucks, and I'll pay you the hundred that Elise owed you."

He scratched his head. "Sorry, can't help you. My friend doesn't work there anymore. He got fired a couple days later. Apparently I wasn't the only one he'd been selling information to."

Kacey crossed her arms. "Oh, c'mon—"

I touched her back. "Too bad. Listen, thanks again, Brandon." I opened the door and Kacey and I walked out into the hallway.

When the door closed behind us, she turned toward me so quickly that she practically pushed me against the wall. "Why didn't you—"

I held my finger up to my mouth and whispered. "Wait 'til we're in the elevator."

We walked down the hall, and when the elevator doors opened and we stepped in, Kacey's face turned a new, brighter shade of red. "He was lying and you let him off the hook! I think *he* was the one blackmailing Dad."

"Look, first, we don't know he was lying. And second, even if he was, it's a long jump from there to the conclusion that he was blackmailing your dad. He's been a good friend to me, and he was right. I owed it to him not to grill him like that. Besides, he wasn't going to tell us anything else the way we were going."

"How do you know? You just gave up!"

I hit the lobby button. "I didn't give up, I just stopped for today. If what he was telling us was true, whoever was calling Elise must have been the blackmailer. Why else would he have been calling your father, too?"

"Why would you think Brandon was telling the truth?"

"Why do you think he wasn't?" I leaned back against the wall and put my hand on my side as the elevator dropped.

"Are you okay?"

"It's starting to hurt. I just need to get home and take a pain pill." I pulled up my sweatshirt and checked the gauze. The blood spot was expanding. There was no use worrying about it until we got back to the house. "What was it about Brandon's story that was so unbelievable?" I said, still looking at the gauze.

"For starters, that he didn't keep the phone number of the guy he found."

I pulled my sweatshirt back down. "Why is that so unbelievable? If Elise calls him out of the blue, and he finds a phone number for her, and he thinks it's somebody she's hooked up with over the Internet, why would he keep it? It wouldn't mean anything to him."

"Okay, but what are the odds that his friend is no longer working at the phone forwarding company?"

"I have no idea, and neither do you. We don't know anything about the guy or the company. It's easy to jump to wrong conclusions when you're emotionally involved."

"Emotionally involved?"

"The minute Brandon accused your dad of taking the money, you were all over him. I could tell by looking at you."

The elevator door opened. Kacey put her hands in her jacket pockets and walked out into the lobby. She continued to walk in front of me as we went through the revolving door to the sidewalk. My side hurt pretty bad, but I did my best to keep up.

Out on the sidewalk, she spun to face me. I straightened my back, which made me wince. She didn't seem to notice. "So, somehow the blackmailer who called Dad ended up talking to Elise. Do you think Elise was in on it? She knew about Chase and could have decided to cash in."

I was glad to see she was thinking again rather than emoting. "I'm not necessarily saying that, although it's a possibility. The flip side is that it's really hard to picture Elise doing something like that to your Dad. She loved him."

Kacey fell back in stride with me as we walked toward the car, which she'd parked in a metered space. I tried to walk as normally as possible, but it was impossible not to limp.

"Who knows?" she said. "As they say 'hell hath no fury like a woman scorned.'"

I walked around the car to the passenger door while Kacey dug in her purse for her keys. She opened the door and looked over the top of the car at me. "What if Brandon was lying, though? He could have been the one blackmailing Dad. Maybe he and Elise were in on it together. Or Elise could have found out he was doing it and was trying to stop him. Either one would make sense."

We got in the car. The windshield was frosted. Kacey turned the key and hit the defrost button. Then we sat back and waited for the windshield to clear.

"But Elise was the one embezzling money," I said. "We know that from the auditors."

"Okay, but that would fit either way. She could have been embezzling with Brandon, or she could have been embezzling to pay Brandon. For that matter, I guess she could have been embezzling to pay anybody who was blackmailing Dad."

I shifted my weight to try to find a more comfortable position. Now my finger was aching, too. "Good point. Then, of course, there's still the most obvious possibility. Maybe Elise was just embezzling the money for herself."

"That wouldn't explain the mystery caller who was calling both her and Dad, though."

"True."

She put the car in gear and pulled away from the curb.

I leaned my head back against the headrest. "There are so many possibilities it's making my brain hurt."

We were cruising down Cedar Springs Avenue when Kacey put her hand over her mouth. "I just thought of something!" she said through her fingers.

"What?"

"If Brandon was blackmailing Dad, do you think he could have killed Elise?"

I laughed, which hurt like crazy. I doubled over and held my side.

Kacey's eyebrows narrowed. "Are you sure you're okay?"

I straightened back up in my seat. "I'm fine. It's really starting to hurt, though."

"We should have waited until tomorrow to go to Brandon's."

"It's okay, really. Anyway, the idea that Brandon could be a murderer is the best argument you could have made to take the heat off of him in my mind. You saw him. I don't think a killer is lurking anywhere beneath that doughy exterior."

"That's what they always say about killers: *He was such a quiet guy.*"

"Whoa, now you're starting to sound crazy. We don't know that anyone killed Elise other than Elise. I'm no private investigator, but I've been in enough investigations to know that often the thing that seems obvious in the beginning isn't what happened at all. Hopefully I stopped questioning Brandon in time that he still trusts me. I'll have other chances to talk to him." I looked out the window. "This isn't the end."

CHAPTER
FIFTEEN

BY THURSDAY AFTERNOON, A week after I got shot, I was feeling pretty good. Rob Morrow had called and made a date for dinner Saturday night, the wound on my side was practically closed, and I seldom needed anything stronger than ibuprofen for the pain in my finger. Kacey and I were at the gun range, and I was practicing shooting with my left hand.

When I was a kid, my dad insisted that I learn to shoot with both hands. When I was a teenager, he even occasionally made me shoot left-handed in local juniors' tournaments, primarily because that was the only way I could get any real competition in my age group. It had been years, though, since I'd done much left-handed shooting. For the first time since I taught her to shoot, Kacey was beating me.

She was not being a gracious winner.

I hadn't been outshot since before I entered the Secret Service, and I wasn't taking it particularly well, even though the score was close. So I was glad when my cell phone vibrated in my pocket and broke things up. I set down my .357 Sig , took off my hearing protectors, and hit the button on the phone. Officer Ferrell's nasal voice was easy to recognize.

"Officer Ferrell, how are you?"

"I'm calling because we got the toxicology report back on your friend, Elise Hovden."

That was news. I didn't even know they had done a toxicology test on her. As if he'd read my mind, he said, "It's part of our procedure for a suicide scene. Did you know anything about Ms. Hovden's Valium use?"

I waved at Kacey to get her attention. She took off her hearing protectors. "I didn't know Elise took Valium."

Kacey raised an eyebrow.

"Kacey Mason is here with me. She didn't know, either."

"The reason I ask is that we didn't notice a pre-scription bottle in the car or at her house, though I can't say we were looking for anything like that.

And she was loaded. Not enough to kill her, but enough to zonk her pretty good."

I shifted the phone to my other ear and propped it there with my splinted hand. "That's strange. Why would she take an overdose of Valium if she intended to kill herself with carbon monoxide?"

"It's not that unusual, really. A person who is going to commit suicide will sometimes take something to calm the nerves first. What's unusual is the amount of Valium she took. She must have been pretty loopy by the time she got into the car."

"Have you checked with her doctor?"

"Since there was no prescription bottle, we don't know who her doctor is. Besides, we're not really doing an investigation. I was curious and just thought it was worth a phone call to see if you knew anything about the Valium."

"Sorry, we don't."

"By the way, I read in the paper that you were quite a hero in Coppell last week. I guess I don't feel so bad about getting flipped by you." He gave an awkward half laugh. "I want you to know that I'm okay with that and there are no hard feelings. You're pretty tough— especially for someone so . . . attractive." He cleared his throat.

I wondered if he thought I'd been lying awake worrying about whether he was mad at me. Then I wondered if he was coming on to me.

"Thank you, Officer Ferrell. I'm glad there are no hard feelings. I was lucky out in Coppell, that's all."

"You can call me Ed."

Uh-oh. I didn't like where this seemed to be going. "Listen, I'm in the middle of something, so I've got to go."

"I thought that maybe—"

I had to interrupt him before he got it out. "Wait, I forgot to ask. What will you be doing next on Ms. Hovden's case?"

"There is no case. It's already been ruled a suicide. We're closing the file."

"Of course. Thank you for calling, Officer Ferrell." There was no way I was calling him Ed. "I've really got to go. Good-bye." I shifted the phone back to my good hand. As I clicked it off, I heard him say, "But I—"

Kacey removed the empty magazine from her pistol. "So, Elise was on Valium. I guess I can see that. She seemed to have some anxiety issues."

I stuck the phone back in my pocket. "We can talk about that in a minute. First, you're not going to believe this. I think Ferrell was going to ask me out."

Kacey cringed. "It makes me feel oily just to think about it." A sly smile lit her face. "Oh, he'd be great for you, though. Congratulations."

"Thanks. You're a real scream. Anyway, at least he said I was attractive."

"Let's see, Rob Morrow . . . Officer Ferrell—" she

held her palms up and moved them as if she were weighing the two men on a scale—"that's a tough one."

"What are the odds of settling down with a guy like Rob Morrow?" I said. "I'm just another woman to him. I'm not going to let myself take him too seriously."

She replaced the magazine on her pistol. "Well then why don't you get out and meet someone real? You never go out; you just sit around the house like a grandma. You're gorgeous, but you never give guys a chance to meet you."

I picked up my gun. "Wait until you're older, dream girl. You're used to walking around campus where there are a million guys your age drooling over you. Enjoy it while you can. It's different when you get out in the real world. Think about it. Where does a twenty-nine-year-old security specialist who's recovering from a drinking problem meet guys?"

"Oh, c'mon. You're just making excuses. My gosh, Rob Morrow came to your hospital room to meet you! With your looks, you could meet guys in a monastery. In fact, that's a great idea. Why don't you come to church with me Sunday morning? There are a million good-looking guys at the church next to the campus."

"Yeah, and all of them are nineteen."

"No, actually there are a lot of guys in their twenties and thirties. And they're not all married, because some of them come in by themselves."

"Sounds like you've been scoping. Where do you get the time to listen to the sermon?"

"I keep my eyes open, that's all."

I checked the magazine on my pistol and turned toward the target. "Anyway, back to Elise. I can see why she would take a pill or two if she was going to kill herself, but why take an overdose before she gets in her car in a closed garage and turns on the ignition?"

"Overdose? Who said anything about an overdose?"

"Ferrell—I mean, Ed—" I smiled—"Ed told me that she had taken much more than a usual dose. Not enough to kill her, but a lot."

"Maybe she wanted to be sure that she got the job done." She pulled out her phone and squinted at the clock. "We're running out of time. We'd better get back to shooting."

I picked up my hearing protectors. "By the way, you don't happen to know who her doctor was, do you?"

"No, but I imagine her personnel records at the Ministry would show that."

I shook my head. "Never mind. Let's put up a couple more targets and I'll show you how a real lefty shoots."

I picked up my gun. As the target rotated into place and I raised my Sig, I thought of the missing laptop and the Valium and the calls to Brandon. I pictured Elise's twisted body in the front seat of her car. Nothing about her death added up.

I sighted down the barrel and tried to concentrate but couldn't shake the feeling that Elise's death and the attempt to blackmail Simon were connected. I squeezed the trigger. The muffled pop must have triggered something in my brain, because it occurred to me that the one person who still might be able to shed some light on this whole thing was the person who'd known about Simon's illegitimate son longer than anyone else. And I was having brunch with her Sunday morning.

CHAPTER
SIXTEEN

THREE DAYS LATER I eased my Camaro up to the wood-shingled guard station at my mother's gated neighborhood in Southlake. I was running late because of my date with Rob Morrow the night before. Well, that's not exactly accurate. It was what happened after the date that had me running late.

Rob had taken me to a new steak place in Victory Park near downtown Dallas. A pack of professional jocks held down the restaurant's corner booths every weekend evening, and the staff treated Rob like a rock star. I was shallow enough to be impressed, and I thoroughly enjoyed the envious looks the restaurant's female patrons shot my way as the maître d' led us to a primo booth in the back.

Rob was everything I could have dreamed: witty, intelligent, self-confident, and of course, beautiful. With curly golden hair that fell loosely over the collar of his long-sleeved polo, he gave the impression of a guy who had leaned his surfboard against the wall just in time to throw on a shirt and pants for dinner. Oh, yeah, and his yellow Ferrari made an impression, too.

He seemed disappointed that I was a nondrinker, which practically forced me to explain that I was an alcoholic—not exactly recommended conversation for a first date. He took it in stride, though. I figured that in his crowd a visit to the Betty Ford Center was as ordinary as a trip to the eye doctor.

Though I was booze-free for the date, my nerves had pushed me to medicate in another way. Before Rob picked me up, I took a couple of painkillers, something I hadn't done for several days. It's not fair to blame the painkillers for what happened. But blaming something other than myself helps ease another kind of pain—the I-hate-myself pain that I felt as I slunk out his apartment door at eight a.m. and grabbed a taxi back to the house.

I was glad that Simon wasn't alive to see that he hadn't really changed me. He should have known that you can't turn trash into treasure by dressing it up in Armani and playing praise songs in its ear.

The taxi ride from Morrow's place to the house had seemed longer than it was, probably because the entire way I was staring at an unpleasant truth. After Simon helped me crawl out of a bourbon bottle, I had convinced myself that my horrible choices in men, and the promiscuous way I acted with them, were behind me. Now, however, I had no choice but to admit that even stone-cold sober—painkillers notwithstanding—I was as capable as ever of behaving like a . . . well, let's just say behaving badly. I couldn't escape the conclusion that I wasn't worth much to anyone, including myself.

As I stared out the cab window, I wondered where I was going. Not in the taxi, but in my life. Nature seemed to have imposed a couple of bleakly unfair rules on me. Everyone who cared about me either died or ran out, and the only meaningful skill I had developed in nearly thirty years was a knack for letting everyone around me down. My thoughts led back to a question I had been asking myself with increasing frequency since Simon's death: What was the point of a life poorly lived, a life with no apparent purpose?

If I had been blessed in any way in my life, it was that I had never been prone to depression, but by the time the taxi arrived at the house, I was about as low as I'd ever been. It's strange, though, how the simple routines of everyday life can sometimes save us from ourselves. I suppose that's another blessing—one that life gives to all of us if we'll let it.

First, I had to pay the cab driver. Then I had to find my house key. Once in the house I had thirty minutes to get ready and leave for my mother's. With one eye on the clock, I turned my thoughts from the gloomy to the mechanical. Gradually, as I showered, dressed, and applied my makeup, my morose thoughts became less like a pistol pointed at my head and more like a vaguely unpleasant haze. They impeded my navigation but didn't completely shoot off my guidance system.

One other blessing of the morning was that Kacey was staying at her sorority house until finals were over. At least I didn't have to look her in the eye as I crept into the house.

By the time I reached the guardhouse in my mother's neighborhood, I was functioning at a level above suicidal. In fact, while the guard searched his list of expected guests, I concentrated on the present and fought my nerves for the second time in twelve hours. Despite our initial underwhelming reunion, I was excited to see my mother again. I had concocted all sorts of plausible excuses for her previous unusual behavior. After all, she had as much right to be nervous as I did. As the guard buzzed me through, the depressing image of Rob Morrow was receding and my hopes were rising for a new and improved mother-daughter relationship.

Beyond the gate were ten or twelve huge houses,

each with at least an acre of wooded lawn. The guard pointed to a two-story colonial just around the curve. "Okay, Ms. Pasbury, it's number 8, right over there." I pulled away from the guard hut, eased the car past several winter-dormant but still immaculately manicured lawns, and stopped at the curb in front of number 8.

The house had to be at least ten thousand square feet, and I wondered what the two of them did with all that space. I stepped out of the car and headed up the stone walk that led to the front door. I had hardly rung the bell when my mother burst onto the porch in a blue silk dress and mink wrap.

"I thought you wouldn't make it in time! Let's go straight over to the driveway. Stanley will pick us up." She grabbed my wrist and tugged me along behind her as she cut across the yard to the driveway.

"Where are we going?"

"Why, to church, of course. It's Sunday."

I looked down at my blue jeans. "Church?"

"You know we always go to church on Sundays."

I shook my hand free from hers. "How would I know that? You've been gone for twenty years!"

"We always went when you were a child; every single Sunday. I would dress you up in your cute little sailor dress, and you would march right up those church stairs. You were so adorable. All the other parents would comment on you."

"You made me wear a sailor dress?"

She sighed. "What difference does it make? I just know that everyone told me how cute you were. Here comes Stanley now."

A black BMW crept up the driveway from somewhere behind the house. As my mother stepped aside to let it move up to us and stop, she said, "One thing will never change. I go to church every Sunday. Even when I lived on the street, I made it to the homeless mission for services."

Since her return to my life, I had already discovered a number of baffling things about my mother. This, however, was one of the most difficult to figure. In every part of her life she seemed to spend far more time on the superficial than the spiritual; yet she attended church as faithfully as a Puritan and apparently thought her presence in the pew somehow painted her soul a more pleasing color. If religion really worked like that, I needed to pay closer attention.

While the type of life I'd lived was certainly no better—flash back to eight o'clock that very morning— I had at least never had the audacity to hold myself out to the world as anything other than a person careening toward damnation. The rotten men and cheap booze (or was it rotten booze and cheap men?) had left little time for the spiritual. That is, until I met Simon. While he had not pulled off a Road-to-Damascus conversion on me, a Bible story told and retold to recovering alcoholics, Simon had nudged me to what could charitably be described as the periphery of the outer edge of faith. Thanks particularly to the alcohol-recovery program, his efforts appeared to be working. That is, until Rob Morrow pulled up in his Ferrari.

Since drying out, I'd become an occasional Bible reader, although still not a churchgoer. Granted, I most often picked up the Bible when my cravings for a Maker's Mark were the strongest, but I picked it up nonetheless. That was progress. On the downside, though, I had not yet learned to view the Good Book as much more than a literary curiosity with a talismanic tendency to calm me when I was twitching in the direction of the nearest bar.

So, struggling under the weight of as much emotional and spiritual baggage as any twenty-nine-year-old should have to deal with, my overriding thought as my mother held open the back door of Stanley's BMW was, *What a stinking hypocrite!* Nevertheless, I got in and slid across the black leather seat to the other side. She got in beside me.

Stanley turned and looked over the seat.

"Stanley, this is my daughter Taylor. Taylor, this is my husband, Stanley. Isn't he cute?"

He ran a hand through his graying hair, which was sparse on top and too long everywhere else, and stuck his other hand over the back of the driver's seat. "Nice to meet you," he said, in a baritone voice that seemed a mismatch for his narrow nose and thin lips.

I took his hand and shook it. It was slender and damp, and when he turned away from me to pull the car onto the street, I wiped my palm on the leg of my jeans.

"If I had known we were going to church, I would have dressed a little nicer." I tugged at the hem of my fitted leather jacket, as if by pulling hard enough I could somehow convert it to a skirt. I'd lived most of my life in inappropriate attire, and my uncanny talent for dressing wrong no longer completely unnerved me the way it had when I was younger. Still, it was a flaw that was unmatched in its ability to accentuate my long list of insecurities. I let go of my jacket and twisted a finger in my hair as I thought about what I should be wearing.

"Your jeans are just fine, dear." My mother pulled her mink wrap around her shoulders. "You know how the kids are nowadays. They wear just about anything to church. You'll probably be dressed better than most of them."

"That's great, but I'm twenty-nine years old."

"Of course you are, but you'll always be my little girl. Did you know that the average American owns seven pairs of jeans? Stanley, turn up the heat, it's like an icebox in here."

Stanley sighed and pressed a button on the dash.

My meeting with my mother had been strange

the week before, but this was downright surreal. She acted as if I were still nine and had just come home from summer camp. I wondered whether she had any concept of the passage of time. Plus, she was a walking Trivial Pursuit game. The pitch and yaw of the conversation left me yearning for solid ground. Like a passenger on a boat in a rough sea, I looked out the window and tried to focus on the horizon.

After driving for ten minutes down a parkway lined with subdivisions with names like Astor Ridge and Chesterfield Falls, Stanley pulled the car into the circular drive of the Calvary Baptist Church. Judging by the size of the building, the height of the sparkling steeple, and the quality of dress of the people entering the church, this was not just any old church in Southlake society.

Stanley glanced back over the seat. "I'll park. You get us a place to sit."

My mother stepped out of the car and slung her wrap around her shoulders with a flair. Without even a glance behind at me, she strode up the stairs with her head held high. I stopped on the second stair and watched her. She was making an entrance, and I may as well have been wherever I had been for the past twenty years. I sighed and followed, increasingly conscious with each step that I was the only adult in sight who was wearing blue jeans.

When she arrived at the door, she turned to me. "For such a young, healthy thing, you certainly walk slowly. What happened to your finger?"

So, she'd finally noticed. I opened my mouth to explain, but she turned away and walked through the door. My shoulders sagged.

We stepped into a huge, carpeted vestibule where people milled everywhere. As we approached the entrance to the sanctuary, a tall greeter with a thick Texas accent said, "Mornin' to you, Mrs. Venable." He handed us each a bulletin. My mother nodded at him with no more sense of recognition than if he were a bellman at a hotel. She walked down the aisle and selected a seat halfway to the pulpit in the center section.

The choir began its opening number, "Holy, Holy, Holy," a song I actually had a faint memory of from my childhood. Before they were halfway through the first verse, my mother began to sing, softly but audibly. I turned to her, my eyes wide, but she was looking straight ahead. I glanced around to see whether anyone else seemed to hear her. No one was looking, but her voice grew stronger with each passing second. Soon, I noticed a few people giving her furtive looks. Others seemed oblivious, though by now her voice was loud enough to be heard halfway to the front row.

I tugged her sleeve. "I don't think the congregation is supposed to sing along with this."

She patted my hand. "Honey, this is church. We're here to praise the Lord. If people don't want to hear it, that's their problem."

Stanley slid into the pew next to me. He must have noticed the horror on my face. He leaned toward me and whispered, "Don't let it bother you. The regulars are accustomed to it."

"Doesn't it embarrass you?"

He shrugged, then pulled a graphing calculator out of his pocket, and went to work on some sort of calculation. Just a hunch, but I don't think it had anything to do with the pastor's theme for the day.

By the time the song ended, my good hand was squeezing the edge of the pew so tight that the blood had left my knuckles. I eased my grip and took a deep breath. When I opened the bulletin, I received a confirmation that God was truly merciful: The choir didn't have any more numbers scheduled for the service.

Although I had been inside some churches since I was nine, I hadn't been to an actual church service. My mother had been right, though, when she said that we attended church every Sunday when I was a kid. As the service unfolded, everything was reasonably familiar. The sanctuary, with its white arches and cryptic stained glass, was far fancier than the church of my youth, but still not as imposing as some of the cathedrals in D.C. where my Secret Service pals and

I had worked functions. The rhythm of the service was similar to those I remembered from my childhood.

As the minister shared a story about a neighbor who was crushed beyond solace at the loss of a child, I thought of the night Dad died. We had relaxed by the campfire and talked, and it had been nice. I learned more about him in that one conversation by the fire than I had my entire life. I learned about the things that haunted him; the marks that war and killing—necessary killing, but still killing—had made on him. I remembered, in particular, one thing that he told me about my mother, who by then had been gone eight years. He said that before her emotional problems won out, she had been a woman of faith, of strength. He worried that he had cheated me of that faith, which he clearly viewed as important.

All of that came before the men with the shotgun arrived, and the talking stopped.

I looked at my mother and tried to picture her in the way Dad had described her, but I couldn't. Each time she breathed, the wrinkles at the edges of her eyes contracted and expanded, struggling to break through the putty of her makeup, struggling to reach the light once again. She had so thoroughly buried her face's strong, solid features that I wondered if I would some-day discover that she was little more than a clown. But Dad had loved her to the end, even after she'd been gone so many years. That was proof enough for me that she wasn't a clown. There was something of substance beneath the tacky façade. There had to be.

She turned to me and smiled, and I thought I noted a hint of real affection in the way the tiny lines above her lip crinkled. We see what we want to see, though, and I was afraid that my emotions were trying to PhotoShop a picture that was as impassive as a still life.

I had trouble concentrating on the pastor's message, but when he began his closing prayer, I lowered my head along with the rest of the congregation. Simon had taught me to pray, but the results had left much to be desired. After all, Simon was dead. If God was much of a listener, he had given a strangely tone-deaf response when he deleted from my life the one man who had mattered to me since my father died. Despite my doubts, though, Simon gave me hope, and sitting there in the pew next to my mother, I raised a hopeful prayer that God would give my mom back to me again.

As we filed out of the sanctuary, my mother looked right past me as she nodded at this person and that. Waiting on the front steps for Stanley to pull the BMW around, she finally spoke to me—but only about the nasal quality of the pastor's voice and the garishness of the song leader's tie.

Once we were on our way back down the boulevard toward their house, she fanned herself with the church bulletin. "Pastor Franklyn is a good man, but sometimes he just goes on so long—and the perfume on that woman next to me! I thought I was going to be asphyxiated." She glanced at me. "Oh, sorry, that was a poor choice of words in light of your friend's suicide."

I kept my eyes on the back of Stanley's head. "It's all right."

"I would have introduced you to some people, but I thought you would be uncomfortable, what with your blue jeans and all."

As she yammered, I picked at a thread that dangled from the seam of my pocket. They weren't even my best jeans. I snapped off the thread.

On the way back to their house, I spent a lot of time looking out the window. I turned occasionally to nod or smile, just enough to look like I was listening. I was thinking, though, about Simon. He worked so hard to sell me on the idea of God, but here I was disappointed again. After all, what good is God if he never, ever gives a person a break?

Dad had always warned me that self-pity was like quicksand. If you let yourself get too deep in it, it becomes nearly impossible to get out. During that ride back to my mother's, though, I quietly wallowed in it. And I enjoyed it. I wondered when it would be my turn; my turn to have an anchor in my life; my turn to have someone who would love me no matter what. Maybe it was too much to ask. Or maybe it was simply that God works methodically just like the rest of us. Even he must need time to fix a mother-daughter relationship as messed up as this one.

CHAPTER
SEVENTEEN

BACK AT MY MOTHER'S house, she escorted me to a large breakfast nook cupped by a bay window. The window looked out over a Texas winter garden dominated by clusters of purple and yellow pansies and a sculpted marble fountain. The breakfast table was set for three, and in the middle was a platter with a variety of fruits and muffins. When Stanley came in from the garage, we sat.

My mother unfolded her napkin. "Stanley, say grace."

He folded his hands in his lap. "Bless this food and bless us, too. Amen."

A Hispanic woman in an apron appeared next to me. "Would you like an omelet, ma'am?"

I raised an eyebrow and leaned over to whisper to my mother. "You have servants?"

"Oh, no, honey. We just decided to have brunch catered. It's a special occasion with you here. This is"— she lifted her reading glasses, which dangled from a gold chain around her neck, and peered at the woman's name tag—"this is Maria."

I looked up at Maria and smiled. "I'll have a cheese omelet with bacon and ham and wheat toast, please."

Maria smiled back at me. "Hash browns?" Her accent was thick.

"Yes, thank you."

My mother adjusted her napkin in her lap. Without looking at me, she said, "My, that is certainly a lot of food. You know, you're getting to the age where most women can't eat as if they're teenagers anymore."

I looked down at my jeans, which were stretched tight over my thighs. I had bought them too tight. I was sure of it.

She took a drink of her grapefruit juice. "When I was your age, I could eat anything that I wanted. You got more of your father's build. He was sturdier."

I fiddled with the cocktail ring on my finger. Was it my imagination, or was it more difficult to get off than it used to be?

Stanley spooned some fruit onto his plate. He seemed to pay no attention to either of us as he stabbed bite-sized pieces of cantaloupe with his fork and shoveled them into his mouth.

"I understand you were a hero again last week," my mother said. She set a blueberry muffin in the center of her plate. With her butter knife she scored four precise lines across the top of the muffin. I was so fascinated by what she was doing that I forgot she'd asked me a question. Holding the muffin with one hand and using the scored lines as a guide, she carefully sawed the muffin into eight equal slices. Then she meticulously arranged the slices in two rows of four on her plate.

By the time she was finished, I was mesmerized. I didn't realize that my face had drifted close to her. When she looked up, our eyes were no more than six inches apart. She gasped.

I jerked back in my chair. "I'm sorry; it's just that I've never seen anyone slice a muffin with such precision."

"Measure twice, cut once; that's the key to weight control. That, and cigarettes." She picked up one of the muffin slices and nibbled it like a mouse gnawing cheese.

"I thought measure twice, cut once was a saying that had to do with woodworking."

She waved a hand in the air. "Maybe so, but it applies nicely to eating, also."

I didn't see how it had anything at all to do with eating, but there was no point in pressing the issue.

"I understand you got shot in the finger." She said it with no more emotion than if she'd been observing that I'd bought a new dress.

"Actually, I got shot in the side. Just a nick, though. It was no big deal."

She pointed at my splint with her fork. "Then what's that?"

"It got caught between a reporter's head and the floor of Starbucks."

She took another nibble of muffin. "You know, when you were a little girl you were so clumsy." She grunted as she chewed, and I wasn't sure if it was a laugh or an expression of disgust. "We used to laugh when you would play in the backyard and get tangled up in your own feet. You had more bumps and bruises than any child on the block."

At that point, I'd had enough. "Well, I couldn't have been too clumsy, Mother. I was all-district in basketball and all-state in softball."

"Were you really? That's wonderful. Nevertheless, you were clumsy when you were small. There can be no doubt about that. I remember it as if it were yesterday."

Maria came in from the kitchen and placed my omelet and hash browns in front of me on a dark blue plate. Garnished with diced tomatoes and parsley, the food was so pretty that I almost hated to cut into it.

I picked up my fork. "I thought you might call me when I was in the hospital." I made a point not to look up. "It was all over the news that day. You must have heard about it, didn't you?"

"I don't think that we did. Did we, Stanley?" Her voice had an unnaturally casual quality. "My memory anymore is so awful. Getting old is no treat, you know?"

Stanley's head was buried in the Arts and Leisure section of the paper. He merely cleared his throat.

"We were awfully busy last week," she continued. "It seemed that we had something every night. I don't know how we can keep up this schedule."

I placed my hands in my lap. "I'm your daughter. I was in the hospital."

She wagged her fork in my direction. "I suppose I have to remind you that you didn't call me, either."

"I was the one who got shot. I think the calls customarily run in the other direction in that situation."

"You're right. I should have called."

I took that as an admission that she had known.

"I guess it will take some time for me to get back into this mothering thing." She pointed at my omelet. "Do you think I could have just a taste of that? It looks scrumptious."

Before I could answer, she had cut off a hunk of egg and placed it on her plate. She then spent at least two minutes subdividing it and moving it around with her fork until it was arranged just the way she wanted it in relationship to her remaining muffin slices.

"You know, I broke my arm once when I was twelve," she said. "Roller skates. Uncle Ralph told me he'd never seen a child take to skating as quickly as I did. He said I always tried to do too much too soon . . ."

As she went on about her natural ability as a skater, I fiddled with the tape on my splint. Maria appeared to my right and poured coffee into my cup. I smiled up at her and wondered whether she had a daughter, and if so, whether they laughed and talked and fixed each other's hair. In fact, I wondered whether she might want another one.

Maybe it was self-centered of me, but I tried again to bring the conversation back to my injuries. After all, the newspapers had called me a hero—and this was my mother! I held up my splint. "My line of business can be dangerous, but I never really appreciated how dangerous until I met Simon Mason. The past year has been crazy."

My mother looked at me blankly, as if she had no idea how to respond to such a rude interruption of her roller-skating story.

Stanley rustled his paper and peeked around the edge. When our eyes met, he withdrew behind it again, like a turtle pulling its head back into its shell. "So, I understand the bullet was intended for that

Morning News reporter," he said from behind a grainy photo of a football player. "What's her name?"

"Katie Parst."

He lowered the paper and squinted at me over the reading glasses that were perched near the end of his skinny nose. "She's the one who's been doing those reports on organized crime, isn't she?"

"That's right, an extortion ring. She's a brave woman. I'd never met her before, but I like her a lot. She stayed with me for a long time at the hospital."

My mother lifted a piece of omelet with her fork, opened her mouth unnaturally wide, and inserted the bite carefully into her mouth, seemingly concerned that some part of the egg or fork might brush against her teeth. This time she chewed and swallowed before she spoke. "I'm sure this Parst woman probably felt a sense of obligation. After all, according to the paper, you saved her life."

"I'm sure she did feel obligated. But I think she likes me, too."

"Of course she does, dear." She smiled and scooped three dollops of cream cheese the size of golf balls from a dish in the center of the table. She placed them on the edge of her plate. Suddenly she picked one up with her fingers and popped it directly into her mouth.

My jaw must have dropped, because as she picked up a second one, she said, "What are you staring at, honey? It's the dairy group." She popped that one into her mouth, also.

I wanted desperately to be back on earth. I lowered my head and concentrated on my omelet.

"It was a terrible thing about Simon Mason's assistant, the lady who killed herself," she said. "Stanley and I saw it in the paper, didn't we, dear?"

His voice barely made it over the top of the page. "I don't remember anything about any suicide."

My mother placed her fork on her plate. "Of course you do. We talked about it, don't you remember? I said that I wondered if Taylor knew her."

"If you say so, dear." He still didn't lower the paper.

"I wonder who I could have talked about that with if it wasn't you?" she said, scratching her head. "Well, did you know her, Taylor?"

"Yes, I knew her pretty well, actually. She didn't like me."

"Why not? Did you do something to her?"

I sighed. "No, I didn't do something to her. She just never took to me, I guess." The last thing I wanted was for my mother to know that Simon's top assistant was in love with him and jealous of me.

Stanley chose that as the time to emerge again from his shell. He put down his paper. "How did it happen?"

"How did what happen?"

"The suicide."

"Carbon monoxide. She apparently loaded herself up with Valium, got in her car with the garage door down, and turned on the ignition."

Stanley took off his reading glasses and set them on the table next to his plate. "Poor girl. Are they certain it wasn't an accident?"

"It was the middle of the night, and she left a note. Kacey Mason and I found her—and the note."

He tilted his head. "You were at her house?"

"Kacey and I had a meeting with her that morning. We found her body. Later, we found the note in the house."

"How gruesome," my mother said.

"Yes, it was pretty gruesome."

Stanley picked up his glasses again. "What did the note say?"

"That's pretty sensitive, with her family and all."

"Of course." He put his glasses on and opened the business section.

My mother picked up her last slice of muffin. This time she slathered cream cheese on it with her knife. "That's certainly a nice house you're living in," she said, just before shoving the muffin in her mouth. Suddenly she seemed to have no concern at all for her teeth. A glob of cream cheese stuck to one of her incisors. I figured I could spend a lifetime trying to make sense out of the eating habits I'd observed in this one brunch.

I resolved never to pay attention to her eating again, unless I was making a video for her therapist.

"It's Simon Mason's house. I'm living there with Kacey. She's a good kid, a good friend."

Stanley looked at me over his paper again. I hadn't even realized he was listening anymore. "You're actually living in Simon Mason's house? You were that close to him?"

"Yes. He was a lot like Dad."

My mother took a long drink of grapefruit juice and put her glass back on the table. She wiped her mouth with her napkin. "Well, it's all water under the bridge. I hope you're moving on. Each day is a new day."

"You're a veritable cliché machine," I said.

"Well, Miss smarty-pants, I'm sorry I couldn't be more original."

"I was just kidding."

She folded her napkin and placed it on the table next to her plate. "It's all right. I don't know why I'm being so sensitive. It's the stress."

I didn't know if she was referring to me or to something else that was causing her stress.

"If you're finished eating, I'll give you a tour of the house." Her voice was suddenly bright again.

Actually, I'd barely begun to eat, but I looked again at my tight jeans and put my fork down. "I can't wait to see it."

Stanley stood up. "If you two don't mind, I've got some work to do. I'll be in the study."

She waved at him. "You go on, dear. We'll just be having a girl talk."

I didn't know what she had in mind, but I had a difficult time envisioning us in a girl talk. So far, the morning had been so much less than I had hoped for, in nearly every way. I could feel my shoulders sagging at the mere thought of a long walk through her house.

Just before we pushed back from the table, she pulled a prescription bottle out of her pocket. She shook a pill out onto the table and sized it up carefully before cutting it in half with her knife. As she placed the pill on her tongue and tipped her head back, I glanced at the bottle, which was almost empty. Valium.

I nodded at the bottle. "What would happen if you took five or six of those?"

"Why would I do that?"

"You wouldn't, but do you know what would happen?"

"Honey, if I took two of them, I'd be asleep in ten minutes. That's why I cut them in half. If I took five or six, I wouldn't wake up for a week."

CHAPTER
EIGHTEEN

WHEN I GOT BACK to the house, Kacey was in front of the television in blue sweatpants and a yellow Tri-Delta sweatshirt. Her feet, in running shoes and white ankle socks, were propped on an ottoman. She wore her hair in a haphazard ponytail. "Well, how did it go?"

I tossed my purse on the couch. "What are you doing here?"

She picked up the clicker and turned off the TV. "When I pulled out my stuff to study for my econ final, I realized I'd left my notes here. So I had to drive over and get them. I've only been here a few minutes."

I kicked off my shoes and plopped down on the couch. "It was disappointing."

"Are we talking about Rob Morrow or about your mother?"

"Both."

"Strike two."

"I don't want to talk about Rob."

She waved a hand in the air. "That is grossly unfair. Everybody in my sorority is waiting to hear about that date."

I shot her a look. She got the point. "So, what went wrong with your mom?"

I sighed. "Let's see, where do I start? First, I didn't know we were going to church, and here I am in blue jeans."

"So what? Lots of people wear blue jeans to church."

"Not to that church. I looked like an idiot, as usual. Then, all that my mother wanted to talk about was herself—and, you know, after twenty years, I was kind of hoping she'd have some interest in hearing about me."

Kacey slid her feet off the ottoman and leaned toward me with her elbows on her knees. "I'm sorry. Wasn't she interested at all?"

"Not really. It was obvious she hadn't given me a lot of thought."

"I'm sure that's not true. She was probably nervous.

Besides, didn't you say she had some psychological problems?"

I laughed. "I'll say. You're not going to believe this. We're sitting in church, and the choir is singing—you know, a choir song. Nobody else is supposed to sing. Well, my mother starts singing along with them—out loud. Other than the choir, she's the only one in the whole building who's singing."

"You mean she was singing to herself?"

"No! She was so loud that people all over the place could hear her. And then, you should have seen how she cut her food at brunch. She approached it like a heart surgeon and then arranged her food in patterns on her plate."

"Sounds as if she has issues. Maybe you're expecting more than she's capable of giving. Maybe she's just not . . . right enough to be what you want her to be."

"I'm not as good a person as you are, Kace. I'm not willing to cut her that much slack. It seems to me like she's right enough to show at least a token bit of interest in her own daughter, but she's just too self-centered to do it. It's not like she's completely out of her mind or anything."

Kacey looked at me sympathetically.

"By the way, their house is a mansion. Must be ten thousand square feet."

"Does she work?"

"No, but her husband—number three, by the way—is a chemical-engineering professor. According to her, he's some sort of genius. She said he works with the oil industry on the side and makes loads of money."

She pumped a fist. "Way to cash in, Hillary! Now, if we can just keep you together with Rob Morrow."

I frowned. I was not going to let her draw me into a Morrow discussion. "I found out something interesting about her. It's probably nothing, but at least it got my attention. She takes Valium for anxiety. I saw her prescription bottle. It was almost empty. She said that she would fall asleep way before she could take as much as Elise took."

Kacey leaned back in her chair. "So, your mother takes Valium, and she was one of the few people who knew about Chase. You don't think—"

I held up a hand. "Look, I'm not much of a conspiracy theorist. I'm sure a million people take Valium, and nine-hundred-ninety-nine-thousand plus of them didn't know about Chase. Elise commits suicide while loaded with Valium; nobody finds a prescription bottle for Valium in Elise's house; my mother takes Valium, and she is one of the few people who knew that your father had a son. It's an interesting coincidence, but it would be ridiculous to draw any conclusions from it. I'm a lot more interested in what my mother said about the effects of the Valium. Elise must have been totally zonked. How did she get herself into the car in the first place?"

"Maybe she got into the car before the Valium had a chance to kick in. By the way, based on what I saw the other night, I wouldn't be surprised if Brandon takes Valium, too."

Now, I smiled. "Nothing that Brandon takes would surprise me."

Kacey got up, walked over, and put her hand on my shoulder. "Seriously, I'm sorry your mother's been a disappointment. I'll bet it will get better between you. She probably just needs time. Are you okay?"

That really made me feel bad. After all, Kacey had lost her mother and father, and here I was whining. It was time to take Dad's advice and hop off the self-pity wagon. "I'm fine. To change the subject, when's your first final?"

"Tuesday. It's literature and should be easy. My last one's a week from Tuesday, so they're ridiculously spread out. I'm a little worried about econ. That's Friday. I'm trying to get an early start on studying for that one."

If she was worried, the rest of the class must be leaping out dorm windows. The girl was a genius.

Despite my efforts she turned the conversation away from herself. "I suppose this all means that Brandon is Suspect Number One." She sounded happy about that. She obviously hadn't forgotten the remark that Brandon made about her father.

"Nice transition. I thought we were talking about your finals?"

"Who wants to talk about finals when we've got a murder to solve?"

"Whoa. We don't know Elise was murdered."

"Well, if she was, I'd say that Brandon is Suspect Number One."

"Maybe. Or maybe there are no suspects at all, because maybe Elise really did kill herself. Or it could be that lots of other people knew about Chase. We just don't have enough information to know."

"Did you ask your mother if she had told anyone?"

"I was never in a situation where I could ask her. She was too intent on pointing out all of her expensive furniture. I'll have to get back over there and talk to her again."

Kacey pulled her cell phone out of the pocket of her jeans and checked it. "Wow, it's two o'clock. I've got to get some studying done." She walked over and picked her econ book off the floor next to the ottoman. "Do you want me to come along to your mother's next time you go? I'd love to see that house. For that matter, if you want me to come along on your next date with Rob, I think I can find a free evening."

I felt my neck getting warm and concentrated hard to keep my voice nonchalant. "Wouldn't that interfere with your studying? I thought econ was supposed to be so hard."

"Listen, Rob Morrow trumps econ every time."

With her textbook in her hand, she walked past me and started down the hallway toward her room. "You just give me a call any time you need a chaperone. I can be available on very short notice."

The sad thing was that she had our roles pegged precisely. Although I was nearly ten years older, I was the one who needed chaperoning. Kacey could have handled Rob Morrow with no problem. With that humiliating thought capping an eighteen-hour slice of life that I wanted desperately to forget, I stretched my feet out on the couch and closed my eyes.

CHAPTER
NINETEEN

I CALLED MY MOTHER the next morning and asked if I could drop by her house that afternoon. When I got there, she answered the door in a yellow bikini. For a fifty-year-old woman she looked amazingly good. Her hair was pulled back in a bun. She had a red-and-blue striped beach towel in one hand; in the other was a beat-up copy of *The Brothers Karamazov*.

I walked into the house and unbuttoned my leather jacket. I wondered whether I should give her a hug. After all, that's what mothers and daughters did, wasn't it? I took a tentative step in her direction. For an instant, she leaned ever so slightly in my direction. Just as quickly, she caught herself and clasped her shoulders, as if to shiver. She took a step back.

I sighed and stuck my hands in the pockets of my jacket. "It's thirty-five degrees outside. Don't tell me you swim in this weather?"

"Heavens, no. Do you think I'm crazy?"

I decided not to respond to that one.

"I was just getting ready to get in the hot tub. It's a great way to relax and do some reading."

I looked at the book in her hand. *"The Brothers Karamazov*? Not exactly hot-tub reading for most people."

"I find Dostoevsky relaxing. I've already read it twice."

"Of course, who hasn't?"

"Dostoevsky was epileptic, you know."

She was already drifting. "Listen, I came by because I've got some questions to ask you. Is there a place where we can talk?"

"The hot tub is a great place to talk. Did you bring your swimsuit?"

I studied her face. Against all odds, it appeared that she was serious. "I don't usually carry it with me in December."

She turned and walked toward the back of the house. Over her shoulder she said, "I know you're trying to be sarcastic, but I choose to ignore it. I am in my peace zone, and nothing can intrude if

I don't want it to. Why don't you just wear one of my swimsuits?"

The most frightening thing about the suggestion was that we were probably the same size. I followed her through the foyer toward the family room in the back. "Your peace zone? Is that some sort of New Age thing?"

"It's Dr. Schiltz's term. He's my therapist. Cute little guy. Bald as a cue ball, but sometimes that can be attractive, don't you think?"

"I hadn't given it much thought."

"I always believed that Yul Brynner was so—"

I held up a hand. "I think you're losing your focus. You were explaining your peace zone." It occurred to me that even the peace zone part of the conversation represented a significant loss of focus, but it was closer to where I wanted to be than Yul Brynner.

"It's my personal place, my quiet place, and I don't need to allow anyone into it."

"Okay, I don't really want to enter your peace zone. In fact, it frightens me a little bit. All I want is to talk for a few minutes. Is there someplace a little drier than the hot tub?"

She snapped the cap shut on her lotion bottle and draped the beach towel over her shoulders. "I don't like to miss my hot-tub time."

"Do you get in the hot tub at the same time every day?"

"No." She gave me a blank look.

This line of questioning was getting me nowhere. "Okay, what do you want to do? Do you want me to wait in here until you're finished?" I was already mentally running through the business calls I could return while I waited for her to achieve a wet peace.

She spotted an un-rubbed glob of lotion on her shoulder and massaged it in. "Oh, no. You can come out and talk to me while I'm in the water. You don't have to get in."

"But won't that disturb your—" What was I doing? I stuck my hands in my pockets. "Which way to the hot tub?"

She picked up a pack of cigarettes and a lighter off the island, turned and walked toward the back door. I hitched my purse on my shoulder and hurried to catch up.

The air was cold by Dallas standards, but the sun was out, and the backyard fence blocked the wind. It wasn't a day at the beach, but it was far from uncomfortable. I dragged a green-and-black lounge chair over next to the hot tub as my mother slid into the frothy water.

I was not going to waste time. Before she finished shifting her weight around to find a comfortable position, I said, "I came over to ask you who else knows about Chase."

She closed her eyes and leaned her head back on

the deck. One knee extended through the surface of the water, which swirled over and around as if it were a rock jutting from a stream. "So that's why you wanted to come over. I thought that maybe you just wanted to see me." She seemed genuinely disappointed.

I sat back on the lawn chair and stretched my legs. "I do want to see you, but I also want to know who else knows about Chase."

She let her knee slide under the water and allowed her arms to float to the surface. She sat there with her eyes closed, her arms drifting in front of her, and I could see that she was rapidly approaching her peace zone. I wondered whether the conversation would continue once she crossed the boundary, or whether I would have to wait until she made reentry.

She opened one eye. "And is it your business to know whom I may have told about Simon and me?"

I crossed one foot over the other. "Yes, it is. I'll explain why later, if you want me to. First, though, I'd like to know: Who did you tell?"

"My, my, you're demanding. Actually, I like that. It's still a man's world. A woman has to be assertive. That's why I admire that Susan Sarandon. She really seems to keep Tim Robbins in line. She's quite a bit older than he is, you know."

I shook my head. "What does this have to do with Susan Sarandon and Tim Robbins?"

"I was just using her as an example."

I folded my arms. "You were going to tell me who else knows about Chase."

Now she opened both eyes and moved her arms back and forth across the surface of the water. "Not a soul."

I raised an eyebrow. "C'mon, you mean that in all these years you've never told a single person?"

"No one except Stanley. He and I share everything. I told him about both of my prior marriages and about Simon and Chase. Total honesty is the foundation of a good marriage."

"It's worked so well for you in the past." That was plain mean, and I wished I hadn't said it.

"So you came over here to be judgmental." She clasped her shoulders again, just as she had done at the front door when I tried to hug her. "I'm used to that."

"I'm sorry. That was out of line. I've got a sarcastic sense of humor and sometimes I don't use very good judgment with it."

She let her arms slide beneath the surface and moved her legs in a flutter kick, her toes pointed perfectly straight. She watched intently as her feet moved the water. I thought of a little girl, playing alone in the water, and for a second I sensed that she had blocked me out—or simply forgotten I was there.

I was certain she could entertain herself for hours there in the hot tub. Looking back, that was the first time I got a hint of the world of my mother's mind—

a world apart from the rest of us, where she lived alone and, for the most part, contented.

"If you have to know," she said, "I never really tried total honesty before. This marriage is very important to me. It's my last chance. If I can't make this work . . . well, I don't want to be a three-time loser."

She had come back to our world as quickly as she left, and I felt sorry for her. It was clear which world was more comfortable for her. I wanted to tell her that I thought I was beginning to understand, but there was no way to express it without the risk of offending her. So I said nothing for a while, and she seemed content to lie there in the water with her eyes closed.

A squirrel scampered across the top of the fence, not twenty feet from us. I watched as it paused and then took an impossibly long running leap into a twisted oak tree in the corner of the yard. It sat on its haunches on a thick limb and looked around, as if wondering why it had bothered.

I leaned forward and hugged my knees. "When you came to the house the other day, I told you that someone was trying to blackmail Simon before he died."

"And you thought I was involved, and I told you I wasn't." She sank lower in the water until only her neck and head were above the surface. "If I had had any interest in something like that, I could have done it long ago. I never even asked him for child support."

That argument didn't move me, since she'd given up Chase for adoption years ago. "If it makes you feel any better, I don't think you were involved. Have you ever told anyone other than Stanley?" With no wind in the backyard, the sun was getting warm. I unbuttoned my jacket.

"No, I'm certain of it. When Simon became famous, I thought about it—actually quite a lot; but I decided that I wasn't going to be that kind of person. And that was that."

"I hate to say it, but that leaves Stanley. He's the only one who could have done it." Of course, that wasn't true, but she didn't know about Brandon, and I wanted to see how she would react to the idea that Stanley could have been involved. I braced myself for an explosion.

She ran her hands through her hair and leaned her head back on the deck again. Her reaction was surprisingly mild. "Stanley wouldn't do anything like that. Besides, he's known about this for nearly four years. Why would he just get around to doing it now?"

"Has he had any financial setbacks lately?"

She smiled. "I wouldn't know. My job is to spend it, not keep the books."

She'd become less flighty as the conversation wore on. I was beginning to wonder whether some of the flightiness was just an act. "Is there any way we can find out?"

For the first time, she turned her head and looked at me. "You're a persistent little devil, aren't you? Listen, I am not going to spy on my own husband. Besides, this is ridiculous. The idea that Stanley would blackmail someone is absurd. For goodness sake, he's rich!"

Looking up at the gigantic second-story balcony towering over the pool, it was hard to argue with that. "Didn't you just say a minute ago that you don't really know what kind of financial shape he's in?"

"No, I said I don't know whether he's had any financial setbacks lately. That's what you asked me. He certainly hasn't told me to stop spending money, if that's an indication."

"Do you know where he keeps his books?"

"In his study, I assume. That's where he does all of his work when he's not at the university."

I squinted at the kitchen window. "Is he here now?"

"No, he's teaching a class."

"Can we take a look around his office?"

She shaded her eyes. "Why, of course you may not! This is insulting, Taylor. Besides, I'm not ready to get out of the hot tub yet."

Despite her protest, I got a strange sense from the tone of her voice that she was intrigued by the idea that there might be a mystery connected with her husband. I pressed on. "Can't you see that this is important? All we have to do is take a quick look around his office.

Maybe flip through his financial records if you know where they are. He'll never even know we were in there. That is, if we go now."

Picking her book up off the deck, she sighed. "If it will keep you from talking about him anymore, all right."

I shook my head. That was it? She was agreeing that easily? Despite her protests, she seemed to view this as an adventure.

She stood up, and the water poured off her body, making her look even more slender, more attractive than she had in the house. Without the thick makeup, she was really a beautiful woman. Beautiful and brilliant and troubled—that was the way Simon described her to me. A part of him had been fascinated by her, of that I was certain. And now it was easy to see why. A flutter-kicking fan of Dostoevsky. Not your average woman.

She grabbed her towel and moved it over her legs. A plush robe was draped over a deck chair next to the hot tub. She slid into it, grabbed her cigarettes, and motioned for me to follow her. "Well, my dear, we're off to the secret world of Stanley Venable."

CHAPTER
TWENTY

WE ENTERED THE HOUSE through a different door than we'd come out. This one opened into a Spanish-tiled hallway, with khaki-colored walls. The hall led past the pool bath and connected to the main hallway that ran from the kitchen to the east side of the house. We passed a game room on our left, with a massive mahogany pool table, and a bedroom on our right, with a queen-sized sleigh bed, before we reached a closed door where the hallway dead-ended. She tried the knob gingerly, as if she weren't certain it would be unlocked. It clicked, and she swung the door open.

The room was forest green with a beamed ceiling and lots of leather. It smelled of cigar smoke. In the back of the room, in front of two large windows, was an ornately carved desk. The desktop was empty except for a framed photo of Stanley with both of the U.S. senators from Texas. The picture faced the door, intended to impress. The entire wall to our right was a built-in bookshelf packed with books of all sizes and shapes. The wall to our left was lined with framed sketches of oil derricks and drilling platforms. Clearly, oil was the professor's real business.

"Impressive," I said. "I wonder where he keeps his financial records."

"In the second drawer on the left side of his desk."

I raised an eyebrow.

She turned her palms up. "What? I like to know where things are."

I smiled, walked over to the desk, and pulled open the drawer. It was full of hanging folders with titles such as Mutual Funds and Hedge Funds. One folder was labeled Mortgage-backed Securities.

I lifted that one out of the drawer. It had a few sheets that appeared to be quarterly reports. "Do you know whether these are the only reports? Or does he keep records on his computer, also?"

"I'm sure that he keeps his records current on his computer. He does everything on his computer."

I checked the date on the top report in the file. It was a year old. "Did you know that he invested in mortgage-backed securities?"

"I had no idea."

"You're aware of what happened to that market on Wall Street, aren't you?"

"I don't live with my head in the sand, darling." She went over to the bookcase and peered at some of the titles.

"Did Stanley inherit his money?"

"No, he grew up poor. He's a real engineering genius, though—chemical engineering. In fact, I've got one of his inventions in me." She pulled a book out, opened the cover, and examined it.

I cocked my head. "What do you mean, in you?"

She looked at me over her shoulder. "Right here." She pulled the sleeve of her beach wrap off her shoulder and pointed to a small purple dot in her skin, just behind her shoulder blade. "He implanted a chip under my skin. In case I ever get lost again, the way I used to."

I walked over to get a closer look. "Lost?" I touched the purple dot with my fingertip. I don't know what I was expecting to feel. Heat? Vibration? I felt only skin.

"Lost like when I was living on the streets." She turned away from me. "He said he always wanted to be able to find me, no matter what."

"You mean it's a homing beacon?"

She closed the book and slid it back onto the shelf. "I don't really know. It's just something that he says will allow him always to find me. He said he invented it."

I crossed my arms in front of me. "That's creepy. Sort of *Blade Runner* type stuff."

"What is Blade Runner?"

"It's a movie. Never mind. And you let him do that?"

She shrugged. "It didn't hurt. He used this little thing like a staple gun. It punched it right in. Besides, you don't understand. You've never slept beneath a highway overpass." She hiked the collar of her robe up and held it there, as if to keep a chill off her neck. Then she turned and looked directly at me. "I'll never allow myself to be out there like that again."

I could see the fear in her eyes and I wanted to reach out and touch her. But I didn't. I just stood there like a stranger. "It must have been awful."

She turned back to the bookshelf. "The parts that I remember weren't so great. Most of it is a blur. Like a movie where the characters are walking in fog."

I was not willing to be a stranger any longer. I took a step forward and touched her arm.

She flinched and lowered her head. "I'm fine now. That was another time."

I let my hand drop from her arm. I thought she might cry, but she straightened her back. "So, I'm bionic, you might say. The woman with the computer chip in her back. That's a bore. Where were we?"

She pulled out another book and flipped the pages. I took the hint that she wanted to move on. I walked back over to the desk. "If Stanley grew up poor, and he's a college professor now, how does he pay for all this?" I waved my hand around the room. "College professors don't make this kind of money."

"Like I said, he's a genius. He's developed patents for the oil industry. Drilling inventions. He's also written some textbooks, but mostly he's made his money from the patents. I get the impression the patents have been sort of like his own little oil wells. He just sits back and watches the royalties flow in."

I put my hand on the desk. "I don't see any computer around here. Does he work on a laptop?"

"Yes, the house has a wireless network. He likes to sit in front of the television and work."

"Do you know where he keeps the laptop?"

"The only time I ever see it is when he has it with him. He must have it with him now."

I opened the other drawers of the desk and found nothing of any interest. On the floor beside the desk was a leather computer case with a brass buckle. I unhooked the buckle and opened it. In it was a small laptop. "He must not have taken it today. Here it is." I pulled the computer out of the case.

She narrowed her eyebrows. "That's not his laptop."

"How can you tell from over there that this isn't his laptop?"

"That's an Apple; his laptop is a Dell." She paused. "That's how I know; he's computing very well."

I just stood there looking at her.

She tapped a finger on her forehead. "It rhymed. Didn't you get it? That's an Apple; his laptop is a—"

I held up a hand. "I know it rhymed, Mother." I sighed. "Why are you so certain he uses a Dell?"

"He told me he owns stock in Dell and that he always buys Dell computers. Believe me, one thing I'm sure of is that Stanley has never owned an Apple."

"Well, then what is this?" I held up the laptop.

"I don't know, but it's not Stanley's laptop."

I was opening the lid when a door slammed at the other end of the house. My mother's back stiffened.

"Hil?" It was Stanley's voice.

Her arms dropped to her sides. "I didn't expect him for another hour, at least."

I put the laptop back in the computer bag and fastened the buckle. Stanley's footsteps moved down the hall toward us. It was too late to get out of the room.

I walked over and stood by my mother, next to the bookcase.

The door opened and Stanley stepped into the room. His silky, cream-colored sport shirt had two buttons unbuttoned, revealing a stringy gold chain and a pasty, hairless chest. With his balding head and slight build, the whole picture made me think of a blinged-up Chihuahua. "What are you two doing in here?" His voice was as flat as his expression.

I opened my mouth, but she beat me. "I was just showing Taylor the way we did the built-in shelves. She's thinking of building a house and wanted to get some ideas. We're learning all about each other. She's as much of a book lover as you and I are."

He shoved his hands in his pockets and stared at me. A crease formed in his forehead, just above the bridge of his nose.

"We both love Dostoevsky." I cleared my throat. "What are the odds?"

He turned back toward my mother. "You're wearing a bathrobe."

She looked down and laughed. "Oh, my, I completely forgot. We came in from the hot tub. Well, c'mon, Taylor, I want to show you some things we did in the bathrooms, too."

Stanley stepped aside as we walked past him. Just before we got out the door, I glanced over my shoulder. He was glaring at me.

When we got to the kitchen, she turned and grabbed my arms. Her face was flushed and her eyes bright. "That was a close one, wasn't it?" She put a finger to her cheek. "Now, how can we find those financial records?"

I took a step back and studied her face. "Are you sure you want to try? He didn't look happy."

"Oh, heavens yes. Did you see the look on his face? That was the most excitement I've had for years." She fanned herself with her hand.

Something didn't compute here. "What happened to, *We tell each other everything*"?

She frowned. "Listen, the truth is that I'm a trophy to him. I know that. He's not the type who ever dated a lot of pretty women. Then I came along." She put her hands in the pockets of her robe. "Sometimes you take what life gives you. That's what I've learned in three marriages."

I reached over and squeezed her arm, but she just stood there. She didn't even take her hands out of her pockets. I let my hand drop.

She straightened her shoulders. "I've got a right to know about his finances. I'm his wife."

"Do you think he would tell you if you just asked him?"

"I doubt it."

"Well, it's worth a try. It's certainly the easy way. That will be Plan A, but let's work on a Plan B in case he's not willing to talk to you about it." I looked around the corner and down the hall. The door to his office was closed. I kept my voice low. "Let's start with the basics. How much did you know about Stanley before you married him?"

"A lot. In the beginning he appreciated me."

"How long did you date?"

"Two months."

"You married a man you had only dated for two months? And now you're telling me you knew a lot about him?"

"I knew he was rich and I knew he was nice to me. That's enough. It's a double improvement over my second husband, who was poor and hit me—until I got smart and started hitting him back."

I could see that catching up on my mother's life was going to take a long time. "Do you think you can find an opportunity when he's not here when you can get on that laptop that we saw in his office? Maybe that's where he keeps his financial records."

"I told you, that's not even his laptop."

I drummed my fingers on the countertop. "Maybe it's his laptop and you just didn't know about it. Maybe he sold his stock in Dell and took a liking to Apple. It's worth looking at. Anyway, do you think you can get your hands on his regular laptop? The Dell?"

A strand of hair had fallen loose from her bun and dangled near her cheek. She twirled her finger in it as she thought. "It would be difficult. He has it with him all the time. I'll see what I can do, though."

"Great."

"You know, Taylor, Stanley didn't have anything to do with blackmailing Simon Mason."

"If you're so sure, then why are you helping me?"

"This is exciting. It's sort of like we're a mother-daughter detective team, isn't it?"

I put my hand on her shoulder. "Yeah, I guess, it is."

"Sort of like *Crime and Punishment*, which is my favorite Dostoevsky book. I sometimes find *The Brothers Karamazov* a bit obscure, don't you?"

I sighed. "Honestly, Mother, I've never read any Dostoevsky. Can we stick to the point?"

She nodded. "You're right. Okay, I'll keep my eyes open and see what I can do."

I checked around the corner again, then turned back to her. "By the way, he's not the violent type, is he?"

She laughed. "Stanley? Oh, honey, he's a pussycat."

I remembered the look he gave me when we were walking out of his study and wondered whether she really knew much about Stanley at all. One thing was certain, though, she knew him better than I did. So I demurred. "Okay. When you learn something give me a call."

She walked me to the front door. Before she opened it, she did something I remember as if it happened five minutes ago. She reached up and put her hand on my cheek. It was warm, and I wanted to take it and hold it there against my face. Before I could say or do any-thing, though, she pulled it away.

"You really should try Dostoevsky, honey. Every well-educated person should be familiar with his work."

"Sure, Mother, I will." And that was that. She showed me a glimmer of hope, and she took it away. As I walked away from the front door, I resigned myself to the idea that this was how things would be. She had only the slightest hint of motherhood to give, and I was getting all that she had. If I was smart, I would accept that and stop wishing for more.

As I opened my car door, I turned and looked over my shoulder. She was still standing in the doorway; just standing there watching me. I wondered why, and I lifted my hand to wave. Before my hand rose above my waist, she turned and closed the door.

CHAPTER
TWENTY-ONE

THE NEXT MORNING TOM Petty was free-fallin' on my car stereo as I headed to my office. Just before the vampires moved down Ventura Boulevard, my phone rang. I hit the button on my Bluetooth headset, cutting off The Heartbreakers and stopping the vampires in their tracks.

It was Katie Parst.

There was nothing unusual about that. Katie had called me every day since the shooting at Starbucks, wanting to know every detail of how I was feeling and how I was healing. And, honestly, I liked that. When she was satisfied that nothing about my condition had changed for the worse in the past twenty-four hours, she turned to business.

"I've got some news. The Southlake Police busted a prostitution ring yesterday."

I honked at a pickup that cut me off as I was turning onto McKinney Avenue. "Just a second. I've got a cowboy here who's trying to play bumper cars." Once I had safely merged into traffic, I turned my attention back to Katie. "Prostitution ring in Southlake? You've got to be kidding me. That's upper-class suburbia."

"You'd be surprised. Not too many years ago they busted a sex slave ring in one of the other high-end suburbs."

The light in front of me turned red. I pressed my foot on the brake. "How would a prostitution ring even operate in Southlake? It's nothing but big houses and shopping boutiques. Are you telling me there were streetwalkers in front of Victoria's Secret?"

She laughed. "Not quite. They operated out of a normal-looking house in a normal-looking neighborhood. I guess I should say 'otherwise normal-looking' neighborhood. The johns would just make an appointment, show up, and take their pick. Some of the girls were as young as fourteen."

I pulled onto the side street that led to my building's parking garage. "That's sick. I hope they put the johns in jail along with the pimps."

A dog launched into a frenzy of barking on her

end of the phone. "Just a second, Taylor. Bandit, no! Sorry, I'm still at home. Our dog is at the back window fooling himself into thinking he's intimidating a squirrel."

When the barking stopped, I said, "What does a prostitution ring in Southlake have to do with me?"

"I've got a source in the Southlake Police Department. I've known her for a long time. She tells me there's a list."

I pulled the car into my office building's parking garage and wound my way down the serpentine ramp toward my parking spot. "A list of what?"

"The johns. Apparently the guys who ran the whole thing kept books: names of customers and in some cases phone numbers. Even some e-mail addresses. I guess they e-mailed notices when they were running a special. As my dad used to say, every job is a sales job at some level."

"Gag me."

"I know. It makes me feel dirty just talking about it. Anyway, I think I'm going to be able to get a copy of the list."

"Whoa, your friend is a really good friend."

"I didn't say I'm getting it from her. Let's just say that I've got my ways. The reason I called, though—and you'll probably think this is crazy—is that I've had this uneasy feeling. Like a premonition."

"What?"

"Okay, it's probably nuts. I know that. And I know how highly you thought of Simon Mason; but I think that his name is going to be on the list."

I pulled into my parking space. "Simon Mason? Using hookers? Katie, I don't know whether to hang up on you or burst out laughing."

"You're that sure?"

"That sure." I pulled into my space and turned off the ignition. "I'm telling you with one-hundred-percent certainty, he was not that kind of man, and he will not be on that list."

"Okay. I'm probably being an idiot. I should know better than to believe in premonitions. I'm sorry I called."

"It's all right. By the way, what would you do if his name were on the list?"

There was silence for a moment. "I wouldn't publish it. It would hurt Kacey. And, besides, I owe you too much. It might come out, but not from me."

I swung the car door open. "I never thought I'd hear myself say this to a reporter, but you're okay, do you know that?"

"Thanks."

"Are the cops still hanging out at your house?"

"Still here. I don't know how long the Coppell taxpayers are going to be willing to foot the bill, but for now no one seems to be complaining."

I locked the door, put my keys in my purse, and

slung it over my shoulder. "You can laugh about it, but I hope you're being careful. I didn't get shot for nothing. I want you to stay alive."

"Believe me, so do I."

"Will you call me?" I headed toward the elevator lobby. No one else was on that floor of the parking garage, and my footsteps echoed off the concrete walls.

"Call you for what?"

"When you get the list. Call me just to ease my mind."

"Sure, I'll call you."

"Thanks. I'll talk to you later." I hit the End button and stuck the phone in my purse. While I waited for the elevator to the building lobby, I couldn't erase the thought in the corner of my mind: What if Simon really was on the list? The rational part of my brain knew that the notion was ridiculous. It also knew that that was what people had thought about many televangelists who were caught up in scandals. Those televangelists were not Simon Mason, though. Simon just wouldn't do it. I was convinced of it.

Nevertheless, as I stepped onto the elevator and punched the lobby button, I was chewing my lip and thinking bad thoughts about Katie Parst for putting such a stupid idea into my head.

CHAPTER
TWENTY-TWO

LATER THAT AFTERNOON I was in my office typing a security plan for a new client, when my mother called. She was panting.

"I did it!"

I hit the speaker button and put the handset in its cradle. "Did what?"

She practically squealed. "I got into his laptop!"

I saved the document I was working on and spun my chair away from the credenza. "You're kidding me? Where did you find it?"

"In his study. It was right where you left it."

"Oh, you mean the Apple."

"Yes, of course, the Apple. I'll never get to his Dell."

"Well, what did you find out?" I rested an elbow on my desk.

"Nothing."

"Nothing? What do you mean?"

"There was nothing on it. Nothing on any of the drives. No documents; no photos; nothing."

I leaned toward phone. "It was a blank computer?"

"Blank."

I ran my good hand through my hair. "Why would he keep a blank Apple computer when he always uses Dells?"

"Honey, I have no idea, but I must say that this was the most excitement I've had for years. Here's how I did it: I waited until he'd been gone to the university for a half hour. Then I snuck into the study. I went in barefoot, but I tied plastic freezer bags over my feet so I wouldn't leave any prints."

I shook my head. "You did what?"

She was practically hyperventilating. "I saw that in a movie—the one with Leonardo DiCaprio and Mark Wahlberg. It's apparently the thing to do."

"Mom, it's your own house. Your footprints are all over it. In fact, our footprints are in his study from the other day."

There was silence for a moment. "It added to the excitement."

I drummed my fingers on the desk. "I'm sure it did."

"I took a closer look at the printed financial statements in his drawer," she said.

"Did you wear latex gloves?"

"Yes."

"I was joking."

Silence again. "You can get a hundred of them for less than six dollars at the warehouse store."

"What a value." There was clattering on the other end of the line, and then a door slammed. "What are you doing?"

"I just walked out onto the porch to smoke a cigarette." The lighter clicked. She exhaled.

"What financial statements did you look at?"

"The ones you pulled out of his drawer and some others that were misfiled in one of the other folders. He had more than three million dollars invested in two mortgage companies. The statements weren't current, though."

I opened the drawer of my credenza and propped a foot on the edge of it. "He could have sold those investments long ago."

"He could have, but I looked them up on the Internet anyway."

"What did you find out?"

"They were high fliers until late last year."

I let my foot fall from the drawer and leaned forward. "What happened then?"

"They went into bankruptcy. The shareholders were wiped out."

I leaned my head back on my chair and closed my eyes. "So, he knew that you and Simon had a son, and it looks like he had a three-million-dollar investment wiped out." I opened my eyes and leaned forward with my elbows on the desk. "Mother, how well do you really know your husband?"

CHAPTER
TWENTY-THREE

THE NEXT EVENING KACEY was to meet with the board of trustees of Simon Mason World Ministries to discuss what to do to wind up the ministries' affairs. Now that Elise and Simon were both gone, the top management of the organization had been wiped out. Even though Kacey had known most of the board members since she was in middle school, she was understandably nervous about attending an actual board meeting. Most of the people on the board were nearly three times her age.

I was sitting in front of the television in the family room when she came in the front door. She took off her tweed jacket and tossed it on the breakfast bar. She had dark circles of sweat under the arms of her light blue blouse.

I stood. "How did it go?"

She plopped onto the couch and kicked off her shoes. "Generally awful. I feel like a used dishrag. How do I look?"

"Not so great. Did you stop somewhere for a swim?" I nodded toward her armpits.

She raised an arm and looked. "Good gosh! I'm glad I kept my jacket on."

"No one would ever know."

"Not unless I smell, too."

I laughed. "Did the sweating begin with your meeting tonight, or your literature final?"

"The final was easy. This is boardroom sweat."

"They weren't mean to you, were they? After all, you're just a college kid."

"No. In fact, they were very nice. Too nice."

"What do you mean?"

She got up. "First, I'm starving. Do we have anything for dinner?"

"Didn't they even feed you?"

"They had a buffet. I was so nervous I couldn't eat a thing."

"I made a bunch of those mini pizza bagels. They're in a bag in the refrigerator. I'll throw some in the microwave for you."

"Thanks, but I'll get them." She walked around the

breakfast bar that separated the kitchen from the family room and opened the refrigerator door.

I watched as she pulled the bag of mini-bagels out of the refrigerator and raked them with her hand from the bag onto a plate. Some of them got caught in the corner of the bag. She shook it, but they still didn't come out. Her face reddened. She grabbed the bag and tore it, dumping several bagels onto the floor.

"Well, at least you got it open," I said.

She pursed her lips and bent over to pick up the food.

"Okay, so I can see you're stressed. What happened? I figured they were going to give you a plaque or something."

"You're not going to believe what they asked me!" She tossed several bagels from the floor into the garbage disposal.

I walked over to the breakfast bar and sat on a stool, facing into the kitchen. "What?"

She stuck the plate of bagels into the microwave and punched a few buttons. The microwave hummed. She turned toward me. "They want me to take over Dad's ministry."

I leaned back on the stool. "You mean they want you to wind up the business affairs?"

She shook her head. "No, they want me to take over. They want me to become a preacher. You know, sort of the next generation of the Mason dynasty."

My face must have registered my surprise, because she said, "Yeah, that was my reaction, exactly."

"But you don't have any experience preaching."

"They said there are people who can coach me. They would bring in a senior pastor for a while to help me transition into it. Everyone kept talking about my press conference after the kidnapping. Name recognition—that's what they kept bringing up."

They had a point. She had captivated a worldwide television audience during that press conference. "I can't say that I blame them. You were pretty spectacular."

"Knock it off, Taylor."

"No, really. You know you were great. Everyone said so."

"There's a difference between answering a few questions outside a hospital and standing on a stage in front of fifteen thousand people."

"Yes, there is, but you could handle it. And, as they said, you've already got the name recognition. That's eighty percent of the deal. The more I think about this, the more I think it's not a bad idea. It's been done before, you know. How about that guy down in Houston? He took over for his dad, and he hadn't ever preached before. Now he's huge."

"I don't want to be a preacher."

"Then don't. They can't make you."

She turned on the faucet and washed her hands. Then she picked up a dish towel and dried them. "I know. But if I don't do it, I'll feel guilty."

"Why would you feel guilty?"

"It's a chance to do something big, something for God. Something like Dad did. And God is just dropping it in my lap. It's like I'm looking God in the eye and saying no."

"How do you know God is dropping this in your lap? Just because it's the board of directors' plan doesn't mean it's God's plan." I was really out of my element at this point. As my recent behavior could attest, no one knew less about God's plans than I did; but she needed support, and it was the first thing that popped into my mind.

The microwave beeped. Kacey turned away from me, opened the door, and took out the plate of bagels. When she turned back to me, she stood for a moment, holding the plate of bagels in front of her with both hands. Then she did something that was long overdue considering all that she had been through. She began to cry. Unlike when she was with me in the hospital, this time she wasn't crying for someone else. She was crying for herself.

I hurried around the breakfast bar and put my arm around her shoulder. "It's okay, Kace. You don't have to do what they want you to do. It's your decision, not theirs."

She put the plate down on the island and wiped her eyes with her sleeve. "It's not about that." A black streak of mascara ran like a gash from one eye down her cheek. She pressed a palm against the side of her head. In a voice that was higher, more childlike than I had ever heard from her, she said, "Why did this happen to us? Dad and I never did anything to anybody."

I pulled her toward me and hugged her.

"I miss him so much," she said. "I just want him to come back. What am I going to do?"

With her head on my shoulder, I wiped my eyes with my good hand. "It just happened, Kace. You didn't do anything. It just happened." I should have had something better to say; something a real sister would have said; something that mattered. But I didn't, so I just held her.

After a few seconds she pulled back. "We both know why it happened, and Dad knew it, too. If it hadn't been for me, he would still be alive." She put her head back on my shoulder. I could feel her shaking.

I ran my hand through her hair. "You didn't kidnap anyone, and you didn't present your father with an impossible choice. They did that. They were evil men."

"Then why are they still alive while he's dead? Why do they still have families, and you and I are alone? Why do they get to win?"

I stroked her head. "I don't know, baby, I don't

know." I didn't even bother trying to keep myself from crying. She was right. We were alone, and it wasn't our fault.

We needed to cry. We had earned the right. We stood there with our shoulders heaving, and I was glad—glad that she was able to cry, that she was finally letting it out.

I remembered how Simon had asked me to take care of her, and I remembered why he had died. And I realized that it all worked together. At that moment, as Kacey and I held onto each other in the middle of the kitchen, I knew that I loved her so much I would do anything, even die, to protect her.

Though I had not spent much time thanking God in my life, I silently thanked him—thanked him for putting me there in that room with Kacey. He had given me something I'd never experienced, something both Simon and Dad had.

He had given me something worth dying for.

CHAPTER
TWENTY-FOUR

WITH AS MUCH TIME as I'd spent with Simon and Kacey during the previous nine months, it was sometimes difficult for me to remember that I owned and operated a full-time security business that had clients other than Simon Mason World Ministries. In fact, I had lost a few of those clients through lack of attention. I'd already decided that one of my resolutions for the coming year would be to get back to business and mend some fences with my client base. The afternoon after my visit to Mom's house, I got a head start on that resolution by meeting a client for lunch at Chili's.

He was one of my favorites—a guy with a quick sense of humor, lots of money, and little real need for the level of security services he asked my company to provide. In some ways I think he just liked the idea of being important enough to require security. He'd always been a drinker, and he played to a caricature. We hadn't been in our seats for two minutes before his gelatinous cheeks were so flushed they practically glowed as he motioned urgently for a waitress. Before long he was scratching his round nose between sips of his vodka martini. "These Dallas allergies are killing me. Vodka seems to help."

I laughed. "I've never heard that one. Whatever happened to Benadryl?" I stared longingly at his martini, but when the waitress asked if I was going to have one, too, I waved her off.

He nodded at my splinted finger. "Does it still hurt?"

"It comes and goes. I'm fine."

"You're a tough one, Taylor. I like that."

"Believe me, I'm not so tough."

"Well, I have been wondering why you haven't stopped any bullets for me. I was one of your first clients, wasn't I? Don't I rate?"

I smiled. "Hank, the security we provide for you is so good that no one would dare try to take a shot at you."

He lifted his glass. "Well said." He downed the martini and motioned to the waitress for another. "What about your side? That's where you got shot, isn't it?"

I touched the spot just above my hip. "It's funny, but that part's been no big deal. Every once in a while it burns a little, but that's about it. It's practically healed."

He looked up at the waitress, who set his fresh drink down beside him. "Thank you kindly, darlin'." He winked at her.

She pretended not to notice and wiped some water off the edge of the table with a cloth that she pulled from her back pocket. "Do you want to hear the specials?"

"Do you know them all by heart? You must be a smart one." He gave her a wobbly smile that exposed the whitest teeth money could buy. Hank was a good guy, and completely harmless, but at this point it was obvious he was completely creeping the waitress out.

"I think we know what we want," I said. The waitress gave me a grateful look.

After we ordered, I folded my arms on the table. "I haven't talked to you for a while. I just wanted to check in and make sure we're giving you good service."

He rubbed a thick finger along the side of his nose. "Everything's fine, just fine. I wouldn't mind seeing a little bit more of you, though. Your people are good, but they're not Taylor Pasbury."

I'd always had a hunch that Hank had a crush on me, despite being at least twice my age and having been married for nearly forty years. I had never encouraged it, but it certainly didn't hurt when it came to ensuring client loyalty. "I'll tell you what. You've got that awards dinner coming up in January. How about if I handle that one for you myself?"

He took a gulp of his martini. "That would be great."

I pointed to the half-empty martini glass. "I'll do the driving, too."

He chuckled. "You know me too well."

As I sat there dreading the prospect of spending an entire evening with a sauced Hank, I heard my phone vibrating in my purse. I pulled it out and checked the number. Katie Parst.

"Hank, would you mind if I take this one? It's a reporter from the *Morning News*."

"Ah, your public. I understand. It must be tough being America's pin-up security girl."

I gave him a mock scowl as I got up. "I'll be right back." I hit the button on the phone and walked toward the front of the restaurant. "Katie? What do you know?"

"I saw the list, and I owe you an apology. Simon isn't on it."

I sighed. "I told you."

"I know, I know. I didn't have a single good reason to think that he was. Reporters aren't supposed to act stupid like that."

"It's all right." I turned sideways and brushed

between two groups of people who were waiting for a table. "Excuse me."

"What? I couldn't hear you."

I switched the phone to my splinted hand and opened the front door of the restaurant. "Nothing. I was just trying to get past some people. I'm at Chili's."

"Sorry to interrupt your lunch, and sorry about the Simon thing, too."

"It's okay—really. Even though I didn't believe it could be possible, I have to admit that I'm relieved. You seemed so certain."

There was a pause on the other end of the line. "Listen, Taylor, there's something else about the list."

I stopped on the sidewalk, just in front of a bench that faced the parking lot. A few feet to my right, a man in a blue and silver Dallas Cowboys jacket flicked an ash off his cigarette, took a drag, and dropped the butt onto the curb. "What about it?"

"Didn't you tell me your mother's last name was Venable?"

"Yes, why?"

"And she lives in Southlake?"

"Yes."

"Is her husband's name Stanley Venable?"

Something tumbled in my stomach. I felt for the bench behind me and sat. "Why do you ask?"

CHAPTER
TWENTY-FIVE

I'VE OFTEN WONDERED WHY I have such a knack for choosing worthless men. For the most part, though, the guys I've dated have merely been lazy, deceitful, or fawning. None of them has ever hit me, and there have been no total sleazes among them—at least not to my knowledge. Upon learning from Katie that Stanley— my own mother's Stanley—had been a regular john for a prostitution ring, the genetic origin of my man-picking problems came into focus. I may have made some bad choices in my life, but I had nothing on my mother. For the past twenty years, her love boat had popped more rivets than the *Titanic*.

Although I had far too much practice in awkward, relationship-ending conversations with men, I had no idea how to break it to my own mother that her husband was a scumbag. When I called her and said I needed to drop by for a minute, I was semi-hoping that she would say she was busy. Sometimes delay for delay's sake is a welcome refuge for social cowards like me. But she wasn't busy. She told me to come around to the backyard when I arrived.

I drove to her house with the top down on my Camaro. Maybe I thought that the wind in my face would somehow blow an idea into my brain about how to break this sort of news. It was one of those unseasonably warm days that visit Dallas nearly every December for a brief time; days that smell of moist soil and wet bark—the air clean and fresh and hinting that somehow, somewhere, something should be blooming. On days like that it was easy to be seduced, to close the eyes and inhale and imagine that spring was just around the corner.

But it wasn't spring, and I wasn't feeling bright. I was about to tell my mother that when it came to marriage, she was, as she had feared, a three-time loser. Despite the car ride, the back of my neck was warm and damp beneath my hair as I stood at her backyard gate mustering the nerve to open the latch. I lifted my hair off my shoulders and let the breeze cool my skin. Then I took off my cotton cardigan and tied it around my waist.

When I stepped into the backyard, my mother

was standing with her back to me, gripping her pruning shears in one hand. A trowel jutted from the back pocket of her faded jeans. Her plain white T-shirt was untucked and smudged with dirt. She turned her head slightly, frowning at a gangly shrub, as if preparing to scold it for allowing itself to go to seed over something as easily endured as a few weeks of cold weather.

She hadn't heard me come in, so I stood and watched her. As she reached down to take hold of a stem, I caught her profile. She wore little makeup, and once again I was struck by how pretty she was. The early afternoon sun lit her cheeks, and her face showed barely a crease, even around her sharp gray eyes. It was stunning that fifty years, some of them undoubtedly harder than I could imagine, could have had such an inconsequential impact on her skin.

She bent over with the shears and snipped, then caressed the stem with her fingers. Her frown disappeared and her lips moved, as if she were whispering to a child or a pet. I wondered what strange entanglement of spirit allowed her to be at peace in the presence of something mindless that sprang from the mud, yet so roiled when dealing with flesh and bone.

She must have sensed my presence, because she straightened up and lifted her chin. "You found me," she said, without turning around.

I felt bad about intruding, about dragging her back from a world where she seemed to fit so much better. "I came through the gate, like you told me."

"I was thinking about you and Chase."

She turned, and the glow lingered in her face long enough to ignite a smile unlike any she had given me since the day I saw her inspecting the vase in our entryway. It was a warm smile, a mother's smile, and I remembered it from when I was small. She had loved me during her good spells; she had loved me when she was able. Seeing that smile, I wanted to pull her down and sit in the grass and talk about important things and inconsequential things. I wanted to talk the way that mothers and daughters were supposed to talk. I couldn't, though. Not now.

I hated what I had to do, and I wanted to cry.

As quickly as the smile had brightened her, the light flickered and went out. She nodded at the sweater wrapped around my waist. "You don't have the hips of a high school girl anymore, dear. That might not be the most flattering look. Accentuate the positive, I always say."

She had snapped me back to reality in a way that was uniquely hers. Eventually I would become accustomed to the irony of her thoughtlessness, but at this point I was still adjusting. It struck me that what I had so far been giving to the relationship was vastly disproportionate to what I was getting.

I loosened the sweater from around my waist and started to drape it over my shoulders, but a mental picture flashed through my mind. In it, my shoulders were as big as a linebacker's. The notion was absurd. At five foot nine, I weighed only 140 pounds. I was learning, though, that a mother's cuts—even ridiculously unfair ones—slashed exceptionally deep. I clutched the sweater in one hand at my side.

"I didn't know bushes had to be cut during the winter," I said.

"It's not cutting, it's pruning. You wouldn't go the whole winter without trimming your hair or your toenails, would you?"

I tried to recall how long it had been since I'd had a pedicure, but I resisted the temptation to look at my feet. The conversation was already crashing. Time to get right to the point. "I've got something to tell you."

She bent over and snipped another stem. "It must be important if you came all the way over here on a workday."

I shifted my weight from one foot to the other. "It is." I looked over at the table and chairs by the pool. "Do you think you should take a break? Maybe we should sit down."

Her back stiffened. "It must be bad news." The pace of her snipping quickened.

"You're right. It's not good. It's about Stanley."

She kept her eyes on the shrub. "What about Stanley?"

"Katie Parst—the *Morning News* reporter who was with me that day at Starbucks—called me today. She's been doing an investigative piece. It led her to something that involves Stanley. It's pretty shocking."

She brushed a strand of hair from in front of her eye. "How long is this buildup going to last, honey? Should I come back in the morning, or are you just going to tell me?"

"Okay, here it is. A prostitution ring has been operating in Southlake. The police busted it and they confiscated a list of the johns. Do you know what a john is?"

She gave me a patronizing smile. "You must be kidding, dear. I lived for part of a year under a highway overpass. There are few things about the seedy side of life with which I am not familiar."

I cleared my throat. "Stanley was on the list. He was paying for sex. Some of the girls were as young as fourteen."

She looked at me over her shoulder for several moments, her expression never changing. Then she turned her back again, lowered herself to a knee, and reached out to select another stem. "Don't be so quick to cast the first stone."

I raised my eyebrows. "I said prostitutes. Did you hear me?"

She snipped the stem in two. "Everyone is always so high and mighty with me. If I find something that's good for me for a change, they always want to tear it down. I'm used to that."

"This has nothing to do with tearing you down. It's about Stanley."

"Don't try that approach. I know exactly what this is about. First you wanted to accuse Stanley of blackmail. Now, this. You resent me so much for leaving you and your father that you'll do anything to get back at me. Maybe it would be better if you just left now."

I shook my head. "That's crazy, Mother. I'm not trying to hurt you."

Her head bobbed as she snipped several stems in rapid succession. She tilted her head, and the sunlight glinted off something moist in the corner of her eye.

I moved over to her and put my hand on her shoulder. "I'm sorry. I really am. But Stanley's not the person you thought he was. If I were you, I would want to know."

She sat in the dirt, reached up, and put her hand on mine. Then she took a deep breath and let it out. "I was the first pretty woman who ever gave Stanley the time of day. He was bookish, not the strong, athletic type like your father. You can see that, of course. So could I. In fact, I manipulated him with it. When I met him, I was divorced again and . . . well, I was desperate."

Her fingers tightened around my hand. "No matter what happened, I was never going to live in the streets again. I may be crazy, but I am not an animal."

I knelt beside her and put my arms around her neck. I rested my head on her shoulder and waited for her to pull away from me, but she didn't.

She sniffled and wiped her nose with the sleeve of her T-shirt. "Stanley was stable, respected. I was willing to do anything for that, even marry a man I didn't love; a man who didn't love me. I invented a make-believe marriage in my mind—one in which we shared everything, knew everything, about each other. I suppose that's the upside of craziness. It makes it easier to mentally pack up and leave. When things were bad, I just transported myself to my imaginary marriage. It was the better marriage anyway." She looked into my eyes. "As you can see, I hardly know the man. I'm a trophy for him, that's all."

As I had learned the day that Kacey and I cried together in the kitchen, one of life's strange mysteries is that the awful moments can also be some of the best. I suppose the chasm that separates pain and pleasure is more like a narrow ditch. Sometimes it's small enough that a person can step back and forth over it, or even straddle it for a while. During this brief time in my mom's backyard, I had been all over it. Kneeling there with my arms around her, I loved her more than I had at any time since she'd returned. More important, as we sat with our arms around each other in the expanse of her backyard, I knew in my heart that she loved me. I'd been waiting to know that since I was nine years old.

I'm not proud of it, but after twenty years of being alone I figured that if my mother—Mom—had to suffer for a while so I could know what it was like to be loved, I wasn't about to feel guilty about it. She owed me, and for these few seconds I was collecting what was rightfully mine. I even let myself hope that this might be the beginning of a different sort of life for both of us, that we might look back on this as a turning point.

But wishing so hard for something can make a person naive. If I had been thinking instead of feeling, I would have deduced that Stanley's hold on Mom was stronger than either she or I imagined—and that breaking her free would not be easy.

CHAPTER
TWENTY-SIX

ONCE THE INITIAL SHOCK wore off, Mom became a woman of action. She planned to confront Stanley that evening when he returned from a conference in Austin. She wanted me to be there and asked me to come over for dinner. I was glad that she wanted me there. We were going to be a team, the way a mother and daughter should. First, though, there was something I had to do. I told her I would be back for dinner, and I hopped in my Camaro and sped back to Dallas.

By the time I got home, Kacey had returned from her second final exam. She was lying on her bed, her head propped in her hands, staring at her laptop. At least she would have been staring at her laptop, if her eyes had been open. Her computer screen was rotating through a series of party pics from her sorority's fall dance.

I knocked on her open door. "Meditating?"

She jerked, and her chin fell off her hand. "Geez, what time is it?"

"4:15."

"Okay, that's not so bad." She stood up and stretched. "Econ is beating me down."

I tossed my sweater over her desk chair. "Look at the bright side. You'll finish the semester well-rested."

"I could sleep all afternoon and that still wouldn't be the case."

I lowered myself to the floor and sat with my back to her closet door. "Do I have news for you."

She rolled over and pushed herself up so she was sitting with her back against the headboard. She pulled a pillow into her lap and wrapped her arms around it. "Okay, let's hear it."

"It's about Mom's husband, Stanley. His name turned up on a list of johns who were using prostitutes in Southlake."

"I thought you said his name was Stanley."

"Do you know what a john is?"

She looked at me blankly.

"It's someone who uses a prostitute," I said. "The police busted a prostitution ring in Southlake. Stanley was on a list of the guys who used it."

She started to smile, then covered her mouth with her hand. "I'm sorry, but it's so ten-o'clock-news. He's a middle-aged man. It's gross, don't you think?"

"It gets worse. The prostitution ring used girls as young as fourteen."

She put her hands over her ears. "Ooh, he's a perv!"

"I'd say that about sums it up."

She lowered her hands. "How did you find this out?"

"Katie called and told me. One of her sources let her see the list. I just got back from Mom's house. I had to tell her."

Kacey put her hand over her mouth again, but this time she wasn't smiling. "Oh, no. How did she take it?"

I spotted a gum wrapper that was lying on the carpet next to the wall. I picked it up. "She cried a little. I cried a lot."

"Real surprise there."

"Oh, shut up. You would've cried, too. I hate to say this, but it was kind of nice—for me, that is. For the first time it was like she was really my mom. I think there's hope." I worked at folding the gum wrapper in quarters, which was challenging with one hand in a splint.

"Of course there's hope. Before long I'll bet you two will be wearing matching sweaters to the mall."

"Funny."

She leaned forward over the pillow in her lap. "Seriously, I'm happy for you. But I hope you're not going to go all wobbly and lose your sense of humor over it."

"I'm just glad that you admit I have a sense of humor. By the way, wobbly?"

"It's a Margaret Thatcherism. I learned it in World History. Very functional word."

"So you aren't just watching boys at that school. Glad to hear it."

"Watching boys and studying aren't mutually exclusive activities. I'm a multitasker."

"Great. Anyway, back to the point, there's more about this Stanley thing. Mom wants me to be there tonight for dinner. She's going to confront him with it."

She tossed the pillow aside and slid her feet to the floor. "No way! Let me get this straight. You're sitting there eating your roasted chicken, and she's going to say, 'So, Stanley, tell me about the fourteen-year-old hooker from over on Southlake Boulevard.' Somehow I don't see that going anywhere."

I tore up the gum wrapper and flicked the pieces toward the wastebasket next to her desk. Her eyes followed the pieces as they floated to the carpet. "Thanks," she said.

"Sorry, I wasn't thinking." I leaned over and used my good hand to sweep up the tiny bits of paper. "Look, I don't know how Mom's planning on raising it with him, but it's going to be something to see, I'm sure of that."

"Can you bring a guest?"

"Forget it."

She harrumphed. I ignored it. With her apparent yearning for adventure, I was beginning to think Kacey might be better suited for my line of work than the ministry.

"So, what are you doing here?" she said. "Why didn't you just stay at your mom's?"

"I want to take another look at Elise's cell phone before this evening."

"Why?"

"The phone number that Elise asked Brandon to trace. What if it was Stanley's number?"

She squinted at me. "Why would Stanley be calling Elise?"

"Because he needed money and he knew about Chase. Mom said she looked at some of Stanley's investment records. He lost a lot of money in mortgage-related securities. Millions. I've been thinking about how all of the puzzle pieces might fit together."

"And you came up with what?"

"No answers, but a few more decent questions. Katie is investigating an extortion ring that blackmails prominent people who get involved with prostitutes. Stanley is using prostitutes. Your dad is being blackmailed about Chase. Stanley is one of the few people who knew about Chase. Elise embezzles money from your dad's ministry, but Elise loves your dad, and it makes no sense that she would embezzle money from him. So, here goes: What if Stanley was blackmailing your dad, and Elise was paying him off? We figured that it could be Brandon and Elise, but what if it was Stanley and Elise?"

"But Dad told you he never talked to the blackmailer after the first call. The guy just went away."

"What if he didn't go away, but your father just thought he did? Your dad told Elise about the blackmail."

Kacey scratched the back of her head. "You mean you think that Elise may have talked to the blackmailer on her own?"

I stuck my hands in the pockets of my jeans. "Your dad would never have cooperated with the blackmailer. He just would have allowed the information about Chase to become public, no matter the consequences."

"And Elise would have figured it would ruin him. So, she might think she was taking care of Dad by paying the blackmailer for him. It makes sense."

"Particularly when you consider that everyone— the employees, the press, your dad—was so busy dealing with your kidnapping at the time. Elise would have been able to handle it without drawing any attention."

She leaned back against the wall. "Okay, that's all plausible, but what does it have to do with Katie's extortion ring?"

"Nothing that I can see. That may be just a coincidence."

"That seems unlikely to me. We're still just guessing. We don't even know that the phone number Brandon traced was Stanley's. It could be anybody's."

I nodded. "That's why I wanted to come home and take another look at Elise's cell phone. Maybe there's something we missed."

She hopped off the bed. "I want to help."

"I thought you were supposed to be studying."

"Hey, my next final's not until Friday. This is way more interesting than studying."

"I remember college. Anything is way more interesting than studying for a final."

"You got that right."

We went to my room, and I pulled Elise's cell phone out of my desk drawer. I scrolled to the outgoing calls directory and moved down from the top. The directory held only fifty calls, and went back only a few days before her death. We had previously checked out the numbers and could identify all but three. One of those had been disconnected. The other two rang with no answer and no voice mail rollover.

The most intriguing call was made the afternoon before we found her dead in her car. It was one of the numbers that rang with no answer. It was the only time that number showed up on the directory.

Kacey shrugged. "It's a dead end. How can we find out who the numbers belong to?"

I turned off her phone. "I'm not sure. My private investigator friend might know. One thing we can do, though, is try to find out if either of the unidentified numbers is significant. I'm going to call Brandon." I pulled my phone out of my pocket. Within a few seconds I had him on the line. "Brandon, it's Taylor."

He was obviously on a speakerphone, and sounded as if he'd been asleep, even though it was 4:45 in the afternoon. "Did I wake you up or something?" I said.

"No, I've been playing in a video game tournament since two a.m."

"You've got to be kidding me."

"I'm not. It's based in China. And I'm in the middle of it, so what do you need?" I could hear his fingers clicking on the game controller. Someone dropped an f-bomb in the background.

"Who's there with you?"

"No one. Those are the online players."

"I've got a quick question. When did you find that guy for Elise?"

"What do you mean, when? After she called and asked me to."

"No, I mean what day and what time?"

"Is this important right now?"

"Yes. Just do me a favor and think."

"Wait a minute."

I heard more clicking. Then Brandon swore loudly.

"Good grief, Brandon. What game are you playing?"

"Would you recognize it if I told you?"

"No."

"Then let's get back to the point. She called me in the evening. I talked to my friend at maybe two or three the next morning. Then I called her when I woke up that day."

"So, you called her at maybe eight or nine in the morning?"

He laughed. "Try one or two in the afternoon."

"Nice lifestyle. Was that the day before she died?"

"Yeah, definitely."

"Do you remember anything else about the phone number or who it belonged to?"

"Nope. Can I get back to my game? I'm playing for money here."

"I'm glad you're so happy to hear from me. By the way, is there any other way you could trace the number now that your friend is no longer at the forwarding service?"

"What friend?"

I paused. "The friend who you said traced the number for you—at the company that set up the forwarding arrangement for whoever the number belonged to."

More clicking. "Oh, yeah. No, there's no way that I know of. You'd have to subpoena the records from the company, but only a court can do that."

"Thanks, Brandon. You can go back to your game now."

"I never left it."

I clicked off the phone.

By that time Kacey was chewing her lip. "What did he say?"

"Just a second." I opened Elise's outgoing calls directory again. The last call she made to one of the unknown numbers was at 2:30 the afternoon before she died. Brandon said he'd identified the caller for her at one or two p.m. If she was dealing with Simon's blackmailer, that looked like his phone number. Brandon might be telling the truth after all.

Kacey was practically hopping in place. "Well?"

"There's a call to one of the unknown numbers— the only call to that number—within an hour or so after Brandon identified the guy for her. That must be the phone number that Brandon got. If we can match the person who goes with that number, we might have the blackmailer. That is, if Elise was talking to the blackmailer at all."

"Or, we might have some guy she met on the Internet. Or Brandon might be lying."

"Would you get off Brandon for a minute? It looks like he's been telling us the truth. Anyway, we've got some information worth checking out. Wouldn't it be something if that number belonged to Stanley? I can ask Mom what his cell phone number is. It's almost too much to believe, though, that my own mom's husband could be involved in this."

"Why? The guy uses fourteen-year-old hookers in his own hometown and you think he's not sleazy enough to be involved in something like this?"

"Excellent point. By the way, we don't know if his hookers were the young ones."

She folded her arms. "Oh, that helps. Listen, if he's got any brains, he didn't have the calls forwarded to his regular cell phone. He might have two or three phones. That's what guys do when they're having affairs, you know. They get secret cell phones that their wives don't know about. That way they don't have to worry about receiving an embarrassing call while their wives are around—or having their wives sneak a look at their call directories on their main phones."

I put my hands on my hips. "How do you know that?"

"One of my sorority sisters told me there was a rumor that one of her professors was having an affair, and he did it that way."

"Well, if you want pertinent information, ask a Tri-Delt, right?"

"Yep. Hey, I've got an idea. Tonight at dinner you can have Elise's phone with you. Have it set up to speed-dial the mystery number. While you're eating, stick your hand in your pocket and hit the speed dial number. Maybe Stanley's phone will ring."

"Oh, c'mon. What are the odds? Besides, I thought you said he probably had a second phone?"

"Maybe he doesn't. Or maybe he'll have the second phone with him. What's the downside? You might get lucky. Can you imagine if his phone rang in his pocket? It would be an instant investigative classic. You could get it made into a TV episode."

"It wouldn't hurt to try. They won't even know I'm doing anything."

Kacey tapped a finger on her cheek. "Be sure to turn the sound off on Elise's phone, so it doesn't beep when you push the speed dial."

I pulled out Elise's phone and turned off the sound setting.

"Okay, this is too exciting," she said. "Are you sure I can't go?"

"Quit asking."

She touched my arm. "Whoa, I just thought of something else. If Stanley's phone does ring, does that mean he killed Elise?"

I stuck Elise's phone in my pocket. "It would sure make him a prime suspect, but could wormy little Stanley be a cold-blooded killer?"

She folded her arms. "I don't know, but I don't like the idea of you being there with him if his cell phone does ring. If he killed Elise, what makes you think he wouldn't kill you and your mom, too, if he thought he was caught?"

I looked her in the eye. "I'm not Elise."

She smiled. "Good point."

CHAPTER
TWENTY-SEVEN

AT 6:45 I PULLED up to the curb in front of Mom's house. Before I got out of the car, I double-checked the phone to make sure I had programmed in the right speed-dial number. I had intentionally worn an old pair of pleated khaki pants that were roomy enough that I could get my hand in my pocket and hit the button without anyone noticing. I wouldn't be fashionable, but as they say in the world of architecture, form follows function.

The last thing I did before I opened the car door was check to make sure my .357 Sig was firmly tucked into the inside pocket of my purse. It occurred to me that I was preparing for the possibility—albeit highly unlikely—that I might have to shoot my own mother's husband. I shook my head. The idea was too bizarre to dwell on.

Slinging my purse over my shoulder, I headed for the front door. Mom must have been looking for me out the window. She opened the door before I rang.

"Oh, honey, it's so nice to see you," she said in an unnaturally loud voice. She held a finger up to her mouth, and whispered, "He's in the den. I'm ready to stick this pig."

At least she was enthusiastic—and she didn't even know yet that Stanley might be more than just a creepy slime bag. I didn't see any advantage to telling her my plan. I touched the outside of my purse and felt the reassuring bulge of my pistol. "What's for dinner?"

"Spaghetti—confetti." She paused. "It's almost ready."

I stared at her.

"It rhy—"

"I know."

She swept her hand to motion me toward the dining room. "I hope you don't mind, but there's no cocktail hour planned. We're just about ready to eat."

Now, here were two great examples of the different worlds in which she and I lived. First, of course, there was her bizarre rhyming. Besides that, somehow Kacey and I always seemed to overlook the cocktail hour on weeknights as we microwaved our frozen dinners.

"That's fine with me. I don't drink anyway, and my lunch got interrupted, so I'm plenty hungry."

The dining room was long and ornate, dominated by a mahogany table with a gold inlay, which sat beneath a crystal teardrop chandelier. A huge blue, red, and gold Persian rug covered the floor to within a foot of the walls. An elaborately framed impressionist landscape overlooked the room from the wall behind the head of the table. Three places were set—one at the end of the table beneath the painting, and one on each side. The china and crystal were gold-rimmed and expensive. It was an impressive spread for spaghetti. And for a college professor.

"You'll be here." Mom pulled out the chair to the left of the table head. "You may as well go ahead and sit down. I had the caterers come again. I didn't want to be bothered with cooking tonight. We have too many other things on our minds."

I sat, unfolded my napkin, and placed it in my lap.

"I'll get Stanley," she whispered. "He doesn't know anything's up." She walked out of the room.

I reached into my pocket and felt for the correct speed-dial key—the 3. For the tenth time, I tried to figure what could go wrong. As Kacey said, the plan seemed risk free. If his phone didn't ring—and I was realistic about the long odds—neither of them would even know I'd dialed the number.

Muffled voices came from another room, but I couldn't make out what they were saying. Then the voices stopped. A clock ticked in the entryway. I put my hands in my lap. Outside, in the distance, a car horn honked. I turned and looked at the door to my right, which led into the kitchen. A faucet opened, and running water hummed and splashed into something. It calmed me to hear any sound in the house, even a kitchen sound. Maria was preparing to serve us. Everything must be okay.

Still, there was no sound from the side of the house where Mom had gone to get Stanley. I placed my hands on the edge of the table. I wondered how long I should wait. What if he—

Footsteps came down the back hall, and a moment later Mom and Stanley entered the dining room.

This was the first time I'd seen him without a jacket. I was a bit surprised by the loose layer of stomach that folded over his pleated slacks. It gave his upper body a bell shape beneath his silky blue shirt. He held out a hand when he entered the room. "Nice to see you again, Taylor. We always seem to have a good meal when you're here." He gave Mom a look. "Believe it or not, we don't always have a chef. Your mother is still trying to build some enthusiasm for cooking."

I suspected that he would have held that comment

if he'd known what was about to hit him. I looked at Mom to see how she would react. She ignored him, pulled out the chair directly across from me, and folded her napkin in her lap. Stanley sat at the head of the table, to my right. Within seconds Maria, whom I recognized from our Sunday brunch, came wheeling into the room with a steaming serving cart. She filled each of our plates with spaghetti, asparagus, and garlic bread.

"This looks great." The smell of garlic was warm and deep, and I was starved. I hoped Mom wouldn't force the action before we had a chance to eat. I picked up my fork.

Mom frowned. "I'll say grace." I set the fork back down next to my plate, placed my hands in my lap, and bowed my head.

"Dear Lord, we thank you for bringing us together . . ." It quickly became apparent that when Mom prayed for a meal, she wanted God to know she meant it. She had already given thanks for the mild winter weather, the bounty of the fall's harvest, and the peace of the season when she lost me. I wondered whether she was going to revisit the Protestant Reformation.

It occurred to me that this was the perfect opportunity to speed dial without drawing attention. I opened one eye. Stanley was sitting upright, head unbowed, but his eyes were closed.

Thanks to Simon and the 12-step program, I had been reintroduced to prayer during the past year. Admittedly, my progress had been spotty. Nevertheless, the occasion called for all the assistance I could get. Besides, my head was already bowed, and I had always considered myself an opportunist. I was more to the point than Mom: *Lord, if Stanley did it, please make this work. I reached into my pocket, felt for the 3 key, and held it down.*

It had been unrealistic to think there was any chance that a cell phone was going to ring in Stanley's pocket, and it didn't. Mom was now talking about life-sustaining spaghetti, and she even requested blessings on Maria as she served us. The only noise other than her voice was the steady ticking of the entryway clock—until I heard the faintest sound from the side of the house where Mom had gone to get Stanley.

I turned my ear in the direction of the sound. It was a tune, one that I recognized: "Music of the Night" from *Phantom of the Opera*—a cell phone's ring tone. I opened one eye and peeked at Stanley. He didn't seem to have heard it. Mom was oblivious, now entreating heaven for peace in troubled times. I reached in my pocket, hit the End button, and waited. Within a second the music stopped.

I never really expected this scheme to work. Now that it had, I couldn't believe my good luck. I was practically giddy. As Kacey had said, this was the stuff that legends were made of. Then I began to doubt. Maybe it had been my imagination. I felt in my pocket for the 3 key and held it down again. Mom's voice became louder and fell into rhythm with the ticking of the clock as she built toward a climax. I strained my ears, focusing on the hallway. There it was: "Music of the Night." I opened an eye and peeked at Stanley again.

His eyes popped open.

He turned toward the hall but caught me out of the corner of his eye and stopped. Just then, Mom ended with a flourish, "In the name of Christ our Lord, the savior of the world, and our hope for eternity, amen."

I kept my eyes on Stanley. I clicked the phone off and set it on the table next to my plate. He gave me a perplexed look. Then a red wave began to spread from his neck, up past his jaw, and into his cheeks.

Mom placed her hand on her fork. "Well, let's eat." She looked at the phone on the table. "Are you expecting a call, honey?"

I tapped a finger on the table. "No. I think Stanley might be, though." I pressed the speed dial button again. Within a few seconds the music drifted into the room, more easily discernible now that Mom was no longer praying.

A drop of sweat appeared on Stanley's forehead. It hung there for a moment, then it released and slid quickly down to his thick, dark eyebrow where it disappeared. He swiped at his eyebrow with the back of his hand.

Mom wrinkled her forehead. "What's going on?"

I hit the End button and the music stopped. I kept my eyes on him. "Mom, I think it's time we had our talk with Stanley. Would you like to go first?"

CHAPTER
TWENTY-EIGHT

I'VE SEEN LOTS OF people get caught doing things they shouldn't. Reactions are as different as personalities. Some people are aggressive, some are cool thinkers, some are contrite, ready to take their medicine. Stanley was none of those. He was pathetic.

I kept my mouth shut about the cell phone while Mom hit him with the prostitution. At first he denied it, of course, but when Mom gave him the details about Katie's investigation of the extortion ring and the list she had gotten from the police, he caved. Then, as her voice grew louder and louder, he began to sob.

It was a sickness, he said. He needed help. It was purely physical, nothing more. Mom meant the world to him. Without her, he may as well be dead.

I wanted to puke. Instead, I shoveled spaghetti into my mouth while Mom beat him farther and farther down in his chair. I figured that my time for questioning would come soon enough. I had no intention of going hungry for this worm.

In the meantime Mom impressed me. She was emotionally needy but she wasn't stupid. She lambasted him. Before long he was blowing his nose into his table napkin. He had never been good-looking. Now, sitting there with his pointy nose running, his narrow eyes puffy, and his sallow cheeks blotched with red, he was one of the least attractive men I'd ever seen.

The only time he showed even a hint of spine was when she brought up the fourteen-year-old hookers. His usually low voice practically squeaked as he denied that he knew there were any girls that young. He pointed out that it was Southlake, for goodness' sake. He thought it was a reputable place. As soon as he said it, his eyes made it clear that he knew he had chosen his words poorly. "I feel awful. It's tragic that this happened," he added hurriedly.

I couldn't take any more. I threw my napkin down as I rushed my last few chews and swallowed. He practically cowered when the napkin hit the table. "Tragic? Happened? You've got to be kidding me! It didn't just happen. You did it! Tragic is what happened to those fourteen-year-old girls who were preyed on by a sick, middle-aged man. With a comb-over!"

Okay, the part about the comb-over was a cheap shot, but it just popped into my head. I wasn't going to let it break my rhythm. "The only tragic thing about this is that you didn't catch some sort of disease! That's what you deserved."

Mom's eyebrows narrowed. It was obvious I'd raised a subject she hadn't considered. She glowered at him. "You don't have a disease, do you?"

He couldn't have made himself any smaller. "Of course not. Anyway, they require condoms."

I threw my hands in the air. "Spare us the details!"

"Okay, I'm sorry." He sniffled and wiped his nose with his napkin again.

I looked down at the phone on the table, which I had almost forgotten. I picked it up. "Before we go any further with this, I've got a few questions for you, myself. Do you mind, Mom?"

She shook her head.

"Then follow me." I pushed back my chair and moved around the table toward the hallway.

Mom took a drink of water as she stood. She wiped her mouth, folded her napkin, and dropped it next to her plate. "Where are we going?"

"You'll see."

Mom followed me into the hall. Stanley lagged behind, and I looked at him over my shoulder. "C'mon, Stanley, don't get lost back there."

He hung his head. Sweat pooled above his eyebrows now and beaded on his cheeks. He had brought his napkin with him from the table and he blotted his face every few steps.

When we got halfway down the hall, I stopped and held up the phone. "Let's see, now, we should be getting close." I pushed the 3 button and held it down. Within a few seconds, "Music of the Night" drifted down the hallway.

Mom turned an ear toward the music. "What's that?"

"We're about to find out." I followed the music down the hall to a door that was cracked open. I recognized it from the day we had found Stanley's Apple laptop. It was his study. Just as I pushed the door open, the music stopped. I hit the End button on the phone.

We walked in and stood in the middle of the room. I hit the speed dial again. The music came from behind the desk. I followed the sound to the top desk drawer, which was partially open. I pulled open the drawer. In it was the Apple laptop.

I pulled the laptop out and set it on the desk. The music stopped again, and I turned to Stanley. He was no longer crying. His eyes moved from the laptop to the phone that I held at my side. "Where did you get that phone?"

"I'll tell you what, under the circumstances why don't I ask the questions? You do the answering."

He just stood there looking at the phone in my hand, as if it were a moon rock. I held it up higher to give him a good look. He turned his head away.

"Why the sudden affinity for Apple laptops? Mom said you were a Dell man."

He wiped his forehead with the table napkin. "Many of the students use them. I thought I should be familiar with . . . with how they work . . ." He avoided looking at the phone in my hand, even when I pushed it closer to his face.

I glanced at Mom. "You'll be interested to know that I just speed-dialed a number from Elise Hovden's phone. She's the woman who worked for Simon Mason and committed suicide, remember?"

Mom nodded. "I remember, but I don't understand. How did you get her phone?"

"I picked it up from her house the day we found her body. It had some phone numbers on it. She called one of the numbers the afternoon before she died. I just dialed it. It rings to your husband's laptop."

Mom crossed her arms and frowned at Stanley. "Was she another one of your women?"

I held up a hand. "No, it wasn't like that. Wait, though, there's more. A couple of days before she died,

Elise had asked a friend of hers to trace a phone number for her—a number that was supposed to be untraceable, because it was set up through a forwarding service. The phone number that just rang on Stanley's computer was that untraceable number. There was only one problem for Stanley. The untraceable number got traced, right to his new Apple."

He shifted his weight from foot to foot but didn't respond. His brow was furrowed, as if he were working through a difficult math problem.

I decided to go all the way and see if he could be bluffed. "You may be wondering why Stanley would set up an untraceable number for Elise Hovden to use. You see, Mom, he was blackmailing Elise. Or to put a finer point on it, he was blackmailing Simon Mason through Elise. It was just too tempting for you, wasn't it, Stanley? Knowing about Simon's son and all. Katie Parst thought Simon was being blackmailed by the extortion ring she was investigating, because they blackmail people who get caught up in vices. She figured Simon must have gotten involved in gambling or prostitution. It wasn't those people, though, it was you."

Now I crossed my arms, and the three of us stood there—Mom and I looking at Stanley; Stanley, his eyebrows narrowed into a V, looking back at us.

He took a deep breath and let it out. He walked around the desk and lowered himself into the desk chair. "You're right. I was trying to blackmail Simon, but it's not what you think. I didn't get a nickel out of it."

He opened a drawer on the right-hand side of the desk and pulled out a Colt .38 short-barreled revolver. I stretched my arm in front of Mom and pushed her back a step. Rather than point the gun at us, though, he simply laid it on the desk in front of him.

Up to that moment, events had progressed far better than I could have hoped, but when I reached over to feel for the purse that was supposed to be slung over my shoulder, things took a turn for the worse. There was no purse, which meant there was no .357 Sig. In the drama of the moment at the dining room table, I had left my purse sitting on the floor next to my chair.

It's not the sort of move I'll be mentioning in my security company's marketing brochures.

So, there we were: three of us in the room, and only one of us with a gun. Unfortunately it was the wrong one. I took a step to my right, positioning my body more squarely between Stanley and Mom.

Stanley looked me in the eye. He was no longer whimpering. "Before we go any further, here, why don't you answer a question for me? What's to keep me from just taking Elise's phone back from you right now and calling you a liar?"

I held up my hands. In the unsplinted one, I was clutching the phone. "Look, there's no need to do anything stupid. If you want the phone, you can have it."

Behind me, Mom sucked in a breath. "Don't give it to him. He's bluffing. He's not going to shoot anyone." It was a position that was undoubtedly easier for her to take while I was standing between her and the gun.

Stanley moved his hand over to the revolver. His fingers trembled. He didn't pick it up. He merely rested his hand on the grip. "Everyone calm down. Hil's right, I have no intention of shooting anyone."

I motioned toward his hand. "Then, why the gun? Where I come from, that's what they're for—to shoot."

He drummed his fingers on the grip. "I was just making a point. If I were as bad a guy as you're making me out to be, I would just shoot you and take the phone from you right now."

Mom peeked out from behind me. "Stanley! She's my daughter!"

I did a double take. Despite her well-protected position, it was kind of nice to hear her say it.

"It's okay, Mom." I lobbed the phone across the desk to him. He sat up straight and reached out girlishly with both hands. He barely got a finger on it. It fell to the floor beside his chair.

I rolled my eyes.

His neck reddened, and I wondered whether he had ever caught a ball in his life.

"Just one problem, Stan," I said, as he bent toward the phone and kept one eye locked on me.

"What's that?"

"That's not Elise's phone."

He just looked at me.

I shrugged. "You don't think I'd be stupid enough to bring it with me, do you? I just programmed the number into my phone. My service contract's up anyway. You can keep it if you'd like. I can pick up a new one in the morning."

"Good one, Taylor," Mom whispered from behind me.

He left the phone on the floor and straightened up in his chair.

I nodded at the gun. "Would you really have shot us? Or were you going to load us up with Valium and stick us in the car in the garage with the engine running, like you did with Elise?"

The hand that was next to the gun clenched. I glanced around to determine whether there was anything close enough to pick up and throw. Other than Mom, I didn't see a thing that I could get to. I moved my right foot back a half step and flexed my knees. I would lunge at him if I had to. There was nothing else to do. I opened and closed the fingers of my good hand.

Behind me, Mom's breathing quickened. Stanley tapped his finger on the desk. Something, a bug probably, smacked several times against the window behind Stanley's head. He leaned forward in his chair. I moved up on the balls of my feet.

Then, old .38-caliber Stanley did something that, in retrospect, should not have surprised me. He reverted to form. He lifted both hands away from the gun, buried his face in them, and began to bawl. "I . . . didn't . . . kill . . . her." The words came in bursts between snorts.

It says something bad about me, I'm sure, that I would have respected him more if he had just picked up the stupid gun and taken a shot at us. Instead, Mom and I waited for at least five minutes as he grunted and hacked and blew. If Mom hadn't been ready to jettison the guy before, I sure hoped she was finished with him after this display.

By the time he got a grip, I was tapping my foot on the floor and looking at my watch. He raised his head from his hands. "I guess you think I'm not much of a man."

It was incredibly hard to pass on that one, but I did. "It doesn't matter what I think." I motioned with my thumb over my shoulder toward Mom. "That's your wife, remember?" I turned and looked at her.

I'm not the best at identifying defining moments in anything, let alone my strange new relationship with my mother. I didn't have to be a family therapist, though, to spot something troublingly worthy of note in what she did next. With the gun on the desk now looking far less ominous than it had a few minutes earlier, she emerged from behind me, walked over to

Stanley, and wrapped her arms around his neck. "Don't worry, darling. We'll get through this together." She stroked the stringy hairs that were flattened damply against his scalp.

My eyes must have gotten as big as dinner plates. "What are you doing?"

She pressed her cheek against his forehead. "Can't you see he's suffering?"

I shook my head. "Wait a minute. Prostitutes; Elise Hovden dead in her car; the gun on the desk. This is no time to lose your focus, Mom."

She batted her eyes. "But we haven't heard his side of the story."

He smiled up at her and wiped his nose with his hand.

It's not every day that a girl gets a chance to stand valiantly between her mother and a revolver, only to have her mother, as soon as the danger is gone, comfort the jerk who pulled the gun in the first place. She could not have given me a clearer snapshot of my place in her world.

In the meantime, Stanley was still sniffling. "The people running the prostitution ring . . . were blackmailing me . . . I was afraid they would kill me . . . I went to her house to talk . . . but I didn't hurt her. I would never hurt that poor girl." He buried his head in Mom's chest, which caused her to accelerate her cooing and head stroking.

As he soaked the front of Mom's Burberry cardigan, I had a silent talk with myself. *What did you expect? That she would punt him and move in with you? That you'd have girl talks with bowls of popcorn in front of the fireplace?* The sad thing is, as unrealistic as it seems, that is exactly what I had hoped for. And why not? Was it so wrong just to want a mother? Millions of people have them. Why did I have to be different? I ran a hand through my hair. *You didn't have a mother before, and it looks like you don't have one now. Only fools allow hopes to turn into expectations, Taylor. Now, get over it.*

I walked over and picked my phone up off the floor. Then I sat on the edge of the desk. I watched as Mom stroked his head several more times. When I couldn't take it for another second, I said, "So, Stanley, why don't you tell us what happened at Elise's house?"

CHAPTER
TWENTY-NINE

BEFORE STANLEY TOLD US his story, I did some office rearranging. I told him I'd feel a lot more comfortable sitting behind the desk, with the revolver back in the drawer. By that time he was a real puppy dog, but I still took the precaution of flipping open the gun's cylinder. It was fully loaded. I dropped the bullets into my hand and stuck them in the pocket of my khakis.

He stood alone, hands at his sides like a chastened schoolboy, while Mom and I wrestled two leather wing chairs over from the other side of the room and positioned them in front of the desk. Then I walked past Stanley and sat in the desk chair. Just as he and Mom were about to sit in the wing chairs, Mom remembered that the caterers were still downstairs. She headed for the kitchen to pay them.

As she reached the door, I opened my mouth to ask her to bring up the desserts, but thought better of it. That would have been a bit flippant, even for me, although I'm not sure why I cared. In any event, I was glad that I'd eaten a few mouthfuls of spaghetti before the fireworks started. At least I wouldn't have to sit through the rest of this soap opera on an empty stomach.

While Mom was downstairs, Stanley and I sat facing each other across the desk. I couldn't think of a single reason to try to ease his discomfort, so I just stared at him. Before long he was looking at the bookshelves, apparently deep in thought. I assumed that he'd rather look at anything but me. When Mom came back into the study, she was carrying a bottle of water for each of us. When she handed one to Stanley, he unscrewed the cap and took a long drink.

I leaned forward and rested my forearms on the desk. "Okay, Stanley, what were you doing at Elise's house the night she died?"

He fiddled with the cap on his bottle of water. "It started when I got in with the wrong people—"

I sighed. "So you're really the victim? I assumed as much."

Mom frowned at me. "You asked him to tell the story. Are you going to interrupt him with smart remarks or listen to what he has to say?"

He gave her a pathetic look.

This was going to be torture. "Go ahead."

"They told me that if I didn't come up with fifty thousand dollars, they would let 'some people' at the university know that I had been using prostitutes. I had no idea some of the girls were as young as you say. They didn't seem young."

I practically gagged at the mental picture that statement conjured. I blinked and glanced at Mom. She just sat there with her eyes fixed on his face.

He wrung his hands. "I didn't have fifty thousand dollars. In fact, I was already in debt up to my ears."

Now Mom's mouth fell open.

"It's true. I've made some bad investments. And the oil industry has come up with new drilling technologies. My patents aren't generating the money they used to." He turned toward Mom. "I was going to talk to you about it."

The color drained from Mom's face. "When were you going to talk to me about it? After we got kicked out of our house?" She gripped the arm of her chair, as if on the verge of pushing herself to her feet. This was good. I was hoping she would lay into him. She relaxed her grip, though, and her voice got soft. "Where will we live?"

That one sentence, and the fear with which she delivered it, gave me more insight into my mother's psyche than all of my experience with her since she stepped back into my life. At that moment I understood that there was one nightmare that trumped all others in her life. She had lived in the streets, and it terrified her. She had no intention of doing it again, and she would make any deal, strike any bargain, to avoid it.

He shook his head. "Don't get all worked up, Hillary. We'll lose this house. That's almost certain. But the patents still have some value. They're just not easy to sell. It will take time. Cash is the problem. We're cash poor. Besides, I'm working on a project that will dwarf all the other patents combined." His eyes brightened. So did Mom's. "It involves coal—"

I rapped my knuckles on the desk. "Excuse me. Can we get back to the subject? Elise Hovden is dead. What did you have to do with it?"

He held up his right hand, like a Boy Scout. "I had nothing to do with that. I swear it."

"Then what were you doing at her house the night she died?"

He wiped his forehead with his sleeve. "You were right, I was blackmailing Simon Mason. He wasn't paying me, though, Elise was."

"Did Simon know about it?"

"No. Not according to her, anyway. Two days after I talked to Simon, she called me—on the number you just called this evening. She must have gotten it off Simon's phone. I set it up to be untraceable. I didn't even want to have a phone for it. That's why I got the laptop, just to receive the calls. Anyway, Elise said that

Simon would never pay me. That he would let me ruin him. She wasn't willing to let that happen."

I tilted my head back and pictured Elise—the tight blonde curls always falling in front of her eyes; the turned-up nose that made her look so much younger than she was. I had never met a person whose looks were a worse indicator of her personality. Despite her perky exterior, Elise was an energy sucker. The moment she stepped into a conversation, oxygen seemed to leave the room and everyone began looking for an excuse to talk to someone else. I was sorry for her, and for the many times she must have been made to feel unwanted. No one should have to go through life like that.

I hadn't liked her much, and I would have felt more guilty about that if she hadn't hated me. The story Stanley was telling, though, made me think of her not just more sympathetically, but more kindly. She had loved Simon and had apparently been willing to sacrifice for him. I'd seen good men—Dad and Simon—make sacrifices for others. Sacrifice counted for a lot in my book.

Stanley took another drink from his water bottle. "Everything proceeded smoothly enough. She had paid me twice: thirty thousand in cash, total. She left it in places I prearranged. Then one afternoon she called me again, but this time she knew my name."

"Thirty thousand? More than half a million was missing from the ministries' accounts. And Simon told me the blackmailer demanded two hundred thousand."

"I only asked for fifty."

That didn't add up, but I didn't want to get in an argument over it. I wanted to hear the whole story. "You said you only got thirty thousand from Elise. I thought you needed fifty?"

"She was paying me in installments. It had to be that way. If you withdraw ten thousand or more in cash from a bank at one time, the bank has to report it to the government. So she took out smaller amounts over time and accumulated it. The third installment was due two days after she died. It would have been the last twenty thousand."

"What happened to the other four hundred fifty thousand that was missing from the ministries' accounts?"

"I had nothing to do with that. She was taking it on her own."

Now, this was a wrinkle I hadn't expected. Apparently I had been too quick to nominate Elise for sainthood.

He ran a hand across the top of his head. "She never told me how she identified me. What she did tell me was that she had been found out. She said she'd been embezzling the money to pay me. I hadn't known that for sure, but it was the obvious explanation for how she was coming up with the cash. She offered me a deal that she said could save both of us."

"What kind of a deal?"

"She said she had embezzled more than the amounts she was paying me. Much more. She had stashed the money in a numbered account in the Cayman Islands."

"What was she planning to do with the money?"

"I don't know. She said I could have it if I'd just leave the country and never come back. That way she could tell everyone the whole story. She would tell them she had only embezzled the money to pay me off, to save Simon Mason. I would be the bad guy, and she figured she would skate with the authorities since she hadn't personally benefited. She said she had the information about the account and would give it to me, but I had to act fast."

By this time Mom's head was practically on his shoulder, and I could see that he was just about finished reeling her all the way back in.

"What did you do?"

"I had no choice. I agreed to the deal. I knew that if she gave my name to the police, the guys who were blackmailing me would kill me. Believe me, they are serious people, and they weren't about to sit around and wait to see if I would talk."

Suddenly Mom stood. "You were going to leave the country without me?"

I leaned back in my chair and smiled. It had apparently taken her a while to digest it, but she'd picked up on the one part of the story that most impacted her. Maybe she was going to spit the hook after all.

He reached over and touched her arm. "I was going to send for you as soon as I got the money and settled somewhere. If I brought you along at first, it would risk involving you in this whole mess. I love you too much to put you in jeopardy."

She stood there for a few moments, then sat back down and put her hand over his. The hook was set again, and it was clear she would suck in anything he tossed in her general direction. I decided she was a lost cause. I needed to remain focused on getting the facts.

"Who were the people who were blackmailing you?" I said.

"I don't know for sure. I never met them. I responded to messages they left for me at work. I did what they told me."

"None of this required you to go to Elise's house. So, why were you there that night?"

He crossed one leg over the other. It was apparent he was feeling more confident. "She insisted that I go there to pick up her laptop. She said it had the information about the account on it."

I gave myself another mental pat on the back. So the missing laptop had been important. "Why couldn't she just give you the account information over the phone?"

"I don't know. Maybe she was afraid someone could listen in. All I know is that she insisted that it had to be done the way she instructed. She held all the cards. I did what she told me to do."

He shifted his weight in his chair. "I went to her house at midnight. I had a plane ticket to Caracas, Venezuela for the next evening. You can check with the airline."

"What happened when you got there?"

"It went just the way she planned. I told her I was flying to Venezuela. I showed her my boarding pass, and she gave me her laptop. That was it. I was only there about fifteen minutes. She was fine when I left. Early the next afternoon, I saw on the news that she was dead. I was stunned—there was no reason to think she was going to kill herself. But I admit I was also relieved. My problem had been solved. I canceled my flight to Caracas."

"Where's the laptop?"

He got up and walked over to the bookshelf. Kneeling, he opened one of a series of cabinet doors that ran from wall-to-wall beneath the shelves. He pulled out a few folders from the front of the cabinet and placed them on the floor. Behind them was a safe that was built into the wall.

"Where did that come from?" Mom said.

"It was in the house plans, dear," he said, without looking up.

She screwed up her face but said nothing.

After dialing a combination, he opened the safe and pulled out a Dell laptop. He stood up and held it out to me. "Here it is."

I got up and took it from him. "What did you do with the money from the Cayman Islands account?"

"There was no Cayman Islands account—at least not that could be identified from that laptop."

"I don't get it."

"Your friend Ms. Hovden was apparently scamming me, too. There was a ten-digit number on the computer, but it didn't match up with any account at the bank she identified. Or any other bank I could find in the Cayman Islands. It was just a random ten-digit number that didn't correspond to any account anywhere."

I couldn't help but smile. I never would have given Elise credit for being that shrewd. "When did you find that out?"

"I checked on the account the next morning."

I sat back down at the desk and placed Elise's laptop in front of me. "It must have been a huge disappointment. You thought you'd just had a half million dollars dropped in your lap, huh?"

"I'll admit that that amount of money would have solved a lot of problems for me." He looked at Mom. "For us."

Mom hugged her shoulders and didn't respond. From the look on her face, it was apparent she was confused. Who wouldn't be?

"So, what happened to Elise?" I said.

He shrugged. "I don't understand the question. She killed herself. You saw her."

I drummed my fingers on the desk. "No, that makes no sense. If she intended to kill herself, why would she bother to go through that whole dance with you?"

He closed the safe and the cabinet door. Then he stood and faced me. "Maybe she was depressed all along and she just wanted to be sure that her name was cleared, so people wouldn't think she died a common thief. She assumed I was going to disappear, and everyone would blame it all on me."

That made no sense either. She surely would have waited to tell everyone about Stanley before she killed herself. Or at least she would have explained things in the suicide note. I pulled my phone out of my pocket and began to dial.

"Who are you calling?" Mom said.

"Michael Harrison, at the FBI. Blackmail is a federal offense, so he's just the person to handle this."

Stanley held up a hand. "Wait!"

I lowered the phone. "Wait for what? You don't think we're just going to forget about this, do you?"

"Don't be rash, dear," Mom said. "If you ruin his life, you're ruining my life, too."

"I'm not ruining anyone's life. Your husband blackmailed Simon Mason and was at Elise's house the night she supposedly killed herself. I don't think that's something we can just keep as a family secret."

Stanley lowered his head and said in a soft voice, "If you turn me over to the FBI, I'm a dead man."

I swiveled my chair in his direction. "That's a bit dramatic, isn't it?"

He shook his head. "No, it is not. You saw what they tried to do to Katie Parst. If it becomes public that I was blackmailing Simon Mason, and I'm tied in with Elise Hovden's death, they will kill me. I can assure you of that. They're not going to wait patiently to see whether I tell the police what they were doing to me."

Mom gave me a doe-eyed look. "Taylor, you can't do this."

Though I had to admit that the people who shot at Katie Parst were dangerous, it seemed to me that if they had been professionals, she would be dead. Besides, I couldn't stand to see Stanley use the danger that he, himself, had created, to try to wiggle out of this. I waved a hand in the air. "Mom, nobody's going to kill him. He's just trying to save his skin! Can't you see that?"

He sniffled and looked at Mom. "Hil, I'm telling you as surely as the sun will rise tomorrow morning that these men will kill me." He blinked twice, for effect. "They're evil."

I leaned back in my chair. "Oh, good grief!"

Mom got up, walked over to him, and put her arm around his shoulder. "No, Taylor, you need to listen to him. They're bad people. You know that."

"Mom, we don't even know who they are! In fact, we don't even know if they exist! He may be making this whole story up just to try to worm his way out of trouble."

He looked at me as if my suggestion hurt him. "How could I make up such a story?"

"Easy. I told you that Katie Parst was investigating an extortion ring. And even if I hadn't, you could have read about it in the papers."

"You didn't tell him about Katie Parst tonight," Mom said. "I've been sitting right here."

Honestly, we'd talked about so much in the past half hour, I couldn't remember if I'd told him about Katie's investigation or not. One thing was certain, though: I was getting deathly tired of this whole conversation. "This is crazy." I picked up the phone and began punching in Michael's number.

Stanley took a step toward me. "What if we could catch them?"

I stopped dialing. "Catch who?"

"The people who were blackmailing me."

Mom's eyes brightened. "Yes, what if we could?"

The left side of my brain told me not to let this discussion go on even one second longer. I moved my thumb back over the phone keys.

"They'll kill him," Mom said—as if I hadn't already gotten that point.

The right side of my brain looked at my mother and saw fear in her face. I knew it wasn't fear for Stanley's safety, per se. It was fear of being without Stanley, fear of being alone. That was one fear I understood well.

I stuck the phone back in my pocket and opened my mouth to say something I knew I was going to regret:

"And exactly how would we go about catching them?"

CHAPTER
THIRTY

I BELIEVE IT WAS Forrest Gump who said, stupid is as stupid does. I could make a solid argument that my mother and Stanley cooked up the stupidest plan I'd ever heard. But if I did, I would only be calling myself a name. Because three nights later, the Saturday before Christmas week, I was at the mayor of Southlake's house, strolling up the front walk in a black cocktail dress and four-inch heels. I was doing my part to catch Stanley's blackmailers.

It would be perfectly reasonable to question why a person trained in security at the highest levels of the United States government would allow herself to be sucked into a harebrained scheme to try to entrap the mastermind of what looked to me like a two-bit local extortion ring. The only thing I can say is that it was a testament to just how badly I wanted my mother back in my life. Despite a boatload of contrary evidence, she believed her husband, and there was no convincing her otherwise. I could only conclude that her fear of being alone outweighed her revulsion at Stanley's sleaziness. What motivated her, though, really didn't matter. If I wanted to have a relationship with her, I had no choice but to let their screwy plan play out.

Walking toward the mayor's front door, I had the eerie sense of having been magically miniaturized and transported into a Christmas-themed arcade game. Everything around me sparkled, because everything in the huge front yard, whether living or inanimate, was encased in white Christmas lights. To my right, a brightly determined Santa mushed his flickering reindeer in a trajectory that was destined to mash Rudolph's nose into the thick lower limbs of a massive oak tree.

Behind me valet parkers in khaki pants and Santa hats with flashing red balls on top jogged from the street to the house and back again. They jangled keys like Christmas bells as they opened and closed doors and zipped cars up and down the circular drive. Inside the house, clusters of elegantly dressed men and women stood near the windows in dazzlingly lit rooms, laughing and talking and gesturing with cocktail glasses.

Because of the unseasonably warm weather, and I wore only a light silk wrap around my shoulders. In my good hand, I carried a beaded black clutch, which contained my phone, a lipstick, a pack of chewing gum, a wad of tissues, and my .357 Sig.

Stanley was the primary architect of the plan, and it was subject to second-guessing on so many levels that I eventually just gave up and kept my mouth shut. I figured that once the plan failed, I would have demonstrated my willingness to go the extra mile for Mom and would be free to call Michael Harrison and ask him to send in the grown-ups.

In a nutshell the plan was this: Stanley contacted his blackmailer and got a message to the Boss, informing him of the numbered Cayman Island account that Elise had fortuitously dropped in Stanley's lap. Stanley pretended that he was afraid to access the account, and offered to cut the Boss in on the money if the Boss could arrange to have someone pick up the money and get it safely back into the United States. Stanley insisted on meeting the Boss in person, though, because if he didn't know the Boss's identity, he would have no way of ensuring that the Boss wouldn't just keep all of the money once he had accessed the account. After all, it was nearly a half million dollars.

To my complete shock Stanley said that the Boss agreed to the arrangement, which confirmed my suspicion that this was a small-time operation all the way. The "drop" was to occur at the mayor's annual Christmas open house where there would be lots of people milling around all evening. The Boss was to find Stanley and introduce himself. Stanley would slip him a flash drive containing the account number and bank name. According to Stanley, the Boss made it crystal clear that if it was a trap, others would be under instructions to kill Stanley before he had a chance to ring in the New Year.

My role was to keep an eye on Stanley and Mom from a distance, and if possible discreetly photograph anyone Stanley talked to for any significant period of time. I had no illusions. There were countless ways it could, and undoubtedly would, go wrong. But there would likely be scads of men at the party who were young, handsome, and well off; so despite the distraction of Stanley's plan, the evening still stacked up to be far more promising than an ordinary night in front of the television.

I checked my watch just as an elderly gentleman greeted me at the door and offered to take my wrap. Nine o'clock sharp. If they weren't already there, Mom and Stanley should be arriving any minute. His Honor the mayor was a relative novice to politics, having recently sold his software business for a gazillion dollars and turned his attention to the public good. The house was gigantic, even by Southlake standards, and a bevy of servants fluttered from room to room carrying trays of champagne and hors d'oeuvres. I didn't have to wait long to spot Mom and Stanley. They were standing in the formal living room to my right, surrounded by a group of middle-aged women.

Mom was looking elegant from the neck down, in a long cocktail dress and sequined jacket. As usual, though, her makeup was slathered on. She gestured wildly with her hands as she talked, and with her thickly painted face, she looked like a puppet whose arms were being controlled by an unseen, manic master. Stanley stood to the side of the group in his shiny Italian tuxedo, his face as pale as putty. I tried to catch his eye, but he looked away.

I opened my clutch to make sure my phone was set in camera mode, but I hadn't yet figured out how I could discreetly take pictures. The house was so full of people that just obtaining a clear view of Stanley required constant maneuvering.

I asked one of the waiters to bring me a tonic with lime, and then stood in the foyer watching Stanley out of one eye. With the other eye I scoped a six-foot-three-inch, tuxedoed version of George Clooney. I spent as much time jockeying for position to see George's ring finger as I did maneuvering for a clear camera shot of Stanley. Eventually George straightened his red and green holiday tie, revealing a platinum wedding band. I sighed and turned my full attention to Stanley.

For the next two-and-a-half hours, I made small talk with a startling number of men of various ages who were (a) stupid, (b) wimpy, or (c) boorish. It was as if someone had stenciled *Available* on my forehead while I wasn't paying attention. They came at me one at a time—like ninjas in a low-budget martial arts film. As I fended them off, I sidled from one side of the house to another, trying to keep Stanley in sight.

I realize how inconsistent it is for me to say in one breath that I looked forward to a party full of eligible men, and then, in the next breath to scoff at their efforts to gain my attention. Especially since they were right, I was available. I hadn't heard a word from Rob Morrow since I had allowed myself to become another first-date notch in a bedpost that must have already been carved like a totem pole. All I can say in my defense is that when it comes to men, I'm conflicted. In the long run, though, what I really want is someone as good as Dad and Simon, a subset that is stacking up to be troublingly small.

In any event, just as I emerged from the restroom after my fourth glass of tonic, Mom tapped me on the shoulder. "Stanley needs to see us," she whispered.

"Where is he?"

"We can't talk to him in here. No one is supposed to know you're with us. He wants us to meet him in the backyard."

"In the backyard? Is anyone out there?"

"No, that's why he wanted to meet out there. Apparently something has gone wrong."

I gave her a sideways look. "Imagine that."

She scowled.

"When are we supposed to go?" I said.

"Right now. Follow me."

She went first, and I followed at a discreet distance. We wound our way through the huge informal living area and down a back hallway, past the pool bath to a door that led to the pool deck. That's where I caught up to her. Mom turned around and checked the hallway. It was empty. She opened the door quietly and we stepped out onto the deck. Mom eased the door shut behind us.

The pool light was on, but no one was outside. "Where is he?"

"We're supposed to meet him just outside the gate." She walked along the Italian stone fence next to the pool until she came to an iron gate. "This is it." She grabbed the handle and swung the gate open.

I unzipped my clutch and put my hand on my pistol as we walked through the gate. "I don't know about this, Mom. You'd better let me go—"

Something hard came down on my forearm, knocking the clutch from my hand. I swung one leg back to put myself in a leverage position. I saw movement in the shadows to my left, and I threw my elbow sideways. It connected with something solid, and I heard a yelp. Then I felt a heavy thud against the back of my neck that knocked me to my knees. I tried to lunge at something moving in front of me, but my legs seemed to float away from the pavement just before everything went black.

CHAPTER
THIRTY-ONE

IT WAS THE DREAM again. The one by the campfire with Dad. Everything played out as usual. The guys entered the camp. They blasted Dad with the shotgun. I shot them both and stood over the big guy, waiting for his eyes to pop open. Then I wondered: Would it be his eyes, or Dad's eyes, or Simon's? I longed for the days when my nightmare was predictable. I watched his face and waited . . . and waited.

Then his face became blurry, and it faded away.

Roaring in my ears. Muffled. Monotonous. A moan. My head hurt. I blinked. Everything black. Licked my lips; like a tongue over a nail file. Something rough on my face, brushing my cheeks. My head . . . what an ache. Bag of rocks inside my skull. I blinked again. Everything still black.

My shoulder hurt, almost like my head. I was on my side. I stretched my leg and it bumped into something. Then the moan again. I kicked. There was the moan again. Stimulus-response. I was getting the picture.

I shook my head. Have to focus. Time to wake up. "Mom?" My throat was drier than my mouth, my voice barely a whisper. I coughed. "Mom?" With a little more oomph. The only response was another moan.

Beneath me was prickly stubble. Cheap carpet. It scratched my legs. Everything around me vibrated. My whole body was vibrating. I took a deep breath and my nostrils burned. Gasoline fumes. Then I got it: We were in the trunk of a moving car.

I pushed myself up. My head slammed into the trunk lid. That didn't help. The car hit some bumps, which popped my head against the metal again. I felt around my face with my hands. What was scratching my cheeks? It was a hood that felt like a potato sack. An elastic band secured it around my neck. That was easy enough to stretch. I pulled the hood off and blinked several times.

As my eyes adjusted, something glowed yellow-green above me. It was the safety release for the trunk. That was something good, and I knew I was thinking again. No matter the situation, things could always be worse. Dad told me that. The safety release and my untied hands told me something, too: Whoever threw us into this trunk was an amateur. We had a chance.

I moved my fingers around my scalp to see if I had a fracture. There was nothing but a lump at the base of my skull. It ached but didn't seem serious. Since I'd been out for a while, I was sure I had a concussion. There was nothing to be done about that.

My eyes grew accustomed to the dark. It was amazing how much the glowing safety release illuminated the boxy trunk space. I looked over my shoulder. Mom was lying on her side in the back of the trunk, her knees bent. I reached back and pushed her with my hand, but all she did was groan again. It was a fairly deep trunk, maybe a full-size American sedan.

I found Mom's face with my hands and patted it through the hood. She pulled her head away but didn't say anything. Once I found the elastic around her neck, I pulled the hood off. Then I squeezed her ear. She yelped.

"Mom! It's Taylor."

She opened one eye, then closed it again. "My head hurts." It was surprisingly easy to hear her, considering we were bouncing along in a car trunk.

"Mine, too. They must have whacked us with something. You're more awake than I thought. Let me feel your head." I moved my fingers over her scalp. She wasn't bleeding. "Whatever they hit us with must have been cushioned somehow. Neither of us has a fracture. They probably didn't want any blood."

"We're in the trunk of a car?"

"Yes."

"Will we suffocate?"

Good question. I thought about it for a second. "We should get enough air for a while, anyway. I don't think these things are built that well."

"They're going to kill us, aren't they?" Her voice was amazingly matter-of-fact.

I looked up at the glowing emergency release. "I don't know, but it's not the type of thing that I'm inclined to wait and see. I'm going to open the trunk lid and we're going to roll out onto the road."

I heard her shuffle her legs. "How fast are we going?" she said.

"I don't know."

"Are there cars behind us?"

"I don't know."

"That's a nice plan, dear."

I smiled. At least she was retaining her sense of humor. "Would you rather wait and see where we park?"

"No."

"Then get ready. I'll open the trunk and take a look before we go. If there are cars behind us, we may not have to do it. We can just flag them down. I've been listening, though, and haven't heard any traffic sounds.

I'm guessing we're out in the country." I felt the splint on my finger to make sure it was still in place and no more damage had been done.

"How do we do this?" Mom was moving around now, adjusting her position the best she could in the cramped space.

"Cover your head with your hands. Tuck your legs up under you, and as soon as you hit the road, roll. Let your momentum carry you until you stop. This is going to hurt. You might even break something."

"Maybe they're not going to kill us. Maybe we should just wait and see where they take us."

"Bad idea. If you want to be alive tomorrow, you're going to have to trust me on this one. You can do this."

"I don't know if I can."

I reached behind me and grabbed her arm. "You have to do it. It's the only way. Now, listen to me, as soon as we stop rolling, we're going to have to get moving. These guys are going to slam on the brakes and come looking for us. Hopefully there will be someplace to hide. I'll check it out when I open the trunk."

"I'm afraid."

"You should be. I'm afraid, too." I shifted my position to where I could look over my shoulder at her. "I will not leave you, Mom. Do you understand me? When we stop rolling, I will find you. If you're hurt, I will help you. Whatever it takes, I will get us out of this, but you have to do what I tell you."

Her breath on my neck became short and choppy. We needed to get going. She wasn't likely to become any calmer with the passage of time. "Are you ready?"

"Yes."

Rolling back over, I reached up and pulled the safety release, gripping it tightly with my good hand to keep the trunk lid from flying up. The lid thunked open. Air rushed in through the opening, and I held the release lever tight to keep the trunk from opening more than a few inches. I knew that the driver might be looking at a dashboard warning light at that very moment, telling him the trunk was open. The smell of damp earth and stale manure filtered into the trunk. My guess about being in the country had been right.

At first it was difficult to make anything out, but it was clear that there were no headlights behind us. I tried to remember what the weather forecast had been and recalled that it had been for warm temperatures and cloudy skies. Once we were out on the ground, the clouds would be great, making the night much darker. For now, however, the lack of moonlight wasn't helping me figure out where to go once we hit the ground. I squinted down at the narrow road and realized we'd gotten two lucky breaks. The road was asphalt, which would provide a softer landing than some of the alternatives, and it was steeply crowned, so it would dissipate the shock and funnel us to the shoulder after we hit.

As my eyes adjusted to the surroundings, scraggly shapes emerged near the side of the road. I made out a spattering of short, twisted mesquite trees. The car slowed somewhat and a beer can clattered past on the road, apparently tossed by the driver. That was another stroke of good luck. Once we got out, I'd rather be matching wits with someone who'd been drinking.

The car slowed even more. I knew that if the driver realized the trunk was open we would only have a few seconds. I turned back to Mom. "We've got to go. Ready?"

She nodded.

"Watch me and do exactly what I do. I'll find you after we're on the ground." I scooted to the edge of the trunk and let the lid fly open. The trunk light came on, and the sudden brightness startled me. I blinked hard and lifted myself over the lip of the trunk. Then I rolled out and tucked into a ball. My right shoulder hit the road, but I was already rolling. The asphalt tore my cocktail dress and my skin, but I managed to keep my head and my splinted finger clear. The momentum spun me at an angle to my left, down a short embankment and into a soggy drainage ditch. The tires of the car screeched.

When I stopped rolling, I tried to ignore the pain from my shoulder and the scrapes on my legs and arms. I turned and looked back at the car. It veered to the side of the road about fifty yards away from me and stopped. With the trunk wide open, and the trunk light on, it was easy to see Mom. She was still crouching there, squinting into the night. She wasn't coming.

She had pulled off her jacket. She held it up so I could see it, and tossed it out of the trunk, into the ditch on the side of the road. In case I hadn't seen, she pointed toward it. She was leaving the jacket for me.

I reached up and clutched my shoulders in my hands. Something caught in my throat, and I moved toward her but stopped myself. I couldn't help her by heading that way.

I turned and scrambled on my hands and knees along the ditch away from the car. After about ten yards I came to a spot where the ground was more level. I dove into the field that adjoined the road and rolled behind a narrow mesquite tree. The car doors slammed. I flattened my face against the ground. Damp straw stuck to my cheeks and hair. I lifted my head and peeked around the tree. Two men ran around to the back of the car. They stopped face-to-face with Mom, who was still peering out the back of the open trunk.

I closed my eyes. Don't shoot her, don't shoot her.

When I opened my eyes again, she was edging back in the trunk, away from the men. They were saying something to her that I couldn't make out. My silent plea changed. Don't look this way. Don't look this way. She kept her eyes straight on them. She had no intention of giving me away.

The driver was at least six feet four and as broad as a chest of drawers. Now I understood why I had so little chance when they popped us at the party. As he talked to Mom, he waved a hand, and I could see a beer can in it. Then he lifted his other hand to wipe his face with the sleeve of his blue-jean jacket. In that hand was a semiautomatic pistol.

The next thing he said, I heard easily, because he shouted it with his face within a few inches of Mom's: "Where did she go?"

Mom cowered. I held my breath. She pointed to the opposite side of the road from where I was.

Unfortunately he was big but not dumb. He pointed to his pal, who was equally tall but as lanky as the mesquite tree I was hiding behind. "Turn the car around—" was all I heard. He pointed to the opposite side of the road. He pushed Mom's head down and slammed the trunk shut over her. Then he turned and began walking—directly toward me.

He hadn't bought what Mom was selling. He was closing quickly. I had a choice to make: hunker down and hide, or move and risk being seen.

When I was a little girl, I used to have a dream, over and over, in which a giant was terrorizing our town. He ended up standing outside my bedroom window with searchlights illuminating his head and shoulders. I would hide under my desk in my dark room and tell myself that I was very small and there were a million places he could look and a million people he could find instead of me. Invariably, within a few seconds, he turned toward my second-story window, which was just at his eye level, and looked straight at me. I trembled as he reached out his giant hand—a hand big enough to pick me up like an ordinary person would pick up a lizard or a chick—and crashed it through my window. That's when I would wake in a sweat, my heart pounding.

I was never going to hide beneath my desk again.

I looked to my right, toward the middle of the field. The next closest mesquite tree was ten yards from me. I was glad my dress was black. I would be hard to spot as long as I stayed low and quiet. I belly-crawled to the tree and slid in behind it. My legs were burning from the dirt and gunk that I knew must be accumulating in the scrapes in my skin. Wet soil clung to my arms in globs, but generally my hands and arms hadn't taken nearly the beating that my legs had.

I lifted my head just enough to spot the giant. He was at the side of the road, looking into the ditch. His partner had turned the car around. The headlights now illuminated the road but didn't reach as far to the side as my little tree.

The giant didn't have a flashlight, and I whispered a word of thanks for that. I knew that if I could put just a little more distance between the road and me, they would never find me on a night this black. As

I put my hands beneath me to crawl again, the wind gusted across the field from the road. It was the perfect covering noise. I looked back over my shoulder. He was squatting now, his eyes focused on something in the ditch.

Pushing myself to my feet, I scrambled across the field toward the next mesquite, which was another thirty yards or so from the road. My back was to him. If he saw me, and if he knew how to use that gun, I wouldn't even hear the shot before it dropped me. The scrawny tree seemed to move away from me as I ran. When I got within a few feet, I dove behind it, rolled onto my back and listened. Nothing but the wind rustling the limbs.

I rolled over onto my stomach. The giant stood with his hands on his hips, looking directly at me. He swore. I scanned the ground around me for anything I could use as a weapon. There was nothing but damp grass and straw. My best bet was to rip a branch off the little tree.

I shook my head. That was panic talking. A mesquite branch couldn't win a battle with a semi-automatic. I had to think. My only chance was to run. I would stay low and zigzag and hope he wasn't any good with the gun. Whether I was fast enough to outrun him, especially while I was zigzagging, we would just have to see. I closed my eyes and got right to the point: Please God; please God. I opened my eyes and kicked off my shoes. Pushing myself into a low crouch, I looked toward the road.

He was walking back to the car. I dropped back onto my stomach. I knew I didn't deserve the break I'd just been given, but I figured maybe Dad and Simon had enough stroke upstairs to have put in a supplemental word for me.

The giant yelled something to his partner, who had been walking the opposite side of the road. His partner turned and made his way back to the car. Within a few minutes they had gotten in and turned it around again. They sat there for a while, facing down the road away from me. I assumed they were talking over what to do. I sat up with my back to the tree and took stock of my situation, glancing at them over my shoulder every few seconds.

My legs were badly scraped, my shoulder ached from where it had slammed into the pavement, and my head felt like it was encased in a steel drum. My legs and arms worked, though. My feet came out relatively unscathed, and the pain at least meant I could feel my body parts. As Dad used to say, there are positives in every situation, no matter how bleak. The people who survive are the people who see them and use them.

I had no cell phone. I assumed it was in the front seat of their car or lying with my purse on the side of the road somewhere between where I was standing and

Southlake. I scanned the horizon. No houses, no signs of life, not even an animal. Not a single car had come down the road. It looked as if I would be walking.

I picked up my shoes. Four-inch heels weren't going to be worth much out here. I knocked the heels off against the trunk of the tree. Then I hiked up my skirt and stuck the heels in the waistband of my panties. They might come in handy as weapons. I put the shoes, sans heels, back on. As soon as they drove off, I would check to see if I could walk on them. If not, I would toss them away.

The car's engine revved. I peeked around the tree and watched it pull down the road. If I was to have any chance of finding where they were taking Mom, I would have to track it as long as I could. Fortunately the landscape was flat as a board. I came out from behind the tree and took a few steps on the heel-less shoes. My ankles wobbled. The shoes were no use at all. I kicked them off.

I walked at an angle back toward the road, and soon the car was so far in front of me that there was no danger they could see me in their rearview mirror. I moved out onto the pavement and looked back down the road in the direction from which we'd come—the direction of Dallas, I assumed. Then I turned and looked at the car's taillights heading in the opposite direction. My eye caught Mom's jacket, lying in the ditch to my right. I walked over and picked it up.

I held the jacket to my face and smelled it. It had the unmistakable fragrance of her perfume—pretty horrid, but it was Mom. I felt my eyes filling and wiped at them with my hand. Leaving her jacket for me was motherly, wasn't it? I chose to believe that it was.

I looked up the road. The taillights were still easily visible. I had no illusions that I could catch them, or even track them for long, but at least I might be able to see if they turned off the main road before I lost them. That would help the police. Of course, getting the police out here would take a long time, even if I had a phone and could call them right then. I had no idea where I was. How could I expect the police to help in any time frame that would matter to whether Mom lived or died?

I looked at Mom's jacket and then at my bare feet. The jacket could help, but not in the way she probably imagined when she threw it out of the car. I sat down in the middle of the road and tore the jacket down the middle seam. Then I wrapped one half around each foot, tied each half off, and stood up. Not exactly Adidas, but not bad.

I took a few quick steps and reached down to make some adjustments to cover the pressure points. After a few more tentative steps, I started to jog. My legs and hip ached, but by the time I'd gone a couple hundred yards, things began to loosen up. Even my head began to feel better with the movement. I was desperately thirsty, but that would have to wait. I tried to think about something else.

Within a few minutes the car's taillights, which were very far down the road now, brightened. I moved over to the ditch and crouched, ready to bolt back into the field if they turned around. Instead, they made a right turn and headed at a ninety-degree angle to the road I was on. I stood next to the ditch and squinted into the night. They traveled half a mile or so and turned left, moving away from me for a few seconds. Then the taillights went dark. They had stopped.

There was still not another car in sight. From the narrowness of the road and the roughness of the asphalt, I gathered I was not exactly on Main Street, even by rural Texas standards. This late at night there was no telling when another car might come by. I kept my eye on the spot where the taillights vanished and made a mental note of a row of tall trees, probably a windbreak, just beyond. It wouldn't be easy to find the spot, and I didn't want to waste time trying to locate them when I got in the vicinity. Just as I was about to start jogging again, a yellow light came on near the car. It appeared to be a light from a house or a building of some sort. They had moved indoors.

I took a deep breath and set out down the middle of the road at an easy pace that I thought my feet could handle. The air was cooling, but the jog would warm me quickly. Assuming that the place where they stopped was a mile-and-a-half or so away, I figured I could reach them in less than twenty minutes if my feet held out.

As I fell into a rhythm I chuckled when I thought what a picture I would make if a car did come down the road. A long-legged woman in a shredded, muddy dress, with a cocktail jacket for shoes. Just out for a jog on a country road at who-knows-what-time in the morning. No one was likely to pick up this hitchhiker.

Nevertheless, I desperately hoped for a pickup to come by—preferably one with a good old boy and a shotgun in the cab. I was going to save my mother or die trying. And if no one came along to help, I was just going to have to improvise.

CHAPTER
THIRTY-TWO

BY THE TIME I reached their car, my footwear had shredded, and I was running barefoot in the grass on the side of the road. Mom's jacket had served its purpose, though. My feet were in reasonably good shape, although they stung like crazy where my stride had brought me down on burrs.

When I got within a couple hundred yards, I stopped, wiped the sweat from my face with what was left of my tattered dress, and surveyed the area. The car was parked in front of a relatively new, two-story log cabin with an elevated porch that appeared to run all the way around the building. The backyard sloped away, so the porch was just a few feet above the ground in the front, but looked to be ten feet or so off the ground in the back. I figured that the back of the house must have a walkout basement, with the floor of the porch forming the roof of the walkout.

From the size of the cabin, I guessed we were on a high-end hunting lease, which explained why the road had been so empty. The house was lit up as if they were throwing a holiday party. I couldn't see anyone through the windows, and I had no idea whether they had met others there.

Keeping my distance, I moved around the side to the back. The porch extended farther from the house in the back, creating a large deck on which sat a huge double-winged gas grill that I could see from the slope when I stood on tiptoe. I wondered if there might be a propane tank I could use somehow.

As I suspected, the basement of the house walked out onto a concrete patio beneath the deck. The windows in the basement were dark. That could be the most opportune spot if I needed to break in. I continued around the back, staying twenty yards clear of the deck, until I rounded the corner and moved back up the hill on the opposite side of the house.

The terrain sloped upward so steeply that when I neared the front of the house I could easily step up onto the porch and swing myself over the cedar rail if I wanted to. Four rustic rocking chairs sat in a row on the porch on that side of the house. A dozen or so western items hung from the outside wall as decorations. There were horseshoes and steer skulls, and near the back corner two things that particularly caught my eye: old-fashioned, steel-jawed traps with jagged shark-like teeth that could clamp onto a leg or foot and do serious damage.

When I reached the top of the slope, I turned the corner, dropped to my knees, and crawled along the porch line in the front of the house. Here the porch was only a few feet off the ground. The earth was slightly muddy, but by that time I could have rolled in a pig sty and it wouldn't have made much difference. I had a shredded dress and shredded legs, and grass or straw clung to virtually everything else. I stopped for a second, sat, and rubbed mud on my face and neck. If I was going to sneak around, I might as well be as hard to spot as possible. Besides, if these guys saw me the psychological effect couldn't hurt. They were sure to think I was a lunatic.

When I got to the front window, I peeked over the edge of the porch. The big guy was standing with his back angled to the window. He was talking on a cell phone. The side of his face was flushed, but I couldn't tell if he was angry or drunk or just ruddy. In his hand was a 9mm pistol, which he waved in the air as he spoke. I crawled back around the corner and sat with my back to one of three log posts that held up the front of the porch.

It was time to formulate a plan. They weren't going to sit in this house forever, knowing that I was loose and might bring help. On the other hand, they were likely worried about police cars and SWAT teams. It would never occur to them that I was crazy enough to arrive on my own.

I analyzed the information I had. In the house were at least two men. One had a gun, and it was a safe bet the other must, also. Both were considerably larger than I was, but the skinny one didn't look too imposing. In an ideal world he would be the one I tangled with, if necessary. On the other hand, I had to avoid getting close to the giant or I was likely to die—and so was Mom.

I assumed Mom was still alive. We were in open country, and a loud sound would travel for miles. If they'd already killed her, I'd have heard the shot. In trying to rescue her, though, I faced two huge disadvantages: I had no idea where she was in the house and no idea of the floor plan.

It was time to face facts. My chances of pulling this off alone were slim, but I had no way to call for help. Even if I did, Mom might be dead by the time it arrived. I thought about the jacket she threw out of the trunk for me. I was not going to leave her here to die alone.

I peeked over the porch at the traps on the wall. They were the only halfway decent weapons available.

The trick was to come up with a plan that would allow me to take advantage of them.

I studied the traps in the indirect yellow light coming through the window near the back of the porch. The larger of the two must have had an eight-inch jaw spread—probably designed for coyote. Those jagged teeth were as illegal as a hand grenade. Before I could figure out how to use the trap, I had to get it in my hands. I ran my fingers around in the dirt beneath the porch until they closed around a stone about the size of a tennis ball. If I was going up on the porch, I at least wanted some sort of a weapon to buy a few seconds if I got surprised.

I grabbed the porch rail and pulled myself up and over. My bare feet hardly made a sound when they came down on the wood plank floor. I edged along the wall toward the back corner of the house until I came to the first of two windows. It was dark and small and appeared to look out from a bathroom or laundry room. I took a quick look and confirmed that it was a slender bathroom with a tub and shower. I continued past it and reached the traps, which were only a few feet from the second window.

The light from the window illuminated the traps. Each hung from a metal hook and was tethered to the wall at the bottom by a leather strap tied around a thick nail. I untied the strap on the larger trap and lifted it from its hook. Its weight surprised me as I eased if off the wall. The first thing was to determine whether it worked. The porch wasn't the best place for that. I eased back toward the front of the house to a point where the porch was low enough that I could swing myself back over the rail to the ground.

My feet squished into the mud as I landed. I sat with my back to the porch post and laid the trap on the ground. On each side of the circular trap was a stabilizer leg that stuck out about four inches. The legs could be spiked to the ground to hold the trap in place. In the center of the trap was a metal trip plate. When the trap was in the open, loaded position, any pressure applied to the trip plate would spring it, slamming the jaws shut.

The jaw spread was large enough to break a man's ankle in an instant, if I could just figure a way to lure someone into it. I grabbed the jaws and pressed my weight down on them to load it. It clicked into the locked position. Now, would it snap shut? I wanted to test it, but those heavy metal teeth would echo like a gunshot when they snapped. I would have to trust that it would work.

Holding the trap by one of the stabilizing legs, I pulled myself up over the rail again and edged down the porch. When I reached the last window on that side, I peeked through the glass. It was the kitchen. Skinny Man was sitting at the table, facing away from a huge window that overlooked the back porch.

From my angle I was looking at his profile. He was alone in the room, smoking a cigarette. Just behind him and to his right was the door to the back deck. On the table in front of him was a beer can—and a Beretta 9mm semiautomatic. I needed that gun.

I flattened my back against the wall. There was little time to think. Dad used to tell me that sometimes the best battle plans were the simple ones born of opportunity. On the other side of the wall I was leaning against was a pistol. It was a weapon I desperately needed, and it was sitting on a table in front of a guy I thought I could take. That was an opportunity I couldn't pass up.

I ducked beneath the glass and moved around the back corner of the house, where I slid along the wall until I was next to the picture window. Skinny Man's back was no more than five feet from me. I scanned the kitchen through the window. A door led from the kitchen to a narrow hallway that seemed to open onto the family room in the front.

The only thing separating Skinny Man and me was a fraction of an inch of glass. The question was, what was the best way to get through that glass? The back door was almost certainly locked, and it was several steps away from him. I couldn't give him time to pick up that gun.

I lifted the trap by one of its legs and waggled it like a softball bat. With its heft, one good shot to the head would neutralize Skinny Man, at least for a moment. I looked at the picture window, then down at the trap. I leaned back against the wall. My eye caught a wrought iron deck chair about ten feet away.

I looked through the window again. Skinny Man took a sip of beer, then a deep drag on his cigarette. He tilted his head back and blew smoke toward the ceiling. I leaned the trap against the wall and stepped lightly across the deck to the chair. Picking it up was not that easy with one hand in a splint, but I was happy that it was good and heavy.

I took a deep breath and exhaled. Holding the chair waist high, I ran toward the picture window. When I got within a few feet, I pivoted, swung the chair behind me, and slung it at the back of Skinny Man's head.

The glass exploded over him. The chair grazed his shoulder and crashed to the floor. I picked up the trap, hopped over the window sill, and uncoiled my best softball swing.

Skinny Man felt for the gun but it clattered to the floor. He threw his chair back and spun toward me, but he was too slow. My swing was true. His timing was unfortunate. The trap crashed into his head, and the trip plate crushed his nose. A coyote's foot could not have sprung the trap more efficiently.

The jaws snapped shut. The teeth crunched into his jaw.

He let out a bestial howl and clawed at the jagged metal. He shook his head, trying to fling it off his face. Each time he slung his head from side to side, blood flew across the room in a stream.

I lunged for the gun on the floor. When I got my hands on it, I didn't even bother aiming at him. He was thrashing on the floor, shrieking and rolling from side to side, still trying to claw the trap from his face.

I knelt behind the table and raised the pistol toward the door that led to the front of the house. Then I waited.

Within seconds the giant bounded through the door, his gun hand bobbing with each frantic stride. With all that movement he couldn't have hit me if I were an elephant. An amateur, in too big a rush to find out what had happened. And he was an instant from paying dearly for it.

When he saw me, his eyes widened. His feet skidded on the tile as he tried to stop. He fired two wild shots while I sighted down the barrel. This shot had a purpose, and I was shooting left-handed so I took my time.

When I squeezed the trigger, he spun sideways, his gun hand flailing. His pistol hit the floor and slid across the room to the base of the refrigerator. He grabbed his shoulder and yelled. Within seconds a dark circle soaked the arm of his denim shirt.

"Where's my mother?" I leveled the gun at his chest.

He scowled.

I counted, "One, two . . ."

He cocked his head, like a pet trying to understand a command.

"Three." I aimed the gun at his thigh and squeezed the trigger. This time, without the crunching glass and clattering chair, the gun sounded like a cannon going off in the kitchen.

He dropped to the floor and howled.

I wagged my head. "Now, you understand, right? When I count, that's a very bad thing for you. I'm going to ask you again. Where's my mother?"

He stopped writhing long enough to point to the door that led to the front of the house. "Out there!"

I walked to the refrigerator and picked his pistol up off the floor. With each step I left a smear of blood on the tile from the scattershot of broken glass imbedded in my feet. I was in for some serious pain later, but for now my body was pumping so much adrenaline I could have walked on hot coals. I lifted each foot and brushed away the blood and the larger pieces of glass.

I looked down at my ragged dress. No pockets, no purse. There was nothing else to do with the gun. I hiked my dress above my waist. The heels from my shoes were still in the waistband of my panties. I pulled them out, tossed them on the floor, and replaced them with his semiautomatic. As I tugged my hemline down, I noticed the sink next to the refrigerator. My throat felt like a sandal that had been left out in the sun for a week. I hit the tap and slurped from the faucet, keeping one eye on the doorway into the kitchen.

When I'd drunk enough to hold me, I wiped my mouth with the back of my arm and turned toward the giant. He was staring up at me from the floor as if I were some sort of demon woman. I was okay with that.

It occurred to me what a horrifying sight I must be to this poor schmuck. I looked at my reflection in the backdoor glass. My feet were bare and blotched with blood-streaked mud; my hair stuck straight out on one side; my filthy dress was torn in at least ten places and bulged with the outline of the pistol I had secured. Diagonal streaks of black mud smeared my face and neck, giving me a Bengal tiger look. I smiled.

By that time Skinny Man had passed out, lying on his side with his legs tucked up to his waist. Blood oozed from his face onto the tile. The giant's pant leg had a dark, growing stain the size of a softball. He held his leg in his hands and moaned.

I bent over Skinny Man and patted him down for additional weapons. I was hoping he had a cell phone, but he had nothing. I wasn't about to get as close to the giant. I pointed my pistol at him and told him to pat himself down, nice and slow. I made him roll from side to side, so I could get a good look at his pockets and pant legs. He pulled a cell phone out of his jeans pocket. The slide top was dangling, busted when he fell. I motioned for him to push it across the floor to me. I picked it up and pushed the buttons. It was dead. I straightened my back. "Where are the phones?"

"What phones?"

"The phones in this cabin. They must have phones, don't they?"

"There aren't any. This place is for hunters. They bring their cell phones."

I tossed his phone to the floor. "You keep an eye on your buddy until I get back. Have you got any other friends in the house?"

He shook his head.

"You would tell me, wouldn't you? Because if you're lying to me, when I come back you're going to regret it."

"I'm telling you the truth, lady. We're the only ones here." He glanced at the back door.

"Yeah, you'd like to get out the back, wouldn't you? But on that leg, you wouldn't get very far before I caught you. And I'm not a cop, so I don't have to worry about a bunch of rules. You've got one good leg and one good arm left. If you want to keep them attached to your body, you stay where you are. Got it?"

He curled into a ball and nodded.

I walked to the door that led from the kitchen down the hallway. I cupped my hand around my mouth. "Mom!"

"I'm in here! I'm tied up!"

I turned and watched the giant's face. "Is anyone

in there with you, Mom?" His expression didn't change, and I knew he had been telling me the truth.

She didn't hesitate. "It's just me. There wasn't anybody else but those two."

As I walked down the hall to get Mom, for the first time I thought of Stanley. I wondered where the Boss had taken him, and whether he was already dead. Fortunately I knew just the person who could tell me. He was sitting on the floor in the kitchen with bullets in his arm and leg.

I was confident he would talk. I had plenty of ammo left, and I was in no mood to be patient.

CHAPTER
THIRTY-THREE

WHEN I TURNED THE corner into the living area in the front of the house, Mom was sitting on the floor in the corner with her back to a heavy oak trophy cabinet. Her arms were tied behind her, and a yellow nylon rope stretched up and threaded through a hole near the top of the cabinet. If she moved more than a couple of feet she would pull the cabinet down on top of her.

"You came back," she said.

"I told you I wouldn't leave you." I set Skinny Man's 9mm on the floor, bent over, and worked at the knot. It was challenging with a splinted hand.

She looked me over. "You look like Rambo."

"It's been a tough night." I tugged at the rope.

"Did you kill them?"

"No, but at least one of them may wish I had."

She glanced at the door that led to the back of the house. "I heard a crash before the gunshots."

"I took a shortcut into the kitchen."

After I slipped her hands out of the rope, she sat on the floor rubbing her wrists.

I don't know what I was expecting—maybe for her to throw her arms around me and thank me. After all, hadn't everything changed in the moment when she left her jacket for me out on the road? I stood above her and waited.

She looked up at me. Her eyes softened, and she opened her mouth to speak. I felt myself leaning toward her.

Then she closed her mouth again. She sat for a second, looking straight ahead. "I suppose you're mad at me for staying in the trunk." She pushed her hair back off her shoulders and reached a hand up toward me.

I clasped her arm and helped her to her feet. "You were afraid. Who wouldn't be?"

She brushed at the mud that I left on her arm. "It wasn't fear, just common sense. You're twenty-six years old. Your body can do things mine can't."

"I'm twenty-nine."

"Of course."

"You left your jacket for me. It helped. Thank you."

"It was cold." She brushed her arm again. "I don't want you to think I was afraid. Bouncing along that road would have killed me."

"They were going to kill us anyway."

"Maybe they were just going to hold us for a while."

Surely this wasn't going to be it—business as usual—a discussion about whether jumping out of the trunk and coming back to save her life was even necessary.

Something clattered in the kitchen.

I turned my head toward the door. "I've got to check on them."

"I'm coming with you."

Maybe that was her way of saying she wouldn't leave me, either—or maybe she was just afraid to be alone. Let's face it, who could possibly tell what she was thinking? "Okay, but stay behind me."

I moved across the room and down the hall. When I got to the kitchen door, I held my hand out behind me. Mom stopped. In front of me the giant was sitting on the floor where I had left him. He looked up at me. The empty animal trap was next to him. Skinny Man was nowhere in sight.

I figured he must have crawled out the broken window. He wasn't likely to hang around here when I had all of the guns. I didn't really care. The way his nose and jaw looked, he wouldn't stay free for long without being identified.

Something about the look on the giant's face, though, made me pause. I stayed in the hallway and raised my gun in both hands. The giant had taken off his shirt and made a makeshift tourniquet for his leg. That was fine. It saved me the trouble. I didn't want him to die, I had some questions for him. With my finger on the trigger, I studied his face. He kept his eyes fixed on me, and barely even blinked. That's when I knew Skinny Man had not gone out the window.

I looked the giant in the eye. "Where is he?"

The giant blinked several times but didn't say anything. Still, he kept his eyes on me.

I lowered the pistol and aimed at his good leg. "One, two—"

He shifted his eyes rapidly to a point just inside the doorway to my right. If his eyes were telling the truth, Skinny Man was not more than four feet from me, just around the corner. I wanted to shoot through the wall, but it was made of heavy logs. A bullet wouldn't go through, at least not straight. Shooting with my left hand was about to come in handy.

He would be expecting me to come through the door at eye level. I dropped to one knee, shoved my hand low across the threshold, and squeezed off a blind shot, aiming up and to the right. I yanked my hand back.

From around the corner came a low grunt. A six-inch butcher knife clattered to the floor just out of my reach. Behind me, Mom gasped. Next to the door there was a thud as something larger hit the floor.

I looked back at Mom and mouthed, "Stay here."

I moved back a few feet and took a deep breath. With two quick steps I dove low and on my side through the doorway. As I slid into the room, I aimed back at the spot next to the door. Skinny Man was on one knee, his hand stretching toward the butcher knife. I squeezed off two shots as I skidded to a stop against the leg of the kitchen table. One hit him in the leg, the other opened a hole in the side of his chest. He crumpled face-first to the tile.

My back was to the giant, and he was close enough to grab me. I rolled away and popped up on a knee, the gun pointed at his face. He curled into a ball again and covered his head with his hands.

I let out a breath and stood up.

Mom leaned against the door frame and gaped, but she was not in a position to see Skinny Man, who was just around the corner to her right.

"Don't come in, Mom. This isn't pretty." I walked over to Skinny Man and kicked him in the side. He didn't move. I bent over him, grabbed his hair, and turned his face up. It was bloody and gashed from the animal trap. His eyes were fixed. The second bullet must have gotten his heart. Beneath his arm, blood pooled on the tile.

"Why didn't you just stay where you were?" I said. I let his face drop back to the floor. He was a man who deserved killing; there was no doubt of that. But why did I have to be the one? I'd already dealt with years of nightmares. This would be the same. He had no right to put that on me.

I straightened up and looked at the giant. He had moved back into a sitting position. His head drooped to the side, and I could tell that he was watching my feet from the corner of his eye. He couldn't even bring himself to lift his eyes to look at me. He was beaten.

I moved over and stood a few feet away from him, just far enough that he couldn't reach me, but close enough that I towered over him. My anger at Skinny Man's stupidity spilled over. I pointed the gun at the giant's head.

"When were you going to tell me about your friend and the butcher knife?"

I jabbed the barrel of the gun toward him. He covered his head and closed his eyes.

"I asked you a question!"

"Please . . ." His shoulders shook.

This wasn't the first time a man had begged me for his life. The last time was at the campsite with Dad when I was only seventeen. I made the wrong choice then, and I'd paid the price ever since. Killing Skinny Man was bad enough, but it wasn't murder. I was not a murderer.

I let the gun drop to my side. I walked over to the table, and slumped into a chair. When I finally spoke, my voice was so soft that it surprised me. "I've got some questions for you. I don't want to hurt you any more. Do you understand that? I don't want to shoot you again—but I will if I have to."

He winced.

I rested the gun on my knee. "You were supposed to kill us, right?"

He nodded.

"Put a bullet in each of our heads, was that it?"

He nodded again.

"Then bury us somewhere out there?" I motioned toward the shattered back window.

He lowered his head. "Yes."

"I'm sorry; I didn't hear you."

"Yes."

"Who is your boss?"

"We don't have a boss. We were hired just for this job."

"Look, we know you work for a gang. We know about the extortion ring. Now, tell me who's in charge."

He squinted up at me. "I don't know what you're talking about."

I waved the gun toward him. "We know all about how you guys operate and we know about the prostitution bust in Southlake."

He grabbed his leg and grimaced. "Lady, I'm telling 'ou, I don't know what you're talking about. We were hired to do this job. That's all."

I looked over my shoulder at Mom. She had stepped into the room and was staring down at Skinny Man.

I turned back to the giant. "Then who hired you?"

He moved his good hand in the direction of his front pocket. I pointed the gun at his chest, and he froze. "I'm just trying to get comfortable. It hurts."

"You can get as comfortable as you want. Just keep your hands where I can see them. Now, you were about to tell me who hired you."

He looked at me for a second, and I could tell he was debating which held the most danger for him, telling me who hired him or keeping quiet. I desperately wanted not to have to shoot him again, but I was beginning to wonder if he had an inverted learning curve. I pointed the gun at his good leg. "One—"

He held up his hand. "Stop! I'll tell you." He shook his head. "You are a crazy woman! Do you know that?"

With the gun still pointed at his leg, I arched one brow. "Last chance."

He wiped his forehead with his good arm. Then he turned and nodded toward Mom. "Her husband."

CHAPTER
THIRTY-FOUR

I THOUGHT ABOUT TAKING the giant back to town in the car. He needed a doctor, and we had no way to contact one. I had checked the car thoroughly for our purses and phones. They weren't in it.

Eventually I decided he was simply too big to handle. So I marched him, both of us limping, into the family room and held the gun on him while Mom tied him to the cabinet with the same rope that had held her. While she worked at securing the knot, she stood as far away from him as possible, extending her hands as if she were handling a dead fish.

He was already getting woozy and couldn't have been any more passive. At one point he even lifted his hands higher to give her an easier angle to tie them. I worried that Mom might not get the knots tight, but with his wounds and the weight of the cabinet looming over him, getting loose was likely to take more energy—and more ambition—than I figured he had left. Besides, even if he did get free, he would be easy to round up.

I told him to stay still and gave him a towel to press on his leg and a bottle of water from the refrigerator. Before we left, I promised I would send the police for him as soon as we got to town. He would suffer for a while, but it was a better deal than he had intended to offer Mom and me. We'd have been buried in the back by now.

I knew that if we stopped at a police station on the way into Dallas, we'd be answering questions until noon. I also knew that Stanley must have been expecting a call from his two jobbers to let him know they'd taken care of us. In fact, they might have already called him to tell him I got loose. He could be planning to catch the first flight that morning to somewhere far away. We needed to get to him as soon as possible.

Anyway, I had a better idea than the police. Once we found the highway, I figured out that we were about twenty miles south of Dallas. We drove nearly all the way to downtown on I-35E before we found a gas station with a dilapidated outside pay phone. I had taken all of the money from the giant's pockets and wallet before we left the cabin. I dropped two of his quarters into the dented-up phone, which hung at a precarious angle from the brick wall of the station.

Standing in the haze of a yellow parking lot light, I swiveled my head as I punched in Michael's number, checking out the area around me. I half expected someone to dash around the corner of the building and pull a gun. It had been that sort of night.

Michael is probably the only non-partying person in Dallas who would answer his cell phone at 2:30 a.m. on the second ring.

"Hello?" His voice was scratchy.

"It's Taylor. Are you asleep?"

I heard shuffling and a click and could picture him sitting up in bed and flicking on the lamp. Now his voice was crisp and clear—the usual Michael. "Are you all right? Where are you?"

The concern in his voice was obvious. After what I'd been through, that was nice. I looked at my reflection in the station window. "I'm not half-bad—for someone who's been knocked out, thrown in the trunk of a car, and taken to the country to be shot."

"Don't joke around. It's 2:30 in the morning."

"I'm not joking. I killed someone tonight, and I left another guy tied up in a cabin south of Dallas. They were hired to murder Mom and me."

Now I heard lots of rustling. "I'm getting dressed. Where are you?"

"At a gas station next to downtown. Mom and I are okay. I'm a little bit beat up, but I'll be fine."

"Who beat you up?" That was a different voice—low and hard.

"Calm down, Michael. Fortunately I did most of the beating. It's just that I ran into a window and some other things along the way."

He chuckled. "They had no idea what they were getting into."

"I'll take that as a compliment. Listen, Mom's husband hired the guys to kill us."

"You're kidding me. How do you know?"

"The one who's still alive told us. We need to get over to Mom's house in Southlake to pick up Stanley before he finds out things went bad."

"Do you want me to call the Southlake police?"

"No need. Stanley will be easy enough to handle. Besides, I want to ask him a few questions before the cops take over. Is that okay with you?"

"Sure. It sounds like you earned the right to ask him a few."

I gave him the directions to Mom's, and we agreed to meet at her subdivision gate in Southlake in an hour.

As I sped past the dimly lit hulks of the Dallas skyline, I enjoyed the thought of what Michael would want to do to Stanley when he got a look at me. This was one time when I might have to be the moderating influence. What an interesting twist. First, though, Mom and I would stop at Simon's house, which was on the way. I needed to get my feet cleaned up before they got infected. A pair of shoes wouldn't hurt, either.

By the time we got to Simon's, I had learned that driving twenty miles with two pistols in the waistband of my panties was a uniquely uncomfortable experience. With each bump and turn in the road, the gun grips rubbed me a little bit more raw. As soon as I pulled down the driveway to the back of my house and stopped, I lifted my skirt, pulled the guns out, and put them in the glove box.

When I got out of the car and stood on the pavement, my muscles screamed, but not nearly as loud as my feet. I lifted one foot with my hand. It was a sticky mess of dried blood and dirt. I cartwheeled my shoulder and quickly determined that was unwise. I would have to get by with as little movement as possible for a while.

As Mom got out of the passenger side, I motioned for her to follow me while I limped to the backyard gate. Once through the gate, I stopped. The porch lights were off, and the house blocked the light from the street. I waited a few seconds to give my eyes a chance to adjust. Then I edged my way around the back corner of the pool, got down on my knees, and groped in the landscaping. Within a few seconds, I was holding the buried house key.

Mom and I moved up the porch steps together. I fumbled in the dark to get the key in the lock. When I turned the knob, I looked over my shoulder at Mom. "We need to be quiet. If Kacey's here, we don't want to scare her to death."

"It's nearly 3:00 o'clock in the morning. Where else would she be?"

"She's been staying at the sorority house during finals." I pushed open the door.

Mom walked past me into the family room. I eased the door closed behind us. "I hope none of the neighbors has insomnia," I whispered. "I can imagine what they'd think if they saw me now."

Mom smiled.

I pointed to a chair. "Why don't you have a seat? I'll wash myself off and throw on a pair of jeans and some shoes. Here, let me turn on a light for you." I was reaching for the switch when the lamp on the end table next to the fireplace flicked on.

Stanley was sitting in a wing chair with one hand on the lamp. In his other hand was his short-barreled .38 revolver.

CHAPTER
THIRTY-FIVE

"GREAT TIMING. I JUST got here myself." Stanley motioned with his gun to the wing chair opposite him. "Why don't you sit down?" The gun shook in his hand as he raised it. He ran a finger under the collar of his black mock turtleneck. The lamp shade angled the light downward, illuminating his chest and arm and gun, but leaving his face in the dark, creating an eerie illusion of a headless gunman.

By anyone's standards I'd been through a lot for one night. I was tired and sore and ready to wring Stanley's scrawny little neck even before he emerged from the shadows of my own family room with a gun in his hand. Now, watching his limp-wristed handling of the revolver, I was tempted to just walk over, slap him, and take it away. Despite his trembling hand, though, it was still a .38. It could put a hole in my head the size of a golf ball. This was no time to do something stupid.

"How did you get in our house?"

"I'm a chemical engineer. When you know a little bit about chemicals, it's amazing what you can do to a seemingly solid thing like a window frame."

"How did you beat the alarm?"

"Stop asking questions and sit."

As I walked to the chair, I surveyed the immediate area for something that could serve as a weapon or a shield or both. The only items within reach were a five-by-seven picture frame, a magazine, and the end table lamp that matched the one next to Stanley. The picture frame was my best bet. At least I could frisbee it and distract him if I had to. That would be desperation. I wasn't there yet, but I kept it in mind.

As I sat, I looked back at Mom. She hadn't moved. "Sit down on the couch, Mom. He wouldn't dare shoot us here. He'd wake the whole neighborhood. The police would be on him before he got out the back door." I wanted to be sure he hadn't overlooked that point, just in case he was even more of an idiot than I thought.

Before she could respond, he motioned to her. "No, Hil. You come over here by me. You're not the problem; you're part of the solution."

I had a sinking feeling that things were about to get complicated.

Mom moved her eyes from him to me and then back to him. She blinked several times but didn't move.

"Does that make me the problem?" I said.

He pointed the revolver in my general direction. Although I really didn't believe he would shoot me there in the house, he was waving the gun around like a Fourth of July flag. The hammer was cocked, and I had no confidence in his ability to handle the weapon so cavalierly without accidentally firing it. As the gun bobbed and slid, I shifted my weight in my chair, in a sort of weird choreograph designed to keep my vital parts out of the line of fire. I hoped he would get settled soon. Each time I moved, a new part of my body ached.

"Yes, I hate to say it, but you are the problem." He nodded toward Mom. "When you come over here, honey, would you please bring me one of those throw pillows from the couch?"

"Honey? How can you call her honey? You hired someone to kill her."

He shook his head. "Not true. They had strict instructions not to harm Hil. As I said, you're the problem."

Mom had bent over to pick up a pillow. When she heard what he said, she straightened her back. She turned to face us, and her eyes brightened.

I didn't like where this was going. "We're not buying that," I said. I glanced at Mom, hoping for a sign that she agreed. "Your boys told us that you hired them to kill us both."

Mom held up a finger. "Actually, dear, they never said that."

I threw up my hands. "What? You heard the big guy tell me they were going to put a bullet in our heads and bury us out back."

She closed her eyes, as if picturing the scene in her mind. "No . . . that's not exactly correct. You asked him if they had planned to put a bullet in your head, and he said yes. He didn't say anything about me. They could easily have killed me as soon as they got me to the cabin, but they didn't."

"C'mon, Mom, you're not buying this, are you? The only reason they didn't kill you as soon as they got you in the door was that they were trying to figure out what to do after I got loose! This is no time to lose your focus. It's kind of important."

She walked over to Stanley and handed him the throw pillow. Then she stayed there, standing beside his chair. "You always take that condescending tone with me, and I don't appreciate it. I'm not crazy."

She had picked one heck of a strange time to air the sort of mother-daughter grievance that would typically be hashed out while sitting cross-legged on a canopy bed. Even so, while absurd, the situation still screamed for diplomacy. I leaned forward with my elbows on my knees and softened my voice. "I know you're not crazy. You're my mother and I love you. It upsets me to see your husband—the only criminal in the room, by the way—trying to manipulate you. Can't you see what he's doing?"

Stanley put his hand on her arm. She pulled it away, which gave me hope. "We've got a home, Hillary, whether we have to move or not. And I want you to be there with me. That's all I've ever wanted." He was pressing precisely the right button and he knew it. "Don't you wonder how I knew you would be here?"

An excellent question, which in the surprise of the moment hadn't occurred to me.

"The microchip in your shoulder. Do you remember? I put it there so I would never lose you. I knew where you were tonight. Every minute you were gone I knew exactly where to find you, so I could bring you home. I'll always bring you home."

He was seducing her into a sort of hearth-and-home ether. If I allowed him to get her there, she might float blissfully for a long, long time. I had to nudge things back toward earth.

"Instead of thinking about the microchip in your shoulder, Mom, why don't you feel the bump on your head? They knocked you out and threw you in the trunk of a car." I pointed at Stanley. "And he hired them to do it."

She narrowed her eyebrows and touched the back of her head. She took a step away from him. Maybe the rational side of her brain had not totally shut down.

Stanley pulled a handkerchief out of his pocket and wiped his forehead. "I hate to say this, Hil, but I think Taylor doesn't want you to be happy."

I wasn't about to let him steal my momentum. I clasped my hands in front of me. "Listen, Mom, even if you believed he told them not to hurt you, you know for a fact that he hired someone to kill me. And what about Elise Hovden? He killed her, too. Didn't you, Stan?"

Bringing Elise into the conversation turned out to be a tactical mistake. He stood up. "Okay, that's enough! I'm about to solve my problem." He took the throw pillow and wrapped it around the stubby barrel of the revolver, and for the first time I understood why he wanted it in the first place. The neighbors weren't going to hear a thing.

He took a step forward.

Mom frowned. "What are you doing?"

He held the pillow tightly to the barrel and pointed the gun at my face. "It's not quite as effective as a silencer, but it should be adequate to preserve the neighbors' sleep."

"Stanley, no!" Mom stepped toward us.

I had just locked my fingers around the arms of my chair when another voice came from the hallway next to the kitchen: "Don't move!"

Our heads turned in unison. Kacey was standing next to the breakfast bar, her target pistol grasped in both hands and leveled at Stanley's chest.

The muscles in my shoulders relaxed. I'd shot with Kacey enough to know that if Stanley moved, he was dead.

And Stanley did move. He spun and pointed his gun at Kacey. Before he could fire, she squeezed off a shot. I waited for him to drop.

But he didn't.

He fired his revolver. Kacey dove behind the breakfast bar that separated the family room from the kitchen. Something clattered against the tile, and her pistol slid from behind the breakfast bar and banged against the baseboard under the picture window.

Stanley whirled and pointed his revolver at me. Sweat rolled down his cheeks. His eyes were wild, frantic. He edged backward toward the breakfast bar, his eyes moving back and forth between me and the gun on the floor. If Kacey crawled out from behind the breakfast bar to get it, he would kill her. If she didn't get it, when he reached the other side of the breakfast bar, she would have no chance. He would execute her at point-blank range.

Mom, who was closer to the breakfast bar than Stanley, took a sideways step in that direction. Stanley pointed his gun at her. "Stay where you are, Hillary, or I'll kill you, too."

She froze.

He continued to ease across the room, moving his gun back and forth between the breakfast bar and me. He had already moved around the couch and end table, putting them between him and me.

Kacey was moments from dying. I forced myself to think. There was no time to zigzag; no time to make myself a difficult target. I would have to go in straight and low and fast. Maybe he would miss. After all, Kacey had just shown that shooting a human being is more difficult than hitting a target.

I was too experienced to kid myself. In all likelihood, in a few seconds I would be dead. But Kacey was back there alone, and she was ten times more worthy of life than I was. I glanced down at my mangled dress and cut-up feet. So, this was how I would die—filthy and cut up and charging across a North Dallas family room to try to save Kacey Mason. I smiled.

Simon was right. God did love me.

I put a hand on each armrest and flexed my knees. One final time I looked at Mom. She met my eyes. I could see she understood. I rocked back for leverage. Adrenaline surged into my chest and shoulders. As I hurled my body forward, Mom threw her arms in the air and screamed. It was precisely the diversion I needed. Stanley's head jerked in her direction.

I covered the ten feet to the couch in three steps and drove my shoulder into the end table, like a football player hitting a tackling dummy. It hurtled toward Stanley's legs.

The plan was good, but the distance was simply too great. Stanley spun and pointed the gun at my face. I dove to the side of the end table and reached for his ankles.

The gunshot exploded in my ear. Something slammed into the side of my head. As my body rolled sideways toward the baseboard, I wanted nothing more than to curl into a ball and go to sleep.

CHAPTER
THIRTY-SIX

WHEN I WOKE, DAD was bending over me, his dark eyes narrowed. "Taylor, are you all right?"

I was so happy to see him that I wanted to shout, but I couldn't speak. I reached up to touch his face. But then it wasn't Dad, it was Simon, and he grasped my arms in his hands and pulled me toward him. He held me close, in the way that I had fantasized about so often when he was alive.

I relaxed so totally, trusted Simon so completely, that my body became limp in his arms. He ran his hand over my cheek, and he looked into my eyes, and for the first time in my life I knew that I was worth something. For the first time in my life, I was good enough.

I wanted to shout. I had waited so long, tried so hard, just to be good enough. If this was heaven, I never wanted to leave.

What had I done to change things? I remembered Stanley, and the revolver, and Kacey. Had she lived? I had to know. I was here with Simon, and I wanted to stay, but Kacey was my sister—yes, she was my little sister—and I had to know. It was the most important thing—because I loved her more than I loved myself.

And I knew that I had found the secret.

CHAPTER
THIRTY-SEVEN

I OPENED MY EYES, and I was being held, but by Michael Harrison, not Simon. He had one hand behind my head. Just beyond him, staring down at me, was Kacey. Behind her was Mom.

My eyes moved right past Michael to Kacey. "You're all right? Thank God."

"And, thank Michael," she said.

I turned my eyes back to Michael. The expression on his face was Dad's expression, the concerned one. I had never focused before on how kind Michael's eyes were. Perhaps I'd been looking past him too long.

"You look great," he said. "Going out?"

I smiled. "You don't look bad yourself. What happened?"

Michael nodded toward the breakfast bar. Stanley was sitting propped against it with his eyes closed and his hand over his side. His chest rose and fell in short, labored bursts. Beneath his fingers a wet circle seeped through his black shirt.

"Will he make it?" I said.

"He was lucky. After what he tried to do to you, I was aiming for his head. Sorry about your window." I looked over my shoulder at a bullet hole surrounded by a spider web of cracks in the glass.

A pain near my eye snapped my head straight. I touched the spot. Something oozed between my fingers. "Shot again," I said disgustedly.

Michael laughed. "Not this time. You tackled the corner of the end table with your forehead."

"Michael saved us all." Kacey's face reddened. "I forgot to turn on the house alarm when I came home. Then I missed the shot. I don't know how."

I smiled again. "It's okay. I'm glad you missed. You don't need that weight on your life." I lost the smile. "We'll talk about the alarm later."

I pushed myself up to sit. Michael kept my head cradled in his hand, and I was happy that it was there. It made me feel safe. I needed to feel safe for a while. "How did you know we'd be here?" I said.

He shrugged. "I didn't. For some reason I thought

I should come by and check on Kacey before I headed to Southlake. I saw the strange car in the driveway and then the blood on the pavement."

I looked down at my feet. They were a mess. "I went for a jog."

"Yeah, I can't wait to hear about it. Anyway, I took a look around back and saw you through the windows."

I frowned at Kacey. "You weren't even supposed to be here. Don't you ever study?"

She turned a palm up. "Some of the girls were finished with finals. They were loud, and it was hard to sleep at the sorority house." She smiled. "Easier than here, though."

Mom had not said a word. I looked at Stanley, then over at her. "I'm sorry, Mom."

"You've not got a thing to be sorry about. You were right about Stan the man." She scowled at him. "No worries, though. There are plenty of other fish in the sea." She reached up and straightened her hair.

Despite her effort at nonchalance, I saw the fear in her eyes.

"You don't have to worry, Mom. I won't leave you."

She squinted and turned her head away. When she turned back, her eyes were red. "You came back for me."

I supposed that was her way of saying thank you, that something in the painful web of her past made her incapable of saying it directly. It was close enough. Pressure grew behind my eyes, and I wasn't sure I wanted to choke it back. I blinked twice.

"Here it comes," Michael said. "It was just a matter of time." He dabbed at my eyes with the sleeve of his shirt.

I jabbed him in the side. "We've had a heck of a night."

"It was a real fright," Mom said.

Michael and Kacey turned to look at her.

Mom smiled sheepishly. "It rhy—"

I waved a hand in the air. "We know, Mom."

CHAPTER
THIRTY-EIGHT

DUST ROSE IN A rust-colored cloud behind my rental car and hung there, suspended, as if debating whether to fight its way higher or give itself up to the inevitable fall. In an instant, a chilly West Texas wind made the choice for it, scattering it to the side of the road next to the campsite. I turned my eyes from the mirror and switched off the ignition. My heart pounded. I fought the urge to wheel the car around and drive straight back to the Lubbock airport.

I turned to Mom. "We're here."

She rolled down her window and inhaled. "The air is clean, isn't it?"

She couldn't have been more wrong. It was a filthy place. Not literally, of course, but in my mind it would always be the dirtiest place on earth. The spot where my life changed forever.

I opened the door and swung out my feet. My boots crunched in dry weeds and gravel. *Doesn't it ever rain in this place?* I walked around the front of the car and waited for her.

"This way." I headed down the rocky path to the circular clearing that served as the campsite. The fire pit in the middle, the precisely cut logs configured around it like dining room chairs—nothing had changed.

I walked to the back of the campsite, to the edge of the path that led down between piano-sized boulders to the lake where Dad and I had washed off after the long drive from Dallas. He warned me about rattlers, and there had been snakes—only they'd walked on two feet and carried shotguns.

Mom stood near the fire pit and pulled the collar of her ski jacket tight around her neck. "It's cold up here. Nothing to block the wind."

"I'll build a fire."

To save us trouble, I'd stopped at a quick shop on the way from the airport and picked up a prepackaged bundle of firewood. We weren't looking for an authentic experience. I'd had all the authenticity I could take from this place. Within a few minutes a small flame spread from the loosely clumped tender and licked at the slender bottom layer of logs. We sat close to each other on a log facing the fire. I pulled my feet up beneath me and hugged my knees. In the distance, across the lake and the bluffs, the radio tower still blinked, as it had that night, just before—.

I squeezed my knees tighter to my chest. I didn't want to think about it; but what else was I supposed to think about? We were here, and we hadn't come to sing camp songs. I'd brought Mom with me to show her, to help her understand why I'd turned out the way I had. Maybe it would help—if not her, then possibly me.

We'd made progress, Mom and I, since the night the police and medical technicians carted Stanley out of the Mason house. For one thing, she'd put him behind her quickly. In fact, she hadn't even visited him. If she had any intention of doing so, she would have to hurry. He had confessed to everything, and the folks at Huntsville Prison were awaiting his arrival. The only question was how long his stay would be. The sentencing would take place in February. In the meantime, he was being held at Dallas County Jail's medical ward until he was fit enough for transfer.

Stanley's confession hadn't come immediately. When the Southlake Police discovered two key bits of evidence, though, he and his attorney began looking for the best plea deal they could make. The first item was a single piece of paper seized from a desk in the whorehouse in Southlake. It demonstrated something that none of us would ever have imagined: Stanley wasn't just a john, and he wasn't being blackmailed. He was an owner. Twenty-five percent of the prostitution operation belonged to him. The extortion ring that Katie was investigating had no connection at all to Stanley. It had just provided a timely excuse that he seized upon when he desperately needed an explanation. It bought him time to figure out how to get rid of Mom and me.

The second piece of evidence was less stunning, but just as dark. Elise's computer had been empty because Stanley had erased it. Or at least he thought he had. Fortunately, he was a chemical engineer, not a computer wonk. The police hired an expert who restored Elise's files and found the bottom half of her suicide note. It hadn't been a suicide note at all, but a note of explanation that she assumed would be read after she left town. Standing alone, the first half looked conveniently suicidal. Stanley had seen the possibilities immediately when he picked up her laptop at her house.

He was an opportunist and he used what luck provided him. He'd told the truth, up to a point. She really had threatened to expose him, and she really had offered him money stashed in the Cayman Islands if he would agree to leave the country. But he hadn't gone to her house just to pick up her computer. He went there to kill her. If he could make it look like a suicide, so much the better.

As for the money in the Cayman Islands, Brandon found it hiding in plain sight. After the police solved the case, Brandon asked if he could look at the flash drive I'd taken from Elise's car. It contained only her past two years' tax returns. Brandon studied the returns for hours, looking for a clue. Then he noticed that her Social Security number was different on each return. And he noticed something else—each number had ten digits instead of the usual nine.

Elise was a sharp one. She never intended for Stanley to get the ministry's money. There were two Cayman Islands accounts, not one, and she hid the true account numbers on the face of her slightly revised tax returns. Once Stanley was out of the country, she apparently intended to contact Brandon from wherever she was hiding, disclose the blackmail and embezzlement, and give him one of the account numbers. Stanley's short-notice trip to Venezuela with her computer would have confirmed her story and damned him.

Elise must have figured that with Stanley and a logical explanation in hand, the police wouldn't even bother looking for her. The discrepancy between the embezzled amount and the amount in the single account wasn't likely to pose a problem. After all, who would believe Stanley's story about how much cash she had already delivered to him? The police would just assume he'd spent the missing amount or stashed it somewhere. Elise would be gone, and the money in the second account would be hers.

I had to tip my hat to her. It probably would have worked. If Stanley hadn't decided to kill her.

As for the rest of us, I had worried that Mom would be forced to move in with Kacey and me. Fortunately, though, Stanley was right about the patents. They still had some value. The university was willing to buy them quickly, but at a deep discount. The sale provided enough cash to keep the mortgage company off Mom's back while she sold the house in Southlake and found a smaller place. She expressed an interest in looking for something close to us. I was guiltily ambivalent.

After things settled down, Kacey, Mom, and I spent Christmas Eve together—an unlikely threesome gathered around the tree. Kacey did everything she could to make it work, from teaching herself to cook her first holiday dinner to asking about Mom's favorite Christmas carols and playing them while we ate. Kacey's mother died when she was young, and she wanted desperately for Mom and me to connect again.

In her own dysfunctional way, I think Mom worked at it, too. She brought a garish, red-and-green striped ball for the tree. "Christmas should be colorful," she said, as she hung it at eye level. True to form, her tone left little doubt that the dazzling ornament was an unspoken judgment on our subdued, white-ribbon theme. She also brought identical gifts for Kacey and me: how-to books that contained a new age road map to our inner quiet place—hot tub not included.

I wondered whether it had been just too daunting for her to try to find a unique gift just for me, her daughter. I let it go, though. If I wanted a relationship, I would have to absorb the slights quietly and focus on the big picture.

And I did want a relationship. I became certain of that the moment she left her jacket for me out on that country road.

We attended Christmas Eve service at Kacey's church near the SMU campus. It was a decision Kacey must have regretted. Those around us cast incredulous glances our way as Mom raised her voice in solitary accompaniment to the choir's special numbers. Meanwhile, Kacey and I sank as low as we could in the pew. For Kacey's sake, I resolved to steer Mom to a different church once she was settled.

The day after Christmas, I suggested to Mom that she come with me to West Texas. I wanted her to see the place where it had happened. Initially she objected, but she didn't fight it hard. We decided to make the trip on December 30, because I had to be back to Dallas for New Year's Eve. I'd agreed to meet Michael and some of his friends at a restaurant. It wasn't exactly a date— at least not yet—but I was looking forward to it. Even I could see that I had been taking him for granted.

So, there we were, Mom and I, two nights before the New Year, sitting side by side, staring into the fire at the campsite where Dad died.

The sunlight faded quickly, and stars appeared in the sky, a few at a time. I rested my chin on my knees. "We looked at the stars," I said.

"Who did?"

"Dad and I—that night. We were lying on our backs, right about in this spot."

I picked a stick up from the ground near my feet. "He said that some people like the stars and some people like the lights. He liked the stars." I drew a circle in the dirt with the stick. "He told me I liked the lights. It hurt me when he said that. I wanted to be just like him."

"He was a good man. You are like him, Taylor. Very much like him."

I tossed the stick away. "No, I'm not like him at all. He could have lived. He sacrificed himself to save me. No matter what I do, I'll never be good enough to deserve that."

She brushed her hands over the legs of her jeans. Then she tilted her head back. "Do you wonder why I sing at church when no one else is singing?"

This was so typical. I was talking about my dead father—her dead husband—and she had found a way to bring the conversation back to her. I turned my head away and didn't respond.

She didn't seem fazed. "I sing because despite all the things I've done in my life, God accepts me as I am. Grace is the one thing I don't have to earn. In fact, I couldn't earn it no matter what I did. It's a gift from Jesus. Giving it made him happy, because he loves me more than he loves himself. And if nothing else makes me happy, that does. So I sing because it's the least I can do to say thank you. I don't care a bit what anyone else thinks."

I turned to look at her. She braced her hands on the log and kept her eyes on the fire. "You don't have to deserve what your father did for you. You can't earn it. It was a gift. Giving it made him happy—because he loved you more than he loved himself, more than he loved his own life."

"How could you know that? You weren't there."

Her voice remained steady. "I know what he did. I read the news stories. I've still got them."

I studied her face. She had stopped in the airport restroom and scrubbed off her makeup. I didn't know why. In the flickering light of the campfire, her skin was clear and clean and glowing. She was beautiful, so incredibly beautiful.

"You knew everything," I said, "but you didn't come back. I needed you."

She rubbed the back of one hand with her thumb, as if trying to scrub something off. "I couldn't."

A few weeks earlier, I'd reacted to the same response with contempt. Now I was beginning to understand just how sick she'd been, how troubled she still was. So I sat there, silent, watching the fire.

I thought of Dad, and how much I missed him. And I thought of Kacey and how much I loved her— so much that dying to save her would have made me happy. Mom was right. For the past twelve years I'd been trying to earn something that was free, something I could never earn, no matter what I did. What Dad gave me was a gift, the same gift I would have been happy to give Kacey. The same gift Jesus gave me. That was what Simon had tried to teach me.

I thought I'd found the secret when I charged across the room at Stanley's revolver in a hopeless effort to save Kacey's life. And I had found it, but I hadn't really understood it. Looking at it from the outside, what I had tried to do was make a sacrifice. But looking at it from the inside, from my heart, it was simply love, pure love. Like Jesus' love. That was what made it a gift. That was what made it free. Maybe that was what gave us all the chance to be free.

Mom was too troubled to give me everything I wanted—at least for now. She understood the secret, that much was clear. I wondered, though, if she was capable of giving the gift as well as receiving it. I wondered what personal demons were holding her back.

We sat there looking at the sky, and after a few moments she said, "Not all fathers are like your dad." She hugged herself and began to rock. "What a father does can change you, put you in a dark hole; a hole that swallows you and holds you down in the blackness for the rest of your life."

I had barely any recollection of her father. He died when I was six. I tilted my head and watched her. Her cheek glistened in the fire light. It was wet. I reached over and brushed it with my fingers. "Did your father hurt you, Mom? Is that what happened?"

She straightened her back. "I loved him. I loved my daddy."

My shoulders sagged. "Oh, Mom."

I touched her arm. She flinched.

She ran a hand back through her hair. "I want to thank you for something," she said, and it was clear she was changing the subject, that she wasn't ready to tell me everything.

I let my hand drop from her arm. "What's that?"

She reached over, took my hand in hers, and squeezed it. "You didn't leave me."